THE
COWGIRL JUMPED
OVER THE MOON

Linda Ballou

Wind Dancer Press

The Cowgirl Jumped Over the Moon

Copyright 2015 by Linda Ballou

The Cowgirl Jumped Over the Moon is a work of fiction. Any similarities' to real places, events or persons living or dead is coincidental or used fictitiously.

Cover Design by Karen Phillips
Edited by Kathleen Marusak
ISBN: 978-1-5120093-4-7

Published in 2015 in the United States
Wind Dancer Press

What readers are saying about

The Cowgirl Jumped Over the Moon

"Linda Ballou captures the energy, excitement and adrenalin rush of the Grand Prix jumping world that has kept me in the game all these years." Susan Hutchison

Susie Hutchison was inducted into the 2015 National Show Hunter Hall of Fame, which "honors excellence by providing recognition, education, and appreciation for the achievements of the horsemen and horses who have made the sport of show hunters so rich in history."

"An adventure that captivates, from show arena to backcountry wilderness. Inspirational in the power of the human spirit."

Charisse Glenn - International Endurance Rider and Trainer

I found the adventures of this young cowgirl hero exciting and reminiscent of my own youthful horse adventures. Getting inside the hearts and emotions of Linda's characters was fascinating. Her attention to detail in both the jumping arena as well as her great love and understanding of the outdoors makes for a very realistic adventure with a window into both of these worlds."

Sharon North Pohl, Founder of Willow Pond Ranch and Farm a non- profit Horse rescue and equestrian center.

Oh, doggone it, Linda! You have me weeping through the edit with the kindness you observe in these characters, especially Gemcie's love for Marshal. It's palpable. You are not only talented in bringing scenes and wilderness to life, but also in carving characters from words as they spring to life from the page, in myriad forms, through myriad types. The feelings you evoke through the plot and dialogue are strong and expressive, translating to the heart as one reads this. What a gift!

Kathleen Murusak, Editor of over 1,000 books!

The Cowgirl Jumped Over the Moon

The glowing eyes in the grizzled face of a bear, jaws agape, exposing canines, haunted Gemcie's dream world. She felt the bear's hot breath on her face as she drifted off to fretful sleep, soon interrupted by the rude clanging of a fire bell. Bolting upright in bed, she glanced at her alarm. It was 3:00 a.m. She threw her dressing gown over thin pajamas and marched down the cold metal stairwell to the parking lot. The pavement pricked her bare feet as she stood shivering with six other guests. A man in an official-looking red blazer finally appeared.

"Sorry, folks, false alarm. You can go back to your rooms," he announced.

Back to her room, but not to sleep. Unable to find a comfortable position, she flopped from side to side like a hooked trout. Gemcie had already gone through the ritual of laying out her red wool riding jacket, inspecting her white riding pants for stains. Her stock scarf and pin rested next to her velvet hat. She couldn't take another sleeping pill; she wouldn't be able to get up and be at the barn by 5:30 a.m. There was nothing left to do except lie there, staring into the deep space of her own mind. She prayed that just lying still would glean her enough rest to perform well in the Grand Prix in a few hours.

Caught between the dream state and the waking world, she saw herself on Marshal, her powerful Irish Hunter, approaching the triple jump. He was chargy, tossing his head and grabbing for the bit just before the row of five-foot fences. She tried to set him up, sitting perfectly erect, sinking her weight into the saddle, but she couldn't rebalance him. He lurched over the first obstacle, pulling a rail on the second. He struggled to regain his footing, but couldn't and crashed hard into the third jump, squarely hitting the wood rails. Gemcie saw herself being thrown, bouncing off the standard, catching a jump cup in the back. Badly shaken, she stood up, put her hand to the small of her back, and felt a warm moist spot on her blouse. Marshal strained to get up, but floundered. After three attempts to rise on his forelegs, his right shoulder crumpled under his weight. Finally, he lay still, resting his head on the damp grass stained by his rich, dark blood.

The vet rose from his examination of Marshal then handed Gemcie a gleaming loaded revolver in dream motion. A canvas sheet, held up by field hands to block the scene from the eyes of the curious crowd, flapped in the breeze. Banners atop flag poles snapped in the hot wind. Looking into Marshal's trusting brown eyes, rimmed in red, she saw the foal she raised ripping around the pasture on spindly legs. Unable to pull the trigger, she handed the gun back to the vet. This would be another night of no sleep on a sweat-soaked pillow. Fresh anguish settled into each cell of her body as she anticipated the event taking place in just a few hours.

Finally daylight came. She arrived at the barn feeling lightheaded with eyes raw and scratchy. She loved the world in the morning, vibrant and tingling with sparkling dew diamonds drying in the morning sun, but today she felt nauseous. Inhaling the smell of new-mown grass flying from the triple mower piloted by a Mexican in a straw hat helped rebalance her system. She drew a few deep breaths, held them in for a moment and exhaled.

She liked to arrive before the rest of the crowd so she could have a few quiet moments with Marshal before an event. He was munching on his morning oats, comfortable in a warm dry stall with mounds of fresh shavings. He nickered softly at her approach. His coarse mane stuck straight up, making him look like a punk rocker. He had a lightning-bolt blaze shooting from his forehead to his nose. His ears were a bit short for his massive head. He was thick in the neck like a prize fighter, and possessed an enormous barrel chest. Tail brushed to a glossy sheen, hooves polished, he received all the attention entitled to a champion from the grooms at the Mariposa Ranch before being trailered to the show grounds.

He chewed peacefully while Gemcie swept off the sawdust that had settled onto his coat over the night. The anxious ferret coiled in the pit of her stomach was stilled by the quiet strength of the stallion. She lovingly brushed the firm round mounds of muscles in his rump, feeling their warmth under her hand. It would go well today. Marshal was fit enough for both of them. He would carry her forward over the course in his steady rhythmic stride. Stout-hearted, he would sail smoothly over each jump without hesitation.

"What a good boy," she said, willing his solid strength into her own body as she groomed him.

She liked to walk the course before the rest of the riders arrived so she could focus. Tapping knee-high boots with her crop, she visualized her ride, counting strides between jumps. Banners whipped in a crisp wind blowing over the green field. A course of fifteen, five-foot jumps placed strategically to test the skills of the riders were set in a snaking pattern. Bouquets of bold flowers flanked the standards and dressed up the day. A direct line to the first double looked easy, but she would have to press him forward to get over the ramped oxer. The first combination rested beneath the shade of a sycamore near the grandstand. Riding into the shadows, combined with the squeal of an excited child in the bleachers, could throw him off. She would keep a leg on, holding him steady. The Liverpool was at a least a thirteen- foot spread of shallow water just beyond a low flower box. Marshal had a twelve-foot stride. It would be hard for him to see the distance required to sail just beyond the obstacle without touching a hoof to the rim.

Dominique La Fevre, a bold, aggressive rider in the number-two spot that day, fell into step beside Gemcie.

"Where's Jorge?" Dominique asked.

"He stayed back with Nicky. Her foal has dropped," Gemcie replied, flashing a smile. "She's ready to pop any minute."

"Should be a fine filly. Good sire, and good dame, too," Dominique said.

Dominique's chocolate-drop eyes nestled in long dark lashes betrayed none of her secrets. Spiked short hair framed her face, giving her the childlike appeal of a Dickens urchin that made her look fifteen instead of twenty-five. Her small boyish hips and strong muscled legs were at home in tight riding pants. She tucked a blousy peasant shirt in, showing off a tiny waist. It was impossible to talk to her without becoming mesmerized by her moist, heart-shaped lips.

"Looks like you've got the edge, riding tenth. But this course doesn't look to be as tough as Del Mar," Dominique remarked.

"Yeah, that was a bitch. I'm never riding on grass without studs

3

again," Gemcie answered with a laugh.

"Marshal was sliding so much I thought you were going to take out the Judge's stand," Dominique said.

A half foot taller than Dominique, Gemcie had long elegant strides with limbs that flowed like liquid. Short-waisted and narrow in the hip, with long legs, she had a perfect rider's conformation. Tall for a female rider, she competed well against the men.

"Who are you riding today?" Gemcie asked.

"Judgment."

"He's a handful."

"Yeah, but he's got scope and he's super careful."

"I heard Sandy Stake is riding today."

"She ought to give it up. She looks like a fireplug," Dominique said.

"Yeah, but she sticks like a tick on a dog."

"How did you sleep last night?" Dominique asked.

"Not well. Some clown set off the fire alarm at the hotel."

"What a drag. I never sleep well before an event myself."

"It'll be okay."

"See you later. I've got to get to the warm-up ring," Dominique said, parting company with Gemcie and walking briskly to her trailer.

When Gemcie arrived back at the barn, she was pleased to see Billy, her trainer, standing in Marshal's stall.

"I was beginning to think you weren't going to make it," she said.

"Have I ever missed an event you was riding in yet?"

"Come to think of it, you never have," she said and laughed, feeling more secure with her mentor on the scene. Not that she couldn't ride without him. His training was second nature to her. She didn't have to think about keeping her hands low and steady. When she was a child he had put handcuffs on her wrists while riding, forcing her hands to be still. Gemcie's hot tears of frustration never made Billy let up. Sue Ellen, Gemcie's mother, had become nervous, afraid Billy's treatment was too harsh.

"Aren't you going too far?" she'd asked. "Handcuffs seem a little over the top."

"Don't worry," he'd replied. "She's going to learn two things this way. One, how to stop over-using those hands; and two, she'll learn how to roll off in a ball instead of breaking an arm trying to catch a fall."

Trusting Billy was mandatory for Gemcie and her mother. The result: Not one extra muscle moved during her ride. She kept her body weight-centered, never weaving or bobbing. She left a lot to Marshal, never interfering with his natural forward motion. They did a lot of winning together.

"He looks good. I like that he dropped some weight. He don't need any baby fat slowin' him down out there," Billy said, running his hand down Marshal's front legs, searching for any lumps or warm spots. Pulling a hoof pick out of his back pocket, he signaled Marshal to lift his front leg. Resting it on his knee, he picked the caked sawdust from the hoof to get a better look.

"He's been doing good on that hay mix. Keeps him mellow too," Gemcie said.

"I want you to do about fifteen minutes of flat work before you get into the ring. Supple him up with some haunches into the rail," Billy said. "Don't get him all prancy though; I want him to stretch out."

"I'll finish off with some extended trot."

"That would be good," Billy said, releasing Marshal's front leg from his knee. He straightened up, stretching his torso back and putting his hands on his lean hips. After sixty years of riding, he still held his wiry, six-foot frame erect. He pulled the zipper on his black fanny pack filled with sugar cubes. Marshal's ears pricked at the sound. Billy slipped a few of the sweet treats into a flat palm and let Marshal nibble them from his hand. He gave the stallion several solid pats, rubbing his immense neck with gnarled freckled hands.

Billy had brought at least a half-dozen riders to Grand Prix-level in his career. Even though he trained many horses to Olympic-level dressage, for the last twenty-five years he'd focused on jumpers. He cut his riding teeth in the rodeo on a cow pony he said was his best friend. He posted a picture of him on the wall of his trailer.

"It's true I'm sittin' on the horse and it looks like I'm tellin' him how to rope that calf but fact is, I was just along for the ride. That horse won me a lot a money," he would tease, slapping his blue-jeaned knee as though the joke was on those who gave him credit for being a great trainer.

Marshal trotted softly into the warm-up ring, tuned up from the flat work and ready for the task ahead. Billy started them over some low jumps then moved them up to a line that simulated the angled gates in the ring, finishing with a couple of bigger jumps to sharpen Marshal's reactions.

"Looks like that tight turn after the Liverpool is what's going to give ya the most trouble here today," Billy said. "Footing could get sloppy goin' through there."

Not wanting to over-do her warm-up, Gemcie stopped to watch Dominique ride. Judgment, a powerful, seventeen-hand Hanoverian gelding took some real ability. She didn't have a regular mount, which put her at a disadvantage. It takes time for a rider to know the quirks of any horse. Her form was exquisite, with legs at the girth, chest up, head high. She had spent her childhood under the instruction of the best trainers in Europe. Eventing top horses honed her riding skills to perfection. Her delicate feminine physique belied her tough interior. She pressed hard to win and took chances.

Judgment was shaking his head as she approached the second combination. She clucked her tongue, giving him a solid swipe with her crop to get him over. He lurched over the fence, but seemed to forget about what was troubling him for the next three obstacles. Then he nearly pulled a rail on the triple. A stiff breeze could have tipped the scale as the rail rocked in the jump cup when the horse's bunched rear passed over it. Dominique approached the Liverpool in a wide, sweeping turn, squeezing him up hard. Through sheer mental determination she got him over the thirteen-foot span, pulling him up sharply to make the bending line to the next jump. It was not a pretty ride, but she made it around clean.

"It's six strides up to the first line, four to the in-and-out, a long five down the next line, and a steady seven home," Billy whispered the last-minute instructions as he lifted Gemcie's leg forward to tighten Marshal's girth.

"Gemcie McCauley aboard Marshal," the announcer's voice blared over the loudspeaker.

She trotted lightly into the ring doing a quiet canter around the outside of the course, letting Marshal feel the crowd. When he relaxed, she moved forward to the double combination under the sycamores. He noticed the grandstand, flicking an ear in its direction, but she felt no hesitation from him. He launched from a perfect spot and they sailed lightly through. The next ramped oxer with a six-foot spread he easily negotiated. Some horses get tired in a week of jumping at a horse show, but Marshal seemed to revel in the challenge. He just grew stronger and more confident, seeming to love the excitement. Gemcie let him fly over the course at his pace keeping a loop in the reins so she would not be tempted to interfere with his movements. She trusted him. The forward flow made him happy. Ears pricked all down the triple line, he jumped the oxers as well as he'd ever jumped anywhere. She couldn't have asked for more.

Billy's heart was pounding with pride as he watched them sail confidently over the demanding field of jumps. Gemcie's focus never wavered. Nothing existed for her beyond the moment when she was riding a course. Her alert, blue eyes remained riveted on the line she wanted Marshal to jump. Her mind melded with his. She was fluid, graceful, giving. She embodied everything Billy strove for in a rider. Marshal was majestic, brave and bold. Billy always said, "Marshal has the mark of a champion, the gaze of the eagle, he looks beyond humans, his eyes to the sky." They were going to do it! They were going to take him to the World Cup! At nineteen, Gemcie was one of the youngest riders vying for the Cup. They had already won the last five Grand Prix on the Pacific Coast circuit this year. They were the combination Billy worked for all his life.

As they made the sharp roll back turn to the Liverpool, Gemcie put both legs on, building stride. She held him steady with both reins, looking fiercely to the other side of the water jump. Her timing was a split second off, the leg pressure a hair too much. Marshal lurched as though he'd been goosed. His stride became uneven; his takeoff too long. His front hoof caught on the lip of the Liverpool on the way out. He tripped, landing on his shoulder, rolling tail over nose. Gemcie flew twenty-feet into the air, slapping the ground solidly, and landing on her back. Spread eagle, she lay perfectly still. A communal murmur went through the grandstand as the crowd stood to see what was happening. The field doctor ran to Gemcie with two men carrying a stretcher behind him. He leaned over her, feeling her neck.

"Don't move," he whispered in her ear in case she became conscious.

He felt her pulse and instructed the men to lift her onto the cot.

"Don't move her too quickly and don't drop her legs!" he barked.

Billy gathered up Marshal, who was on his feet, but his focus was on Gemcie.

The stallion's dripping nostrils flared crimson. Billy soothed him, patting him softly on his wet muscled neck. He walked him out, circling the arena.

"It's okay, big fella. It's not your fault, big fella. It's okay, big fella. She'll be fine."

Billy looked on with concern, from a distance, as the doctor clamped a neck brace on Gemcie. He could see Sue-Ellen charging across the field with her breasts threatening to topple out of her spandex top. Breathless and panting, she arrived in a flurry.

"Is she okay? Will she be all right? Please tell me, I'm her mother."

"We don't know yet. She will need x-rays and an MRI to answer that question."

"Mama," came from Gemcie, slowly coming back to awareness.

"Don't worry, honey, I'm with you, darling, she soothed, taking her daughter's hand and holding it close to her heart. "I'm always with you. You know that. Now just be still."

The medics lifted the stretcher and slid it into the waiting ambulance. With red lights flashing, it forced a pathway through the crowd. Billy continued to hand-walk the badly shaken, confused Marshal, until he was calm enough to be put back in his stall.

Chapter Two

Sleep in the cold metal chair next to Gemcie's hospital bed was hard to come by, even for Sue Ellen, who swore she could sleep anywhere.

"If you were dog tired like I am all the time, you wouldn't have any trouble sleeping either," she would say.

The truth was she didn't have time for trouble of any kind. She just kept mushing through whatever calamity came her way. She rose at five o'clock every morning to keep the Smoker running smoothly. She had started as a waitress serving truck-drivers hash and eggs in an all-night coffee shop in Bishop. For the last twenty years, she'd managed the steak house, making sure fresh red roses and white linen cloths graced the tables each night. She didn't have to carry heavy trays or pour coffee into bottomless cups anymore, but she never forgot the ache in her back from being at a dead run for ten straight hours seven days a week.

Shifting her bulk in the unyielding chair, she let her mind drift back twenty years to a Friday night at Tony's where a sea of hungry people snapped their fingers, and called her "honey." She passed the other waitress, heading to the dining room and clicking her heels along the wooden slat walkway to the cook's station, a hundred times that night. Once in the kitchen she stacked steaming plates of clams smothered in garlic wine sauce and mounds of steaming marina sauce onto a metal tray then hoisted it to her shoulder. Each time she passed the dishwashers' station the boys would click their tongues at her saying *ton Tula*. She didn't have time to ask them what they wanted or what that meant. When the crowd thinned out enough for her to catch her breath, she grabbed the other waitress on the way

9

out the swinging door back into the dining room.

"What does *ton Tula* mean?" she'd asked.

"It means, 'You've got nice tits,' you idiot."

Sue folded over, clutching her stomach, bent into a paroxysm of laughter. She let herself fall into the ever-growing pile of used white linen napkins, pulling her girlfriend down with her into the tomato sauce-stained mound. Overcome with the hopeless lunacy of their predicament, they rolled in the napkins, laughing until tears streamed down their red cheeks. Unable to stop sputtering, they might never have gotten up if the manager hadn't come in to the greasy hall between the dining room and the cook's station to find them.

"Girls, get up," he'd said. "Tonight we dance!"

Sue Ellen smiled wistfully at the vision of Adolf raising his arm to expose frayed seams under the arm of the jacket he always wore. She half chuckled, bouncing her chin lightly upon her chest as she day-dreamed about times gone by. She could feel her own warm breath in the cleft of watermelon breasts. Her muscled arms rested on her protruding stomach while her feet, crossed at the ankles, maintained her balance on the frail folding chair.

"Mama," Gemcie said in a voice that reminded her mother of when she was a little girl. Her daughter had often crawled into bed with her late at night frightened by the shadow of the bear she saw outside her window. She swore she heard the lonely sound of his paws scratching on the screen. Sue Ellen let her snuggle, wrapping her own great girth around Gemcie's small, hot body. They would nestle like two spoons in a drawer until morning.

"Don't move, honey," Sue Ellen said, rising from the chair to go to Gemcie's bedside. She put her hand on her forehead, feeling the damp that always accompanied her daughter's restless sleep.

"You always did sleep hot," she said.

"How long have I been out?"

"About a day. The doctor told me to get him as soon as you woke up, so now, just be still."

"Where's Jorge?" Gemcie asked.

She tried to lift her head from the pillow. A bolt of lightning shot through her body from the base of her neck to the tip of her right toe. She moaned and let her head fall back on the thin pillow. The sensation subsided, but panic set in. Gemcie's eyes, wide with terror, glistened with welling tears.

"What's happening, Mama? I can't lift my head."

Her mother held both of her daughter's hands in her own, kissing them with warm wet lips, tamping down any tears of her own.

"The doctor won't know until they take lots of tests, sweetie. Don't be scared. Just try to stay calm and don't move around. I rang the bell for help."

Gemcie relaxed her head on the hard hospital pillow. Being airborne was all she remembered. She had no recollection of the violent pain and her body going slack, overriding the sensation. She recalled a floating feeling and rising above her own body cloaked in a white sheet below her, as she watched two men strap her arms to her side. She observed them clamping on a confining neck brace then loading her into the back of an ambulance with flashing red lights. She heard the siren as the driver negotiated the traffic to Saint Joseph's emergency ward.

Suddenly she saw a vision of Marshal and tried to rise again. A bolt of molten white-hot pain ripped through her frail body, telling her she was not to move again. She experimented with the horror of her reality, twisting ever so slightly to the left. The electric shock of pain jolted her severely. She tried to roll gingerly to the right. Once again, a merciless flash of unyielding pain flattened her.

"I can't move, mama!" she sobbed, trying not to allow her shuddering shoulders to activate the now predictable, electric jolt of hurt.

"I know you're scared, baby, but you have to be brave," Sue Ellen said, tamping down the tears threatening to overtake her.

"Where's Jorge?" Gemcie asked again.

"I sent him home. He was up all night with Nicky before your accident. You've got a pretty new filly waiting for you when you get out of here. Jorge was with you last night. He looked ragged. I told him I would call him the second you opened your eyes."

"What about Marshal?" Gemcie asked, afraid of the answer.

"He's fine. Billy took him back to the Mariposa. He's probably chomping on some fine pasture grass right about now. Don't you worry about him none."

Dr. Travis entered the room, shutting the door quietly behind him.

"Would you mind waiting outside? I'd like to examine your daughter in private."

Sue Ellen left begrudgingly. She wanted to hear what he was saying to the only person in the world that mattered to her. She placed a call to Jorge as she walked past rooms with open doors. She could see patients draped in thin sheets behind white curtains. Visitors huddled over slack bodies connected to tubes bubbling with red and white liquid. The antiseptic smell of the hospital made her queasy. She let the phone ring a dozen times. There was no answer.

The doctor lifted each of Gemcie's legs, gently placing them back on the bed. He moved educated hands up and down her body testing for sensation. The pain was excruciating. She couldn't keep from moaning but forced back tears, awaiting the verdict.

"Will I be okay?" she asked fighting off a swell of emotion.

"We'll need to take some tests before we can answer that question. I know it's hard for you to accept right now, but the fact that you are feeling pain is a good sign. Your job right now is to rest."

The doctor left and Gemcie was alone. She felt like she was in a premature grave, buried alive while breathing. The door to her white cubicle opened silently, seemingly of its own accord. She half expected the bear ghost of her childhood to appear telling her this was just another nightmare. Soon she would wake up in her own bed, feeling grateful it was over.

Jorge stuck his head, covered with a shock of sun-white hair, inside the room.

"Is she gone?"

"Jorge!" Gemcie's heart leapt whenever her boyish husband was near. Ever since they married a year ago, her life had taken on fairy tale dimensions. He had high cheekbones, ice-blue eyes, a tall lean frame, and the carriage of a soldier. His family had sponsored her riding for the last five years. She and Jorge lived in the guest house of his parents' ranch in Hidden Valley so they could be close to their horses. She felt a surge of pride swell in her chest when he slipped his long slim fingers into her own shaking hand.

"I'm so sorry." Squelched tears came in a feverish fury like a tropical downpour. Her face screwed up in a grimace of pain. No sound came from her open mouth as she choked on her own sobs.

"Don't blame yourself. It's not your fault," he said. "You know there isn't a rider that doesn't take a fall now and again." He held her hands in his own, turning them over to kiss her palms.

"You are the best rider out there. You'll have the best doctors and treatment money can buy. You're going to be fine."

Gemcie snuffled into a tissue as he wiped her tears, dabbing away her fear that he could not love a cripple. His father couldn't look a handicapped person in the eye. He felt the Olympics for wheelchair victims were offensive. People with infirmities should be hidden away behind dark corridors, not put on parade. A tender flow of energy between them assured her that her young husband was not like his father. That ferret gnawing with needle-sharp teeth in her belly eased its onslaught.

"What are you doing here? I thought I was supposed to call you," Sue Ellen said, backing into the room carrying a tray overflowing with bagels, lox, salmon and bacon.

"Hi, Sue Ellen. Hope you don't mind if I couldn't stay away from my wife," he said.

"Of course not, honey. I just thought we had a plan," she responded, laughing, seeming a bit too jovial.

"How's my baby? They didn't have much to choose from down there. When they let you out of here, I'll fix you a proper breakfast," she said, plunking the tray down beside the bed, popping a piece of bacon in her mouth.

Jorge shot a cool glance toward Gemcie, letting her know he didn't want Sue Ellen smacking bacon in his ear.

"Why don't you give us a couple of minutes, mom? Jorge has to get back to the barn," Gemcie said.

"Sure thing, honey. I'll just be outside if you need me," she said, grabbing a bagel on the fly.

Jorge stayed for an hour, slipping out the door when he was sure Gemcie was asleep.

"What did the doctors say?" Jorge asked Sue Ellen, dozing in the hall just outside Gemcie's room.

"Not much. They're going to give her an MRI in the morning.

"Call me if there's any change."

"Okay."

"Get some rest, Sue Ellen," Jorge said. "The doctor gave her a sedative."

Beads of perspiration formed on Gemcie's forehead and upper lip during the test to see if her spine was injured. Encapsulated in the metal tube, she drew on all the self-control she could muster not to scream. She desperately wanted to wipe her eyes, but was instructed not to move. Instead, she let the tears flow down the side of her face to pool in seashell ears. It sounded like a giant woodpecker was pounding on her head. Helpless, strapped to the gurney, she tried to calm herself with thoughts about her world outside, while she stared at the top of the white metal tube with still eyes.

Jorge was taking care of everything in that outside world. The filly arrived with a plug in her intestinal tract. Many foals die in the first week from the toxins of their own trapped waste. The vet was able to reach into her anal cavity and disengage the blockage in time. The filly found the mare's teat and was nursing with vigor. Nicky was giving off good milk. Nicky, the foal and Jorge were all doing fine without her help, Gemcie learned. Nelia had named the filly Chantelle, after her award-winning sire, Enchanted.

Gemcie wished she could be there for the imprinting. If a foal is handled in the first week of its life, its training is easier. She had rubbed Marshal's black bullet-shaped body while he was still wet from the womb. His entire frame trembled with the shock of coming into this world. She blew breath into his soft pink nostrils, making herself his second mother. His spindly legs splayed pitifully each time he tried to stand. She massaged his body, making her touch and scent a part of him, and helped him take his first precarious steps.

When the MRI was complete, the nurse wheeled her down the gleaming hospital corridor to her room. She caught a glimpse of a woman in a walker whose gown was open, exposing alabaster buttocks. Her white, emaciated frame looked vulnerable and frail. Gemcie hadn't seen the inside of a hospital in all her years of riding. Billy made sure she knew how to get clear of a thousand-pound animal temporarily out of control. She knew how to roll herself up into a tight little ball, moving away from the horse on impact.

As a teenager she made extra money riding the problems out of trouble horses. She had a lot of close calls riding rogues, hard-headed horses that were over-disciplined, abused, or just mean-spirited. Billy taught her how to, "get up off their back, stop pulling on their face and work them out of their crazy mood." It took patience, horsemanship, and guts. Horses have good memories and they don't lose bad habits in a hurry. No matter, Gemcie got paid for her efforts. That was how she kept her riding career going until she was sponsored by Jorge's family.

Gemcie's thoughts were interrupted when her mother arrived

with arms full in her usual windy flourish. She wore a bold tunic of purples and blues draping her shoulders, exposing deep cleavage. Sue Ellen produced two dozen yellow roses and placed them in a crystal vase on Gemcie's bed stand.

"How we doing, darlin'? I figured you must be getting bored by now. I brought your computer. I had your old videos copied onto CDs. You always liked this one of you and Pie."

She kissed her on the forehead then popped the CD into her computer. The images of Gemcie at six years old, pushing Pie around their first jumping competition, usually made Gemcie laugh until she cried. Pie had been so cantankerous; he'd stopped short in front of the fence, ducked his head, and tried to toss Gemcie to the ground. She did a somersault over his head, landing on her feet in time to avoid being trampled.

Gemcie grinned as she watched the pint-sized version of herself in jodhpurs, field boots, and hard hat marching back to her pesky mount undaunted. She held his head firmly toward her with the rein while mounting, so he wouldn't tear off, or nip at her leg. Pie never missed an opportunity for extracting revenge on the beings that chose to tame him. He never accepted the idea that he should be pressed into their service. Pushed around by babes of an indifferent kind for years, he pinned his ears, baring yellow teeth at anyone who came near.

Gemcie cajoled him with a constant supply of apples, carrots, and sugar cubes. She brushed him and groomed him until he looked like a show pony, making him feel special. She was consistent in her commands, and let him have as much freedom in his movements as she could. He never did stop taking advantage of the opportunity to have his way with a careless rider, but he did stop trampling his young riders.

She took her first victory lap around the arena on Pie waving her ribbon above her head for all to see. Sue Ellen was standing on the bottom rail of the fence waving her cowboy hat as Gemcie paraded by on Pie. Her mother, fifty pounds thinner, wearing a blue cowgirl blouse with white ruffles stuffed into tight blue jeans, was beautiful in a Dolly Parton kind of way. Gemcie couldn't understand why her mother never married.

Sue Ellen saw depression begin to settle over her daughter like a gauzy veil, as she watched the celluloid version of her former vital

15

self.

"Turn it off, mom."

"I'm sorry, honey, I thought it would take your mind off things."

"The verdict is in," Gemcie said.

"You mean the doctor talked to you without me being here? I told him not to do that."

"Mom, it's not up to you what happens."

"Well, what did the bastard say?" Sue Ellen asked, plopping down on the chair by Gemcie's bed.

"I don't have brain damage."

"Well, I could have told you that."

"Thanks, mom. When did you get your medical training?"

"What about your spine?"

"I have a herniated disc."

"Well, that's nothin'. Lots of folks get that. I know Bernie got an operation for that and was fixed up in no time."

"I don't want surgery."

"Why not?"

"Maybe I don't trust doctors as much as you do. The thought of anyone coming near my spinal cord with a sharp blade in their hand is more than I can handle."

"I see your point," Sue Ellen laughed, "but still, they can fix you up pronto."

"I want to give my body a chance to heal naturally. The doctor said 80 percent of the time it will."

"That's going to take some time," Sue Ellen answered.

"Too bad! I'm not having surgery if I don't have to."

Gemcie let her gaze wander out through the window while her mother rummaged for a sandwich in one of her many packages.

"I brought you some real food. This hospital stuff will kill you," she said, unwrapping the turkey sandwich stuffed with tomatoes, avocados, and bean sprouts.

"I'm not hungry now, mom. Just put it on the tray."

"You've got to keep up your strength. Mopin' ain't going to do it."

"I'm fine, mom; I'm just not hungry. Thanks anyway."

The door swung open and Billy entered wearing the usual blue jeans and fitted khaki shirt. He pulled up a chair, took off his straw Stetson hat and rested it on his knee.

"How's my favorite Gemcie girl?"

Gemcie felt relieved to see him. Just having him in the room gave her renewed energy and courage. The closest thing to a father she had, he had given her guidance in more than horse matters over the years. Her real father died instantly when a semi-truck lost control on the grapevine, a mountain pass just outside of Bakersfield. According to Sue Ellen, the truck had a blow-out, tipped and crushed her father's truck with him in it. Sue Ellen wouldn't tell Gemcie any more about her father, just that he was a handsome cowboy who could sit on a horse and sing a tune like nobody's business. Gemcie tried to imagine what he looked like, but there were no photos collecting dust in silver frames. All traces of him were lost in a fire the year after she was born.

"I've been better. Two days in this place would depress anybody," she said, managing a weak smile.

"What's the prognosis; do we know yet?" he asked.

"She's got a herniated disc, and some bruises, that's all," Sue Ellen interjected before Gemcie could respond. "Doctor says she could have surgery and get it over with right away, or she can tough it out, and see if it will heal naturally. Says she'll be riding sooner if she lets him operate."

"Mom, I'm not having an operation!" Gemcie shot back.

"When I had my back operated on, it took as long to heal as if I'd just been patient and let nature take its course," Billy said.

"Either way, we can forget the World Cup," Gemcie said, nearly choking on the words.

"Now don't you be worryin' about that none. You bein' better is all that matters," he said, patting her arm.

"I don't want an operation. Remember Sandy's crash on Sampson?"

"Yeah, she 'bout broke her back."

"She's had two operations. Each time her back got weaker."

"Then don't have one. Me and Marshal will be waitin' for you. When you're ready for us we'll be there. You can't be rushin' gettin' well. Got to go easy on yourself."

"I don't think she ought to baby herself too much. It never did me any good," Sue Ellen countered.

"Sue Ellen, this is one time you can't do the thinkin' for her," Billy said. Nobody could speak to Sue Ellen the way Billy did. She looked down at red polished toes bulging out of her sandals, then back at Gemcie.

"Why don't you stay with me for a while? You will need someone to take good care of you," she said.

"No thanks, mom. Jorge is coming for me in the morning. Nelia has made arrangements for me to stay in her guest room. I will have room service, a physical therapist and be closer to Jorge."

"All right then, I'll come every day to see how you are doing," Sue Ellen said with a hint of disappointment in her voice.

Chapter Three

Lying in the back seat of the Mercedes, Gemcie enjoyed the worm's eye view of the world. Through the open sunroof she watched the glistening leaves of pepper trees flashing by against a lapis lazuli sky. Her pain subsided if she lay flat on her back with her knees up and kept still. Jorge drove slowly down the private road to the Mariposa ranch, trying not to jostle his patient.

"You will love staying in my old room. It overlooks a courtyard filled with mother's flowers and the fountain in the center. I know you will be comfortable there."

"That's great, Jorge, but I don't belong here. I belong with you."

"I know, darling, but I can't take care of you the way Nelia can."

Accepting her fate, Gemcie changed the subject. "How is Nicky doing?"

"You're going to love the filly," he said, flashing a brilliant smile over his shoulder.

"Is she more thoroughbred or warm blood?"

"I'd say she's more like Nicky, high strung, but she's big-boned like a warm blood."

Excited to breathe fresh air, Gemcie couldn't wait to get back to the barn and the sweet smell of horses and hay. Struck by the sight of a vulture on a recently trimmed bough, she stared into its stern yellow eye as the car passed beneath the limb. The sight of its raw, red head with blue wattle dangling below his black beak unnerved her. The wrought-iron electric gate silently wheeled open. Jim the guard waved to Jorge as they passed the gate tower, with its red tile roof and brown square windows.

"Welcome home, miss," she heard him say, but couldn't see his face.

Jorge drove out of the sun into the shade of the oak tree tunnel. Quiet, untouched by history, the solid trees had provided shelter for the Mariposa for over a century. Jorge stopped the car in front of the river-rock steps leading to the entrance of the main house. With hands on sturdy hips, Nelia stood at the imposing front door of the Early California villa. She wore navy blue riding pants with a full leather seat, sweat-stained from many hours in the saddle, and a spandex top covering firm high breasts. The diamond necklace resting on her bronze clavicle sparkled in the sun. She spoke to the servants in Spanish, telling them to get the waiting cot in position for her daughter-in-law, all the while beaming a brilliant smile down on Gemcie.

"You must be exhausted. I have Jorge's old room ready for you," she said.

She snapped her fingers, setting the servants in motion. They carefully lifted Gemcie onto a cot. Once transferred, they carried her up six steps, past the enormous, dark, solid oak door with a tiny grill window. They took her through the arched doorway, down the side hall paved with Saltillo tiles. Gemcie heard the cool splash of the fountain; a metal dolphin spewing a stream of water from its long snout into a terra cotta basin. The pool below it, crowded with lily pads and their yellow flowers, smelled of gardenia. Huge palms spreading fronds in a starburst pattern provided shade for the elephant ferns at their base. Nelia had transplanted banana trees with purple fruit dangling on long stems from her family home in Argentina.

The four-poster bed tiered with white lace took her back to her wedding night. She and Jorge had spent the night there before heading to Hawaii for their honeymoon. Nelia pulled back the embroidered coverlets and fluffed the down pillows. Fresh-cut red roses rested in a vase on the oak dresser. The flowers filled the room with the over-sweet scent of a funeral parlor. Nelia cranked open the wood-frame windows, letting in the fresh cool air from the courtyard.

"Be careful with her. She's not a sack of grain," Nelia said to the men as they lowered Gemcie onto the too-soft bed.

"Now darling, you will have every comfort. You mustn't hesitate to ask for anything," Nelia said.

Gemcie winced back tears, feeling white hot pain shoot through her body as the men deposited her on the bed. "You really shouldn't have," Gemcie heard herself saying.

"Not at all. You are my daughter and you have everything in my power to offer at your disposal," Nelia said, leaning over to kiss Gemcie on the forehead with moist lips. Nelia lifted Gemcie's hand and patted the back of it softly with her own.

Alone with Jorge, Gemcie whispered furtively, "I really want to be in our guest house with you."

"Mama wants to care of you. I'm gone all day. You need attention. It's better for you here. Besides, I'll come and see you every day." He leaned over and brushed her lips with his own then softly kissed the tip of her nose, finally resting his lips lovingly on her forehead.

"The vet is coming to look at the filly. I must go," he whispered.

The solid door slipping into place behind him clicked like a bank vault. Gemcie felt small and helpless as she rolled her head on the feather pillow to look out on the view that would be hers until her keepers decided otherwise. The sensation of being trapped and impotent that stirred within her was as painful as the burning lava that sluiced through her legs. Neither the twitter of the yellow finches in the trees outside her window, nor the gentle marine breeze lifting the lace curtains on her window, altered the dull fear in her heart that she would never be free to leave.

She studied the sounds of life outside her room. The purr of the skip loader in the field down by the creek. Then the clinking of rocks one by one into the scoop as field hands cleared the area to create a turnout in the shade for six mares and their new foals. The cascade of the boulders pouring from the scoop created a clattering river. Gemcie tried to imagine the size of each rock by the density of their sound on impact. Mexican tunes floated in on the breeze from a dust-covered radio. She slept lulled by the sound of the swishing rainbirds that kept the pastures green in the long dog days of summer.

Occasionally, she woke to a screech that sounded like the scream of a woman. She strained to identify the unnerving sound. She told Jorge about the cries, fearing one of the servants was being abused by her peasant husband. .

"It's nothing, darling. That is Esmeralda, Mama's pet cockatoo. She flies free as she pleases, but always returns to the garden."

"She sounds so frightened."

21

"She has no reason to be frightened. She is powerful, able to take care of herself, and is the most beautiful of birds; snow-white with yellow beak and black eyes. Perhaps she will show herself to you one day and you will see her crest unfold like a royal crown."

"I would like that," Gemcie murmured wistfully.

"She will come," he promised, kissing her softly.

Gemcie looked into his glacier-blue eyes, yearning to be closer to him. "It will give me something to look forward to."

"Yes, my darling," he said, patting the top of her head, making her feel like a good dog.

"How is Chantelle? I would love to see her."

"She is careening around the pasture like a maniac. Look," he said, showing her a picture on his phone of the filly leaping with all four feet off the ground.

"She's gorgeous!" Gemcie said, yearning to watch the filly in person. "Can you take me to her?"

"Not yet. Doctor's orders are that you rest and let your body heal. I will bring you pictures of her progress." He kissed her once more and left, closing the door behind him. Gemcie had never felt more alone. She determined she would find a way to get to the stables somehow, as she drifted off to a fitful sleep.

The Mariposa, wedged between the foothills surrounding Hidden Valley, had a twenty-six stall barn, a professional dressage ring, two turnout pastures and many fields filled with bales of hay bundled into tidy rows. The workout track lined by round metal rails wrapped a grassy event field. There were a couple brush jumps with an imposing ten-foot spread, a grass ramp with a log bank that Gemcie loved to jump, as well as a tricky in-and-out coffin jump. A natural stream meandering through the hunt field created a water pond at the base of the windmill that turned lazily in the soft wind.

The dressage ring, groomed each morning with a tractor pulling a drag behind, was protected by a stand of eucalyptus trees providing a wind block and shade. On most days the rustle of blue leaves on enormous boughs swaying overhead had been all Gemcie heard while concentrating on her workout with her horses. The occasional appearance of a screeching red-tailed hawk floating on thermals, scoping the meadow for mice, was her only company.

She would rise at five, lean into the still gray world, and hurry to the barn each morning. She liked to be onboard her first horse in time to see the pink rays of sunrise spread over purple mountains. The chill in the morning air awakened her lungs. She felt energized as she carved tidy figure-eights into the clean palette of sand.

The white wooden rail fence that surrounded the ranch was constantly being painted. Like the Golden Gate Bridge, by the time the workers reached one end of the bridge, it was time to start all over again. Throughout the grounds were ornamental plum, bottle brush, scented pine, and the sturdy oak. The grandest part of all for Gemcie were the horses. Nelia owned prize-winning Andalusians, thoroughbreds, warm-bloods, Arabs, and a few solid quarter horses for the trail. The trail traced the creek bed shaded by sycamores, deep into canyons with gushing waterfalls, hidden from the eyes of strangers. Never in her wildest imaginings while she mucked out wet stalls at the Circle K, her childhood barn, did she dream she would live here.

Nelia ran the Mariposa with the discipline of a military commandant. Invitations to events held at her facility were coveted. Show days saw the lower pasture filled with eighteen-wheelers hauling in the most prized animals from Santa Inez, Del Mar, the Oaks, Flintridge, and other high-end ranches. Shuttles carried select spectators from the parking fields to the grandstands under the shade of sycamores. Dressage riders in black long-tail jackets and bowler hats danced on gleaming, muscled mounts to the strains of Vivaldi. The hunter-jumpers did their rounds in the afternoon.

It was whispered that Nelia lacked sophistication in the saddle.

"She rides like a barbarian," Gemcie heard a well-heeled guest say when Nelia entered the dressage ring on Rex, her burly, warm-blood gelding. Rex enjoyed having his way with her most of the time.

"She's choking up on him. No wonder he tosses his head," a red-haired woman with plumped lips and pale skin whispered into the ear of her friend.

"She has the finesse of a truck driver," the friend with ivory skin and slicked back hair replied, as she smoothed her tidy bun at the nape of her neck.

Nelia must have sensed they were talking about her. Flustered, she gave Rex an impulsion snap with her whip that jolted him off track. She tried to regain control, but he exploded, bucking and tucking his head between his knees. Nearly unseated, Nelia was furious. She lifted her bowler and tipped it to the judges to let them know she was quitting for the day.

"Too bad they can't even pretend she earned a ribbon today," a woman in a long-tailed jacket tittered.

"That horse should make anyone look good."

They snickered into white-gloved hands, taking pains not to let their hostess notice.

"Sorry, darling. You were doing so well," the woman with the bun said as Nelia strode by, letting Rex go on a long-rein.

"I'll take him," Gemcie had said, holding Rex for Nelia while she dismounted.

"What a pig," Nelia spat.

"Maybe I can help?" Gemcie offered.

"What do you know about dressage? I pay you to ride jumpers."

"What could it hurt if I tried?"

"What can you do that no other trainer in this town can?"

"Maybe nothing, but I might see something they missed."

"All right. He can't get worse than he is now," Nelia scowled, removing her black leather gloves. "Be a dear and get me a drink," she said to Jorge.

"It's not even noon."

"Do as I say."

By the end of the day Nelia had lost her testiness, but her bravado during the award ceremonies seemed forced. It looked odd to see heavy black boots sticking out from under the peasant skirt she wore over white riding pants to keep them clean between events. She didn't bother to change from her barn attire for the evening, even though she'd arranged for caterers and live music. She sipped her sixth margarita of the day a bit too gaily, but did not appear to be drunk. The aroma of chicken seasoned with cilantro and chili peppers drifted in from the six-foot grill where they cooked over an open flame. Huge bowls of guacamole, ceviche, and chips kept the guests satiated until the main course was ready. A glowing summer moon rose from behind the crest of the Santa Monica Mountains as a soothing marine breeze drifted down the canyon, arresting the heat of the day.

"You were wonderful today," Gemcie heard a man's voice from close behind her say.

She turned to see Jorge. He had never paid attention to her before, so it surprised her that he'd noticed how she rode that day.

"Marshal was a bit chargy, but we did well, I thought," she said.

"I don't mean with Marshal, I mean with my mother."

"She just needs to lighten up."

"So did Attila the Hun." He flashed a mesmerizing smile.

Gemcie laughed, saying, "Come on. She can't be that bad."

"She's not. She's just used to having her way."

"Like Rex?"

"Yes, like Rex."

The band struck a lively salsa beat.

"Would you like to dance?" Jorge asked.

Gemcie didn't have a lot of experience at dancing, but the pulse of the music shot through her like an electric current. She couldn't say no, especially to the boss's son. Jorge was masterful. He knew exactly how to guide her body through the movements and whirled her about as though she were light as air. At five-eight, Gemcie was not ballerina material, but tonight she felt the picture of petite femininity in Jorge's arms. Nelia stiffened at the sight of them laughing and breathless at the end of each song, but Gemcie didn't notice. All she saw that evening was Jorge's laughing blue eyes.

Gemcie watched Nelia ride Rex the next day. Her position though picture-book perfect was tense. Rex flowed forward too fast and too strong. Gemcie called them to a halt. Rex bobbled, tossing his head trying to free himself from of the constant control of Nelia's strong hand. Gemcie approached Nelia

"May I?" she asked, sliding her hand under Nelia's legs clenched like metal bands around his barrel.

"Your legs are incredibly strong," Gemcie remarked.

"I grew up riding on the pampas," she said as she laughed, flashing perfect white teeth.

"Sounds like fun."

"We rode all day. Jumped everything in our path. It was my life. These wimps try to tell me how to ride. What do they know?"

"Can you concentrate on easing up with your legs and see what happens for me?"

"What happens is a horse shambling about on his own."

"Let's see what happens."

Rex moved more freely, and trained to perfection, he needed little encouragement to do his job. In fact, it seemed to annoy him if anyone felt the need to tell him what to do.

Nelia beamed as she brought Rex to halt. "He is moving forward like a champion."

"You can let go so he can please you. He will be a gentleman if you are not a brute."

"I get the point! You needn't be rude!" Nelia snapped.

"I'm sorry. I didn't mean to offend you. I'm only trying to help."

"Hi, Crash," Gemcie heard a small voice say from far away.

She struggled to pull her awareness back from the recollection, to the surface of her consciousness. All she remembered was the lull of the creek chugging along outside her window before drifting into a drug-induced sleep. A face emerged from the nothingness. She saw Val with warm brown eyes, nestled in auburn lashes, smiling down on her like a guardian angel. Val's skin was even more alabaster than Gemcie remembered, and she had lost the band of freckles across her nose. Her curly red hair blew out on both sides of her face to form a bob of Harpo dimensions. She used to keep her mane subdued in pigtails, but these days it had taken on a life of its own. Val covered Gemcie's slim hand with her own and patted it softly.

"It's so good to see you. I thought you were at school," Gemcie said, struggling to bring herself back to the present.

"I am; I'm on break. I just finished exams."

"Do you like it?"

"I'll like it a lot better when it's over. I've got one semester to go."

"Is your dad still against your being a vet?"

"Yeah, he always wanted a breeder, but I'm just not into making little knockoffs."

"I know what you mean. Jorge and I don't even talk about that. He wants children, but I can't think about that right now."

"How are you doing?"

"You mean when I'm not whacked out on drugs?"

"I mean, how long do they think it's going to take you to mend?"

"Depends upon how fast I can get back to regular exercise."

"You need to stop taking so many pills."

"I know. I'll have to go to re-hab to break my drug habit after this. I'm numb from pain pills."

"You need to get out of that damn bed, even if it's just to get down on the floor, where you can do a few loosening up exercises.

I'll show you."

"Thanks, Val. By the way, you look great," Gemcie said, trying to change the subject. "It's been a year since I've seen you."

"Yeah, that was some wedding."

"Do you want to see what you look like in a dress?"

"Sure."

"Put on the one marked 'Wedding,'" Gemcie said, pointing to the stack of CDs Sue Ellen left to keep her company.

The warped sound of guitars in a Mariachi band came over the speakers. Murmuring voices, clattering silver and the clink of crystal filled the air as servants sashayed through the elite of Hidden Valley, offering appetizers and refills of champagne. Val and Gemcie fell into to fits of titters when Sue Ellen, in a brilliant blue taffeta cocktail dress, filled the computer screen. Her breasts tumbled out of her gown, threatening to fall in the face of the short man talking to her. He leered at her cleavage as she spoke to the pink bald spot on the top of his head. A duffer in a tuxedo sitting behind her ducked to miss the immense bow resting on her behind each time she bobbed in animated conversation.

"Remember those stilettos she was wearing?"

"How can I forget?" Gemcie giggled.

"She nearly toppled over when she danced with Heinrich."

"Yeah, he caught her just before she hit the floor."

Val came into view munching energetically on a Buffalo Wing. She wiped the red sauce dribbling down her chin with the back of her hand. Her auburn hair slicked away from her face exposed bold, honest, boyish features. The only time Gemcie had ever seen Val in a dress was at her wedding. Bridesmaids wore pink satin off-the-shoulder dresses with a sweet bow trailing behind. Jorge's cousins with tapered ankles, tiny waists and pert breasts were visions of femininity in their dresses. Big-boned, with little deviation between hip waist and chest, Val looked like a great pink box tottering down the aisle.

The camera settled on Heinrich, sleek in his tuxedo, nodding to distinguished guests as he passed through the reception line.

"Henry sure knows how to throw a party," Val observed. "First the bubbly, then red wine with the main course, and something even stiffer with dessert.

"It's not just bubbly, it's Dom Perignon."

"Call it what you want. I was plastered by the time the thing was over."

Jorge and Gemcie floated across the screen leading the wedding waltz. She was wearing a winsome lace gown with a form-fitting bodice. Elegant in black tie and tails, Jorge could not have been more dashing.

"You always did clean up nice," Val said. "You look incredible."

"That damn dress was too tight. My tits were shoved up to my chin. I couldn't wait to get out of it."

"Well, if I had Jorge waiting for me at the end of the day, I'd be in a hurry too."

Gemcie realized she was laughing for the first time since her accident.

Nelia, who insisted on taking care of every detail of the wedding, appeared on the screen in a simple yellow gown that took a less than a maternal dip behind, showing off her muscular back. Sue Ellen offered to cater the affair, but barbecued ribs and fries simply were not suitable for a summer afternoon wedding. Instead, Nelia served poached salmon with baby greens in a raspberry vinaigrette. The floors in the great room waxed to gleaming perfection smelled of the rich oils used to condition the wood. The room felt like a chapel, with massive stenciled beam ceilings and prisms of crimson light filtering through the glass roses delicately etched in leaded windows.

Gemcie appeared, marching down the aisle on Billy's arm with her eyes riveted on Jorge.

"You don't even look scared," Val said.

"I had to be brave for Jorge."

"Oh no, this is the part where I cry," Val said just before the video flashed white, and then faded to solid black. "Who edited this, a monkey with a razor blade?" Val laughed.

"Sue Ellen," Gemcie said.

Val was the only one who knew how hard it was for Gemcie to fit in at the Mariposa. They raised their ponies together and cleaned stalls and evented together. In short, they were inseparable until Val decided to become a vet. Gemcie's entire world was the horses before she met Jorge. She never had time to date or go to parties. She was busy preparing for the next event, grooming for the next entry, working the next champion. She had one affair with a farrier named Bobcat, but he was more like a brother than a lover. He kept her company when she had to attend a function that called for a member of the opposite sex to be at her side.

"Maybe when you get out of school, I can talk to Nelia about letting you tend to our horses."

"That'd be good. A gig here would be all I'd need to get my practice going."

"Thanks for coming, Val," Gemcie said, blinking back tears.

"Did you think I wouldn't?" Val returned, squeezing her hand tightly.

"Do me a favor."

"Name it."

"Don't call me Crash!"

"Why not; everybody else does," Val said, dropping the news casually.

"What are you talking about?"

Val squeezed her hand a little tighter and looked down at the floor.

"I'm sorry. I thought you knew."

"Knew what? Damn it; spit it out!"

"Somebody posted a video of your accident on YouTube. It went viral with the headline that says, 'Crash McCauley is knocked out of the running for World Cup.'"

"You know I don't have time for all that crap. Give me the damned computer. Let me see it."

Gemcie went pale as she watched her ride on Marshal. She broke into a clammy sweat and her heart pounded out of her chest as Marshal approached the Liverpool with confident strides. She saw his hoof catch on the rim of the jump and herself flying over his head and landing flat on her back, lying spread-eagle on the grass, knocked-out cold.

He had been moving forward freely, she with him in perfect union. The years of training and practice created the picture of equestrian harmony with her mount. She had felt no fear heading for that fateful jump, but her instincts had betrayed her. The trust she had in Marshal's powerful stride was broken.

"Turn it off!" She glared at Val. "Who did this?"

"I have no clue, but it must have been somebody who was happy to see you knocked off the circuit."

"That could be any rider I ever beat."

"So much for friendly competition."

Gemcie squirmed with humiliation at the thought of everyone in the world seeing her misstep, but it was the acrid taste of fear rising from her belly that scared her the most.

Chapter Four

No position was comfortable long enough for Gemcie to get solid rest. She could stay on her side with a pillow between her knees for twenty minutes, but then she would have to roll onto her stomach. Nelia placed a small portable fridge in her room so she had a fresh ice pack available at all times. When the pain became unbearable, she slipped out of bed onto the floor, placed the ice pack on her lower back and lifted her knees to her chest. The ice would alleviate the inflammation in the nerve long enough to allow her to lie down again.

The spinal fluid settling in the base of her spine during the night created additional pressure, making mornings excruciating. Unable to stand or walk, she had to ring for the servants. Two men arrived with her cot to take her to the swimming pool. Once in the water, the weight of her own muscles lifted off her skeleton, she was temporarily freed from the nagging sciatic pain flowing from her hip to toe. In the last several weeks, the hot molten sensation had subsided to a tingling, as though she had been given ten Novocain shots that wouldn't wear off.

Her right calf and ankle muscles had atrophied. They would not support her weight, even in the water. When she tried to tip-toe across the pool it was as though there were no muscles in her right ankle. The partial paralysis frightened her. As long as there was feeling, no matter how painful, she believed she would recover the use of those parts of her body affected. The numbing and total lack of mobility in her ankle troubled her deeply.

The physical therapist showed her a series of water exercises that she did each morning with the same discipline she applied to her

31

riding. Every two or three hours she would embark on another twenty-minute session of knee-to-chest movements to relieve the pressure on her spine. Lying flat, a pillow under her knees, she listened to meditative tapes directing energy to her injured anatomy, instructing it to heal. She learned how to activate pressure points to encourage energy to flow through her body.

Resting in the sun after her water workout, Gemcie heard the unmistakable purr of her mother's sedan in the drive. A car door slammed, the wrought iron gate clanged shut, and Sue Ellen appeared wearing a sunhat with a mass of bright yellow sunflowers on the brim. Without fanfare she stripped off her flowered caftan, exposing chalk-white skin banded by a two thin strips of bathing suit, to the morning sun. She settled into the low-slung lawn chair beside her daughter.

"Good mornin', darlin', I brought you a present," she said, pulling a package out of her bulging beach bag.

"C'mon, mom, you know I don't need anything."

"Oh yes you do. You've been spending all this time by yourself. You can't tell your old mom you ain't lonely." She plunked a heart-shaped box of chocolates on the table by the pool chaise.

It was true. She did feel horribly alone most of the time. Jorge did come each evening to tell her of his day, bearing fresh roses for her vase, but then he would leave her to join his parents for dinner.

"Rode Nicky today," Jorge told her as he massaged her leg. "She is still heavy from her foal, but she's coming around."

"She is a great dressage horse."

"I wish you were there to help me with her."

"She will teach you if you let her."

Nicky had won many ribbons for the Mariposa. Her filly promised to bring more.

"Maybe Nelia will let my attendants carry me to the dressage ring and I can watch."

"I don't think you are ready yet, my darling. You have to be patient with your body. Mother says you are doing well in the pool."

Gemcie couldn't take her meals with the family. She had to lie on her belly and eat resting on her elbows. It was impossible for her to sit in any fashion.

"Are you sure you don't want me to bring a tray in and eat here with you?" Jorge offered.

"No, this is not your fault. I'd feel silly eating on the floor with you. Besides, I'm sure Heinrich and Nelia love your being there with them more often."

"Have it your way for now, but you will be joining us soon," he said, leaving her to her own thoughts once again.

Her life had become a strange isolated ritual of exercise and meditation. As she soaked in the warming sun, Gemcie fantasized about her husband's six-foot frame, slender hips and flat, muscled belly. She remembered him riding Rex, sitting erect, rigid in the saddle with long legs draping his big barrel. He floated across the arena on the gelding who reached out with extended, elevated strides. The horse's precise movements, after years of professional training and practice, mesmerized all who watched him. For one hour each day Jorge drilled Rex, training the animal to respond to the nuances of weight shifts in his seat and pressure from his legs. The delicate ballet of dressage calls for a direct line of communication between man and beast.

He wore a T-shirt cut off at the midriff exposing almond-brown skin. A dark wet stain between his shoulder blades betrayed the exertion involved in a technique that looked effortless. Gemcie was shocked the day she saw Jorge strike Rex with his dressage whip too fiercely to be called an impulsion snap. She understood that warm-bloods need a wake-up call now and again, but his blow was a lashing out of anger. Jorge struck two, three, then four times, because Rex had bobbled off track. Jorge did not anticipate the imbalance in Rex's movements in time to head it off. Fury overtook him.

"Put that whip down!" Gemcie demanded, crossing the arena to him.

"Mind your own business," snarled Jorge on a now-reeling Rex. Enraged at being chastised, he jerked savagely on the horse's mouth. Unused to such harsh treatment, Rex reared. Jorge rolled backwards, falling with a thud in the sand. Unhurt, but shamed, he jumped up, grabbed the reins to hold Rex in place, while he pummeled his massive neck with his fists. Gemcie took the reins from his hands and placed herself between Jorge and the frightened horse, whose wild eyes rolled white.

"Who do you think you are? Get out of my way," he said, trying to brush her aside.

Gemcie held her ground. "Don't blame him because you can't

33

feel him."

Trembling, Jorge clenched his fists, backed with tense muscular arms.

He calmed down beneath her steady gaze. "I don't know what happened," he admitted, looking past her.

"You are your mother's son; that's all.

"What does that mean?"

"You are so obsessed with yourself that you are disconnected from the horse," she said.

"I don't need pop psychology from you," he said, challenging her with fierce blue eyes.

"I can help," she said calmly.

After a frozen moment staring down at his boots, he'd said, "What could it hurt?" unclenching his fists, letting his stiff shoulders sag.

She worked with him every day for a month, doing exercises to help him become less mechanical, more empathetic in his ride. Nelia watched with increasing concern as she saw him growing closer each day to the young woman who was there for the horses, not for her son. He helped Gemcie with her barn chores, carrying the heavy buckets of special feed she gave to her charges daily. They relaxed together in the lazy afternoons, oiling saddles and cleaning tack in the shade of the oak trees. Nelia had to admit, Jorge, who had never lifted a hand to do chores, was blossoming in this young woman's presence.

Billy came to the Mariposa twice a week to train Marshal and Gemcie in the hunt field. Jorge watched, mesmerized by her grace and fluidity. He admired her finesse and was stirred by her great courage, knowing he did not possess the fortitude to maneuver the powerful stallion over a field of jumps himself. Galloping rhythmically, cleanly to the grassy bank jump, she sailed neatly over and cantered on to the big double brush.

"What a good boy! Oh, what a good boy," she cried, leaning over to pat Marshal vigorously on the neck each time he landed on the correct lead.

"Come on ahead. This time settle in about six strides out," Billy talked her around the course with his megaphone.

Jorge waited by the out gate, holding it open for her and Marshal when her lesson ended. He walked beside her like a well-trained

German shepherd, anticipating her next move.

"I have something I want to show you," he said.

"Let's have a look."

"No, it's not here. I have to take you to where it is."

"Where what is?"

"It wouldn't be much of a surprise if I told you," he said. "Can't you just trust me?"

"Of course."

"Then be here at six tonight, in your riding pants." He smiled broadly.

"Okay," she said, turning her attention back to Marshal, who always got an ice gel brace after a workout. She wondered vaguely about his mysterious surprise, but thoughts of Jorge or anything else were displaced by the concentration required for her to work two horses that afternoon.

Jorge came up behind her while she was putting up the last horse and grabbed her, lifting her off her feet.

"Put me down!" she giggled.

"C'mon. You promised," he said, pulling her away from her chores.

Two quarter horses were tacked and waiting for them. He led the way to the trail that lined the creek and then turned quickly into a steep incline. He charged up through the foliage, rushing for the sky, yahooing wildly as he passed from her sight. Not to be bested, trusting in the horse's sure-footedness, she pressed her mount up the narrow rock-strewn path. Jorge led her on a merry gallop through a meadow speckled with wild flowers, down a ravine where the air was cooled by a stream snaking through the tall grass. They galloped the rim of the mountain to a plateau overlooking the Mariposa. Once there, she could see suburban lights flickering in the distance, interrupted by a black patch that is Lake Sherwood to the north. He hopped off his huffing mount, ran behind a rock and returned with a blanket and a picnic basket filled with goodies and a bottle of champagne.

"What do you think?" he asked with a grin. "This is my secret place."

Behind him, the monster moon beamed boldly down on the Pacific, forming a silver path to the edge of the world. The water danced with the colors of the city lights along the shore.

35

"It seems a person never has to go any farther than this," she said, flush from the heat of the ride.

He poured champagne into the glasses he had hidden earlier.

"I want to share everything with you, Gemcie," he said, gazing into her eyes for assurance. He had come to look to her for courage. She heard a coyote yipping, calling to his lonely kind. She let him pull her to him. She melted into his strength, losing herself to him. She felt weak enveloped in his arms as he kissed her lips and then moved tenderly down her neck, clasping his hands on her firm breasts.

She felt heat rising up her belly as he worked his way down to her navel. Overcome with desire she helped him undress, tearing at his tight riding pants. She grabbed hold of his buns and pressed his hard belly to her. He pulled her to the ground, stripped off her pants and entered her with hard fast thrusts. His deep, forceful penetration sparked her passion. She moaned, writhing with a pleasure she had never known before. She tore at him with a violent longing. He did not relent until they had both reached a sensual crescendo. Once sated, he rolled away from her onto his back and stared up into the star-studded night. A vanilla moon smiled down on their union. When he had caught his breath he turned back to her.

"Will you marry me, Gemcie?" he asked, staring intently into her lavender eyes gleaming in the moonlight.

Gemcie was stunned at the revelation that Jorge wanted to marry her. He was a prince and she a hired hand. How could this be happening? It had not occurred to her that he could actually be in love with her. Yes, they did everything together, and yes, he did respect her abilities as a trainer, but marriage had not entered her mind.

"Yes!" was all she could say, fearing someone would wake her from this dream.

"You won't be sorry, my darling. All that I have is yours."

Shortly after Jorge's proposal, Gemcie was summoned to Heinrich's study. Jorge's father rarely appeared at the barn or the horse shows. In fact, Gemcie barely knew the elegant, withdrawn man. When the war ended he fled his German homeland, settling in South America where he amassed a fortune shipping goods to America. Entirely absorbed in his work, he paid little attention to the inner-workings of the Mariposa. He bought it to keep the stunning woman with panther-green eyes at his side from becoming restless during his long absences on business trips.

Gemcie turned the heavy metal handle on the massive wooden door to his sanctuary, and stepped softly inside. His office, lined floor to ceiling with oak bookcases filled with business chronicles, law books, stacks of Fortune magazines, and volumes of history, smelled of cigars. He was fingering a globe of the earth that rested on a stand near the window overlooking the courtyard. Feeling her presence, he swiveled his overstuffed leather chair about, surveying her with metallic blue eyes before he spoke.

"Sit down, my dear."

Gemcie settled into a comfortable chair facing his massive mahogany desk.

"How old are you?"

"I'm almost twenty."

"My son is just twenty-three. He tells me he is ready for marriage."

"I don't know if anyone is ever really ready for marriage," Gemcie said, flashing an open smile.

"You've enjoyed being a part of Mariposa, haven't you?"

"Yes. It's wonderful, Mr. Schmit. It's everything I could ever want. I am grateful to you and Nelia for sponsoring me."

"Call me Heinrich. My wife tells me you are like a daughter to her," he said as he abruptly stopped the globe from spinning. "She always wanted a daughter."

"I didn't know."

"There are many things you don't know about our family, many things you don't need to know or need to be involved in."

"Yes, certainly, I'm sure of that."

"For instance, the Mariposa belongs to my wife. Should I die it goes to her not my son."

"Makes sense. The ranch and the horses are her life."

He gave the globe a gentle spin and strode to the window, clasped his hands behind his back and stared out into the courtyard below.

"My affairs are complicated. I thought my son would grow bored with the horses, go to law school, travel with me, and learn to handle my business, but he hasn't. He's not prepared to run my estate."

Feeling his disappointment, Gemcie said, "I'm sorry."

37

"He is his mother's son, but he is not too old to change, Gemcie," he said, giving her a warning glance over his shoulder, then continued on without waiting for her response.

"My son has not been tested by life. Nelia has given him everything he ever wanted. That is partly my fault as I have made that possible."

"What is it you are trying to tell me? I know he comes from money and I don't. But he loves me just the same."

"So he has told me. I welcome you into our family, but I want to make certain you are not joining us for the wrong reasons. You understand?"

"I love Jorge, not his money, if that is what you are getting at."

"I've taken the liberty to draw a prenuptial agreement establishing the boundaries of your financial relationship with my family. Naturally, your personal relationship with my son is your own. If you love Jorge, and want your life here to continue as it has been, you will have no objection," he said, turning his gaze upon her, scrutinizing her for her reaction.

Gemcie hesitated for a moment, feeling intensely uncomfortable. The last five years at Mariposa, with the full support and sponsorship of Nelia, had made it possible for her to ride Marshal in all the top events. She believed this happened because of her natural abilities and hard work, but she knew showing horses required huge amounts of money. Self-sufficient all her life, simplistic in her focus on the horse world, she hadn't thought much about marriage, until Jorge asked her. That he loved her was all too wonderful. She couldn't say no.

"I'd like to read it, before I sign."

"Certainly, my dear."

He handed her a document outlining the limits of Gemcie's claims upon his estate. She skimmed it, unable to understand the legalese describing all the assets situated around the globe. Jorge was in line to inherit Heinrich's trucking enterprise along with the monies stashed in offshore accounts. Gemcie was to agree she would receive none of it if the marriage did not survive five years.

"It seems you are betting against our happiness."

"Not at all. Consider this agreement an insurance policy that will encourage you to work out your differences with my son."

It seemed odd to her that Heinrich felt the need for this

arrangement. She had never asked for more than to ride Marshal. Jorge had asked her to marry him, not the other way around. She had no designs on the Mariposa, or any of the family holdings. The horses and riding were all she cared about. She signed the document knowing her love for Jorge was true.

A kiss on the forehead from her mother, who had been sitting at her side for the last hour, brought Gemcie back from her day-dreaming.

"I best be getting back," Sue Ellen said.

"Thanks for coming, mom. I'm sorry I'm not better company."

"It's okay, darlin'. Your old mom is here for you whenever you need a friend. You get your rest. I'll be back tomorrow with bells on."

Chapter Five

A woman's scream roused Gemcie from her fretful sleep. She rolled her head back and forth on her sweat-stained pillow straining to identify the sound. At first she thought someone was hurt, or trapped, and was reaching out to her for help. Opening one eye, emerging from the stupor of drug-induced slumber, she saw the ghost. It was Esmeralda perched just outside her window on the Japanese Magnolia sporting great pink blooms, the more wildly gorgeous for their singular display in winter. The beautiful bird looked directly into her eyes, and thrust its majestic crown forward over its head in a waterfall of white. She was bold and surprisingly tame. She turned in a circle on the bough, spreading her wings to expose yellow plumage. Gemcie felt honored to have her for an alarm clock, but the sight of the bird made her sad. If only she could fly free and leave her body behind.

She got up and shuffled down the dark hall in her slippers in the still morning before the rest of the household stirred. More than once on her way to the pool she had to stop, go onto her back, and put her knees to her chin to alleviate the extreme sciatic pain she endured in the wee hours. She pressed forward to the cool, soothing water that held such relief for her. Once poolside, she slipped into water still crisp from the night air, unmindful of any chill. The instant cessation of the burning in her leg was all that mattered. Soon she was doing systematic laps. The methodical stroking movements took her mind off her pain and set her imagination free to wander.

She saw Marshal prancing in the pasture, twisting his body into frolicsome contortions. He thrust his massive hindquarters high in the air, doing mule kicks, snorting loudly, dancing lightly with hooves seemingly not touching the ground. Vitally alive, vigorous, the picture of equine health, he dashed madly about the pasture testing the limits of his captivity. He could easily sail over the white fence surrounding his playpen, but the thought seemed never to occur to him. Gemcie determined that today was the day she would once again stroke his fine body.

After her swim and a rest in the morning sun, she decided to surprise Jorge. He had shared the last two months' activities with her by bringing her pictures of Chantelle, and telling her of each day's happenings at the barn. The filly was running all the extra weight off her mother. Her legs went so fast they looked like wheels spinning beneath her full-fleshed torso. The thoroughbred in her took over. She was fast, lean, and high spirited. The stable was a quarter mile hike from the main house, but the thought of seeing her in the flesh spurred Gemcie on.

Her heart raced as she walked with the help of a wooden cane down the worn path through the oak grove, across the footbridge. Today it was all new, the smell of fresh-cut grass, the hum of the cicada, the creak of the swaying eucalyptus overhead. Most exhilarating was the realization that walking diminished the pain in her leg. Her ankle no longer gave way with each step. The doctors said walking would be the best strengthener, once she got through the critical stages of her injury. Her heart was soaring with the thought of full recovery in her grasp. She couldn't wait to find Jorge to tell him her news that she was ready to move back into their guest house.

She spied him sitting in the grandstand overlooking the hunt field. She rushed to him as quickly as she could, using the cane for ballast. At first she didn't know which horse he was watching and who was onboard. As she got closer she saw Marshal being worked by someone she couldn't recognize from a distance. Billy was on the ground directing horse and rider over a few fences.

"Keep him straight then just let him go," Billy yelled on his megaphone.

Close enough to see the trim, erect body of Dominique aboard Marshal, Gemcie froze in disbelief. Gemcie was the only one allowed to ride Marshal. His rhythm and movements indelibly melded into her psyche could be affected by another rider.

"Come again, this time stay off his face," she heard Billy say, but the action of what was happening became a blur. A sea of emotion plowed over her like a desert flash flood. Blood raced to her cheeks. Her face turgid, eyes aflame, she grabbed Jorge by the shoulder and pulled him around to face her.

"What is this?" she demanded. "What is she doing on Marshal?"

"I wanted to tell you, but it I didn't want to upset you," he said.

"Tell me what?"

"Nelia wants Dominique to ride Marshal in the World Cup qualifier."

"You can't mean this."

He held his hands on her shoulders and spoke directly into her angry eyes. "You must understand. Marshal is fit. He's ready now. A year from now no one knows what may come. Look at you," he said, dropping his eyes down to his dust-covered paddock boots.

He was unable to finish his statement about her obvious condition.

"And you always do what Nelia says, don't you!" She spat out the words in anger.

Stunned to know that Marshal was to go on without her, she turned away from Jorge, walked to the rail and watched as Billy, the man who had said he would wait for her, coaxed Dominique over the coffin jump. Even though her leg throbbed with new intensity, she crawled between the rails and made her way to Billy with the aid of her walking stick.

Billy signaled Dominique to bring Marshal to a halt when he saw Gemcie approaching. Dominique pulled him up and walked on a long rein towards the oncoming Gemcie. Marshal nickered to her softly. Gemcie marched past Billy to Marshal, grabbing hold of his strong solid neck and hugging him with all her strength. She wanted to melt into his velvet coat and fly away with him. Pulling strength from him, she turned to confront Billy.

"Why didn't you tell me?" She glared at him in disbelief.

"I couldn't," Billy said, "It was part of the deal."

"What deal?"

"That I should work with Marshal and Dominique up through the qualifier. Nelia felt it would be better for you if you didn't know."

Gemcie couldn't see Dominique's eyes behind her mirrored sunglasses, but her petulant lips, pursed into the shape of a heart, hinted at her smug satisfaction. She had been trying to catch a steady ride for the entire season, and through an ugly twist of fate, had landed on Marshal. Gemcie turned and walked back to Jorge.

"I want out of Nelia's house. I am moving home today," Gemcie said, with a trembling voice that gave way to a flood of uncontrollable tears.

Jorge held her shuddering shoulders in his arms, letting her tears dampen his T-shirt.

"Certainly, my darling, I'll see to it."

He put his arm around her stiff shoulders, giving her support as she limped toward the small white cottage with green trim. He opened the Dutch door for her to enter, leaving the top part of the door ajar.

"I will go to the house now and get your things." Feeling her sorrow seemed to make him uncomfortable. He wanted to get away from her as quickly as he could.

Alone, Gemcie crossed to the mantle crowded with riding trophies and pictures of her holding blue ribbons, and swept them off with her cane. They smashed onto the rough-hewn wood floor. Her gaze fell upon a photo of her standing next to Marshal when he was just a foal with her arm around his neck. He came to her waist and leaned on her body for balance. He had a short scruffy tail and shapely haunches. They were standing knee-deep in wildflowers in the meadow by the stream. Gemcie's eyes were on the sparkling silver water stealing through the meadow, while Marshal cast a sideways glance over his shoulder to the camera. She picked up the splintered glass from the silver frame, and placed the picture back upon the mantle of the river-rock fireplace.

Striking a match, she turned the handle on the gas stove and lit the burner beneath the tea kettle. Soon the copper pot hissed, and steam rose from the spout. Gemcie poured the boiling water into her favorite mug, releasing the rich aroma of apple cinnamon tea. Sitting was still uncomfortable, so she took her tea to the floor and lay on the braided rug before the black, still hearth. Exhausted, hurt and confused, she wanted somehow to start over.

There was a gentle knock at the door.

"May I come in?" Gemcie recognized Nelia's voice, but she didn't want to talk to her.

"What do you want?"

"I want you to understand," Nelia said, as she slipped inside the door, crossing to where Gemcie rested on the floor with knees bent. She eased down to the floor, brushing aside the fallen trophies, and sat on folded legs beside Gemcie.

"For five years I've supported your career, given you every advantage. No one is more talented on a horse than you, but life doesn't stop because you are injured."

"I didn't ask it to stop. I just hoped it could wait a little while."

"What if it was Marshal that was injured? Would your career wait for him? He has his own destiny separate from yours. He is in his prime, bred and groomed for this moment. Do you really want to stand in his way?"

Gemcie lifted her eyes from the steaming tea mug that held no answers, and met the intense green eyes of her benefactor. She trembled, unable to keep herself in check. Tears welled and then streamed down her fair cheeks.

"No, I don't want to stand in his way," she stammered, giving way to the wave of emotion overwhelming her.

Nelia took her hand in her own and kissed the tips of her fingers.

"I didn't tell you about Dominique because I was afraid it would slow your progress. You've been doing so very well. Billy will take care of Marshal. I'll tell Manuel he is to do whatever you ask of him. He will run errands, get groceries, whatever you need, as long as you want him."

"Thank you, Nelia," Gemcie said softly, subdued by the force of her reality. "I'd really like to be alone for a while."

"Of course," Nelia said, rising. "Get some rest, darling. I'm sorry I didn't tell you sooner."

Chapter Six

The passing weeks turned to months. The sycamore leaves curled to brown cigars that crumbled under Gemcie's feet on her morning walk while the marine layer still hugged the valley floor. She rose with Jorge, who left at 5:30 each morning to ride four horses before lunch. She loved to be up before the rest of the world got started. Not that she lacked solitude, but there was something stirring about the pearly skies of dawn mixed with crisp fall air. She was able to hike on flat ground for a couple of miles without her walking stick. Her favorite walk took her along the creek past bulrushes where the red-winged blackbirds sounded like electric guitars out of tune. On her rounds she often saw a big blue heron balanced on spindly legs, like a frozen ballerina.

Living closer to the stable now, she found chores she could do standing. Grooming Marshal was her favorite pastime. She snapped a towel all over his body, stimulating the blood to rise to the surface. She used a round grooved curry to lift the dander from his coat then swiped it off with a soft thick brush. His black eyes pooled with tenderness when she rubbed under his chin with the brush. He stretched his neck full length to assist her in getting maximum coverage over the thick muscles of his chest. She brushed his coarse black tail that nearly touched the ground until it floated free in the breeze.

Jorge tacked him up for Dominique for her sessions with Billy three times a week. The World Cup qualifier was coming up fast. It was hard for Gemcie to watch her work Marshal because her style was so different from Gemcie's. A strict disciplinarian, she forced him into a tight frame. Yes, he looked beautiful this way with neck arched, chin to chest, haunches rounded, but it was unnatural for him. Gemcie rode him in a hunter frame, more forward and flowing than what Dominique allowed him.

Billy pulled up in his truck in a cloud of dust. He was late and seemed rushed. Something was on his mind. He walked briskly into the hunt field where Marshal and Dominique were warming up at the trot.

"I told you not to use draw reins on him!" Billy snapped.

"He needs to be more collected!" Dominique responded sharply.

"Well, you can just take that artillery off. My horses are trained, not manhandled into where I want 'em to be."

"He's been tossing his head; I don't want to get hit in the face, if you don't mind." Dominque glared back at Jimmy in defiance.

"Well, I do mind, Missy. Now take them off!" Billy demanded.

Dominique lifted her feet from the stirrups and hopped down in a huff. She undid the cinch and slid off the draw reins that shackled Marshal's movements and threw them aside.

"If I get hurt, it's your fault."

"Stop pulling on his mouth and he won't toss his head. You are not ridin' him right."

"Give me a leg up," Dominique acquiesced, at least for the moment.

Billy cupped his hands for her to use to spring back up on the seventeen-hand stallion. "All right, then, canter 'round a couple of times. Get 'im going in a nice easy rhythm," Billy said, pulling his emotions back into check.

Obviously agitated, Dominique had trouble getting Marshal to relax into a rocking-chair gait. She weighted him with her seat, sitting erect, head high with legs firmly on his sides, attempting to keep him from racing forward. He was high, switching his tail sharply. Angry, Dominique jabbed him with her spur. Marshal exploded in a rolling buck rivaling any Billy had seen in the rodeos of his youth. An expert rider, Dominique stuck like Velcro, riding out the bending, twisting mule kicks designed to get her off his back and into the dust. It was the longest thirty seconds of her life, but she was able to get him back under control. Furious, she circled him sharply, bending his head into his shoulder and forcing him into a tight circle.

"Get off that horse!" Billy yelled.

"Your good ole boy ways nearly got me killed!" she shot back.

"Let loose of 'im, or I'm going to pull you down from there," Billy said, more harshly than Gemcie had ever heard him speak to anyone.

Dominique released Marshal from the hamstrung position she had twisted him into, allowing his head to relax down to the ground. He appeared subdued by this treatment, but Gemcie knew he was confused. Her heart was crying out to him, but there was nothing she could do.

"You are going to have to find yourself another trainer, Missy. You and me are oil and water," Billy said, lifting his hat with his hand, wiping the sweat from his forehead with his sleeve. He stomped off the field without another word. Gemcie watched dumb-founded as the cloud of dust behind his truck disappeared down the gravel road and out the gate of Mariposa. She knew he would not be back. She had never seen him lose his temper with his students or the animals. Though secretly pleased that Marshal had nearly tossed Dominique, Gemcie worried who his next trainer would be and who was going to watch over Marshal.

The qualifier was coming up fast. It was late to call in another trainer. Maybe Nelia would decide to withdraw Marshal from the competition. Gemcie went to Marshal's stall after Dominique put him away. He didn't nicker at her approach. His head was down. He snuffled the sawdust in his stall, seeming to ignore her presence. She stroked the white blaze on his forehead and spoke softly to him.

"I'm so sorry, big fella," she said, knowing that she had betrayed him.

She could feel his melancholy. She couldn't explain to him why she couldn't ride him anymore. He sensed his life had changed, but was unable to fathom why. Assigned to her at birth, he wanted to please. He looked up at her with forlorn eyes, still not lifting his head from the stall floor. He looked like child trembling from the first slap of a disciplining parent. The guilt she felt over his confusion was unbearable.

When Jorge returned that evening she couldn't keep still.

"What is Nelia going to do?"

"She is looking for another trainer."

"Can't she just forget this year's Cup and wait until I'm better? She knows I'm the only one that can ride Marshal to a win."

"Gemcie, we've talked about this before. The Mariposa is not a charity. Nelia wants that prize money. She has paid for Marshal's care and his training for five years."

"I guess that is all I am to her. A paid servant."

"I am sorry to be cruel. You know that I love you and so does Nelia. This has been hard for her too."

She nestled her head on his shoulder and tried not to think about what was going to happen to Marshal if Dominque had her way with him.

The next day when Gemcie returned from a long walk on Nicky, she spotted a new truck in the parking lot. It must be another trainer here for an interview, she surmised.

Curious, she headed for the covered arena to see what was up. Nelia was on the ground watching Dominque put Marshal through his paces while a man in spit-polished riding boots and spotless full seat dressage pants barked out commands.

"Squeeze him up. More impulsion. Let him know you are in charge," came from the stranger with a French accent. Jock Sherone, a top dressage trainer who was new in town, had worked with Dominque in France and taught her in the classical style of fine riders all over the world. Dominque clucked Marshal forward, pressing him into a rounded frame with neck arched so tightly his nose was nearly touching his chest.

"Lovely!" came from Nelia.

Unable to watch the transformation in progress, Gemcie turned away. Needing to be alone she went to the stables and tacked up Nicky. She was able to ride now, at a quiet pace. Rocking softly back and forth on the bare back pad massaged the muscles of her bottom. She let her legs dangle around Nicky's big barrel. It relieved her of the nagging, tingling sensation in her right leg, and Nicky enjoyed getting out. She ponied Chantelle with them down the oak-shaded path that lined the boulder-strewn creek. Tears flowed as she talked herself into accepting that Marshal had to move on in his training without her.

Doing chores around the cottage took her mind off her frustrations. Manuel drove her to town to get groceries. He carried all her bags and pushed the cart while she tossed ingredients for special treats for Jorge into the basket. She'd never done much cooking. Sue Ellen always took care of that chore when she lived at home. Her whole life had been arranged to enable her to become a top rider.

She stood at the tiny sink below her kitchen window overlooking the hunt field, where the windmill blades circled in silence. Clinching a saltine cracker between her teeth to prevent the tears from streaming, she minced onion for chowder. Cleaning, peeling, dicing and chopping ingredients for a dish to please Jorge was relaxing and made her feel useful. She had learned to bake bread. The aroma of the dough rising and crisping over in her oven filled the tiny cottage.

She even enjoyed doing the laundry. The rhythmic chug of the washing machine churning Jorge's clothes, the steaming warmth rising from the dryer, whirling towels dry, all grounded her mind. Folding his warm cotton undershirts and briefs in tidy piles gave her a purpose for that day. To please him she decided to line his drawers with fresh paper. She lifted the dusty old paper to discover a small plastic packet. She held it up to examine it more closely. It was a condom. Gemcie used other protection. A dark shadow of suspicion clouded her mind. It could only be there for one reason.

Jorge returned at day's end hot from putting four horses through their paces. He was doing some of the workouts she used to do for Nelia's horses. He popped the top off a beer, plopped down on the verandah and put his booted feet up on the wooden table. She joined him in their evening ritual of watching the sun set behind the stack of purple mountains that sheltered their world. Leaning on his muscled shoulder she nestled into the golden mat of hair on his chest, smelling his rich musky odor. She felt the solid pounding of his heart on her cheek. He kissed the top of her head and tousled her champagne-blonde mane.

"How's my girl?" he asked.

Eager to see him at the end of the day, she didn't want to ruin the moment, but she needed to confront him.

"It was lovely; I got worlds done. I'm able to take care of our house by myself now."

"But you don't need to."

"I do need to for now." Gemcie hesitated to ask what she felt she had to know, letting her eyes rest on the magenta horizon fast shifting to dark purple stains on the sky. The burnt-red sun slipped behind the clouds before she mustered the courage to ask.

"What is this?" She held up the condom for him to see.

"Where did you find that?" he asked, taken by surprise.

"In your drawer," she said, lifting her head from his shoulder to see if she could see a lie in her young husband's eyes.

"That's left over," he said.

"Left over from when?"

"Do you remember when my father took me on that business trip just before we were married?"

"Yes."

"He believed a young man should have some experience under his belt to know how to keep his wife happy. He gave me the gift of a 'professional' on that trip. Those were to protect you."

Gemcie, now relieved, rested her head back on Jorge's shoulder.

"I'm sorry I haven't been in the mood lately," Gemcie said.

"It's all right, my darling; you have enough on your plate," he said, giving her a gentle massage up and down her spine. She felt satisfied with his answer, but a seed of doubt that was never there before had been planted.

The next morning while scrubbing the remnants of the bacon and eggs on breakfast plates, Gemcie became mesmerized by the rotating blades of the windmill in the hunt field outside her kitchen window. The rush of sailing over the double-brush jumps in the distance was fresh in her mind. She saw herself galloping up the ramped bank, popping nicely over the other side, and cantering calmly to the double brush. If she could show Nelia that she could ride, she would see that Gemcie was the one to take Marshal to the World Cup, not Dominique. Billy would come back. Together, they could get Marshal back on track in no time. Jorge left early that morning with Nelia to look at a mare she was considering adding to the breeding stock.

Her heart raced with excitement as she pulled on green stretch jodhpurs. She hadn't donned her riding habit for months. Stepping into her boots, pulling up custom zippers, she felt the old surge of adrenaline waking her body. Marshal was munching placidly on his morning hay when she arrived at his stall. He barely lifted his head from his breakfast as she brushed the night's straw off his coat, and placed the hunt pad on his back. She finished tacking him up at the rail. She carried her jump saddle close to her body so she wouldn't strain herself lifting it to his back. She cinched the girth in tight from the height of the mounting block.

Marshal let her slip the snaffle bit into his mouth and the bridle over his soft ears. She scratched under his chin, and patted his massive chest. Her heart was pounding as she slipped softly onto his back from the mounting stand. Once into the hunt field, she let him walk on a long-rein. He stretched his neck to the ground, snorting at the dew-covered grass. Soon she had him going at a brisk trot. He felt stiff and choppy. She continued to let him go on a loose rein, hoping he would relax. Worried Jorge and Nelia would return and try to stop her from riding Marshal, she rushed her warmup.

Moving up to a canter, standing in the stirrups taking her weight off his back, she felt the tingling sensation ribbon up and down her leg. Pressing forward, taking her thoughts from her own body, transferring her focus to Marshal's movements, she looked ahead through his perked ears to see where they were going. After a couple of relaxed laps around the arena, she directed him to the ramped bank they had jumped with ease so many times before. He approached it with the same aggressive vigor, but now he tossed his head. Gemcie had trouble keeping him straight, but he went over anyway.

She turned towards the brush jump. A dull pain mounting in her knee pulled at her concentration. She blocked it out, clenching her mouth tightly, heading onto the imposing spread. Her mind fluttered nervously as she faced the jump. Marshal became chargy and unruly, switching his tail. The strong intent that previously ruled her being, now faltered. She saw disaster looming. She tried to keep her focus on the other side of the jump, but it was diverted by the jagged pain ripping through her leg. Marshal took off early, barely clearing the jump, his heels rubbing the brush. He landed with a jarring thud. Gemcie, unseated, nearly flew over his head. Winded and badly shaken, she realized she couldn't hold herself in the perfectly upright position she needed to stay with his movements. They were out of sync! But, more than that, she was terrified that she would fall again. In the last year her body had healed enough for her to ride, but she was not sure this new sensation of being frozen in terror would ever go away. Defeated, Gemcie knew it was too dangerous for her to ride in competitions.

She let Marshal again walk on a long rein while she caught her breath. She gave him a few, solid brisk slaps to the neck to let him know it wasn't his fault. Still trembling, she put him away, kissing him softly on his velvet nose. Slapping her crop lightly on the side of her leg, she stared down at her polished boots that didn't feel right anymore. On her way back to the cottage she met Nelia going to the stables.

"I saw you on Marshal. You looked like you were in trouble."

"I won't do it again," Gemcie said, unable to meet Nelia's intense gaze.

"I know how much you want to be better. These things take time. You can't rush them," she consoled, wrapping her arm around Gemcie's shoulder.

"How did the mare look?" Gemcie asked, to change the subject.

"What mare?"

"The one you took Jorge to see this morning."

"I've been home all morning going through papers with Heinrich," she said.

The ferret in the pit of Gemcie's stomach unfurled, scratching her insides with its needle-sharp claws. She felt light headed and weak.

"I need to lie down," she said.

"Of course, darling, you need to be kind to yourself," Nelia said, feeling Gemcie's ache. She put her arm around her, giving her a hug. She had power over all things at the Mariposa, but there was nothing she could do to make recovery easier for her daughter-in-law.

"I must get to Rex. He hasn't been ridden for three days. He'll be high as a kite for the show if I don't work him today," Nelia said, and continued on to the barn.

The next day found twenty eighteen-wheelers packed into the lower pasture of the Mariposa for the first spring show. The prize horses snorted hot breath, sniffing their new surroundings as they were led down loading ramps. Proud owners filled with anticipation and high hopes paraded past one another in the chilly gray morning, hand-walking their mounts. The horses crunched through the crumbling sycamore leaves that lined the creek, stretching muscles stiff from a long haul. The crisp air of March, after long layoffs, made this the best show of the year. The fine animals were bright, energized, and eager for the event.

Gemcie wore a lavender turtleneck with a matching blazer and black slacks. Her sun-blonde hair bounced in natural ringlets. Cheeks blushed with pink, a swath of dark shadow on deep-set blue eyes and a hint of color on her lips gave her a soft allure. She'd never attended a show in street clothes before. She felt awkward and out of place but determined she would not pretend to be a rider that day. She would greet guests and direct them to the grandstands as they arrived in the shuttle from the parking lots.

Nelia dashed from the barn to the dressage ring, barking last minute orders to field hands. She again wore the peasant skirt over her white riding pants to keep them spotless for her dressage test on Rex. Flower boxes, brimming with blood-red roses, marked the test letters on the ring. Classical guitar music floated from the loudspeakers in the corners of the arena as the judges took their seats in the stand overlooking the arena, preparing for the first ride of the day.

"Where is Jorge?" Nelia almost screamed. "He's riding his mare after me!"

"He left early this morning. I thought he was with you," Gemcie answered.

"Find him," Nelia hissed through her teeth.

Gemcie wandered through the bustling crowd trying to think where her husband might be. He wasn't at the cottage. He wasn't getting Nicky ready to go. Maybe he was at the main house. Her eyes wandered over to the trailers in the lower pasture for a clue. She spotted Dominique's Explorer parked next to the Oaks eighteen-wheeler. She must be riding one of their horses; she wasn't riding Marshal today. Something pulled her towards the trailer. Dust settled on her black loafers as she made her way across the crowded pasture, avoiding getting stepped on by a horse being hand-walked by its rider.

She noticed a slight bobbing of the trailer hitch as she approached the changing room at the front of the Oaks eighteen-wheeler and felt a vicious bite in the pit her stomach. Unyielding, she drew closer. Her hand trembled as she touched the cold metal of the door handle, not wanting to know what was inside, but needing to quell the raging fury of mounting suspicion in her mind. She jerked the door open to see the muscled legs of Dominique clamped around Jorge's waist. Sitting on a camp chair, legs spread wide, jodhpurs around his ankles, he held Dominique in place on his lap. Surprised, but nonplused, Dominque cast Gemcie a haughty, triumphant smile over her bare shoulder. Jorge was too stunned to do anything and just stared at her like a deer in headlights.

Gemcie slammed the door.

53

The world around her, blurred by tears, spun out of control. She ran through the crowd of milling horses, causing one to rear.

"Hey! Watch it! You scared my horse."

"Who let you in here?" Came from another rider trying to avoid Gemcie's mad dash.

Soon, Jorge came running behind her, but she managed to reach the cottage where she grabbed her riding pants and boots, and ran to Marshal's stall before he could catch her. Marshal stopped munching on hay and nickered sweetly to greet her. She held her tears in check as she tacked him up. Unmindful of any pain, she swung up on him without the aid of the mounting block.

Marshal was not allowed to trail. He was much too valuable to risk being rock bruised. Gemcie headed for the trail she rode many times with Jorge to their special place. Marshal, beside himself with excitement, trembled at the chance to be outside. Snorting, prancing, he pulled to be free. Gemcie held him back until they reached the incline that would take them to the plateau overlooking the Mariposa, and then she let him have his way. His great strength unleashed, he exploded up the trail with such power she could barely stay with him. The shoulder-high sage was a blur as he charged ever upward, giddy with his new freedom. With heart pounding, Gemcie ducked low-hanging limbs, fast leaving the world behind. Marshal leaped over a whispering creek intersecting the trail, and lurched up the steep incline on the other side. Ears pricked, black mane flowing, neck glistening with sweat, his ferocious energy unchained, he was finally free to be the stallion he was born to be. Gemcie kept her head low, close to the crest of his mane, clinging to his mighty frame as he barreled up the trail that narrowed when it wrapped the rim of the cliff. She finally slowed him to navigate huge gouges in the trail that threatened to give way if they dared travel too close to the edge. Marshal charged up the last rock-strewn stretch of trail to the plateau overlooking the valley.

Gemcie circled Marshal to allow him to catch his breath and calm down. Still energized, he whinnied out over the canyon, calling to his kind. Gemcie took her feet out of the stirrups, allowed her legs to stretch down, lifted her torso and dropped her head back, with eyes to the sky. She spread her arms out, turning palms to the sun, mimicking Indians on war ponies beseeching power from the Great Spirit. She felt Marshal's energy rising up through her body and the warm sun blessing her upturned face. Tears came like a torrent, running down her flushed cheeks unchecked. She slumped forward over the saddle, hugging Marshal, letting her body drape him loosely. He stood strong, still and brave, with pricked ears attuned to the wind. She let loose the violent coil of confusion inside her, sobbing into his thick mane.

Tears spent, she stared at Hidden Valley spread out below, segregated in tidy chunks of green pastures divided by white fencing. A faded brown church with turquoise spires sitting on a lonesome hill watched over the residents. She saw the windmill in the hunt field of the Mariposa twirling slowly in the breeze that drifted through the canyon each afternoon. She knew her time here was over. This would be the last time she would share a sweet surrender to Marshal's great strength. This world no longer belonged to her. She wiped her face with her sleeve, gathered the reins and began the descent to the barn.

Marshal shambled down the backside of the peak where the footing was loose rock and shale. She leaned back in the saddle, careful not to rock about as he sashayed down the steep descent in a swaying mambo step. Once on the meadow floor, heavy with the spicy aroma of sage, the going was easy. They marched through purple lupine and sticky monkey. She let Marshal take a drink at the creek that softly tumbled over rocks covered in a cloak of green moss, the wild part of him stirred by the scents on the wind.

When she returned to the Mariposa, the trailers had left. She must have been gone hours. Nelia would be furious, but none of it mattered now. She put Marshal up and went back to the empty cottage. She let herself fall face-down on the white linen bedcover. The salty taste of her husband's semen rose in her throat as she sobbed inconsolably. She felt weighted to the bed, not knowing what she would do, what she could possibly say to him when he returned.

She didn't rise when she heard a soft rapping on the door. It opened, allowing a bright shaft of sunlight into the darkened room. Nelia entered, went to her daughter-in-law, sat beside her on the bed, and rubbed a strong brown hand in a warming circle on her back, as she spoke slowly and deliberately.

"You should not have taken Marshal. He could have been hurt."

Gemcie didn't respond. She turned her head away from Nelia.

"I'm sorry, little one that you had to grow up so soon. My son is more like his father than he knows."

Gemcie turned her head to face her, asking, "What do you mean?"

"I wasn't much older than you, but I was heavy with Jorge when I learned that to be a woman is to know sorrow."

Gemcie cast a tearful glance over her shoulder at the woman she believed was the enduring power, the matriarch, the pride of her husband, to see a compromised creature delivering the sad burden of truth she believed belonged to all women.

"Why did you stay?"

"Heinrich has always done what he wanted to do. In exchange for my understanding, he gave me my son and the Mariposa. It is an arrangement that grows sweeter with time."

An overwhelming pity welled in Gemcie's heart, not just for the woman before her, but for herself. This was not a truth she could accept; not now, not ever.

"I can't be like you, Nelia. I am leaving."

Chapter Seven

"How about a job at the Smoker? I can't just lounge around the house all day, I'll go nuts," Gemcie told Sue Ellen, who was busy rustling up breakfast for her daughter.

"I didn't bust my butt for you to end up slingin' hash," Sue Ellen said, placing a plate loaded with sausages, pancakes and eggs in front of Gemcie. "Kate said you could come back to the Circle K and help her with chores there. She needs all the help she can get."

"I don't remember asking you to bust your butt for me."

"Everything I've ever done was for you."

"Yeah, well, try doing something for yourself!"

Sue-Ellen spun around and glared at Gemcie, while wiping her hands on her apron.

"If I didn't know you were hurting inside I'd probably slap the crap out of you. Whose house do you think you're living in?"

*****

Six weeks at Sue Ellen's had been almost intolerable. As a kid, Gemcie never thought much about their arrangement. She just ran out the door each morning, grabbing her jacket off the antique hat rack in the hall that held umbrellas and boots, and headed for the barn. Now when she returned to the Circle K, her childhood barn, she saw the sagging fences gnawed to crescents by horses given to cribbing. Ramshackle jumps lay on their sides. The stalls needed painting, and the roses were dead.

She was brushing the sawdust off the rump of Kate's mare at the tie-rack with a couple of the other boarders getting their horses ready for their workouts.

"Heh, Crash, heard you won't be riding for the Mariposa anymore," came from a slim-hipped brunette.

Although she maintained her composure, Gemcie flushed at the thought that every person she ever met, and some she hadn't, had witnessed her fall.

"That's right. Dominque is riding Marshal."

"I heard that's not all she's riding." This came from the blonde cowgirl picking the packed straw from her horse's hoof.

Both girls giggled with that revelation.

"Who told you that?" Gemcie demanded, on the verge of losing it.

"I couldn't help but see it at the Memorial Day show. She is stuck to him like crazy glue."

Gemcie didn't know how to respond. She wanted to evaporate into thin air.

"I've got work to do," she said, leading the mare into the workout arena. She mounted and tried to tune out the humiliation of the day by focusing on her ride. She put the mare through her paces with sit to trot, post to trot, extended trot and a little side passing. The sound of a red hawk screeching overhead was her only distraction.

She saw a shiny black Mercedes bounce slowly across the rocky creek bottom that every vehicle had to navigate when entering the Circle K ranch. A woman about forty-five in a fresh white equestrian blouse, stain-free jodhpurs and new boots parked the car and strode toward her.

"You're Gemcie McCauley, I believe?" she said with a broad smile.

"Yes, I am. What can I do for you?"

"I saw you ride in the Grand Prix last year. You were great."

"Thanks."

"I heard you're giving lessons now."

"Who told you that?"

"Why, Kate did. I've got a wonderful warm blood I just bought. I've never ridden and I want to start, right away."

"Okay. Why don't you tack up and I'll be with you in a minute?"

Gemcie found Kate working her filly in the round pen.

"I've never given lessons."

"There's no time like the present."

"That woman is green as spring grass."

"That's right; she's not going to know much of anything about riding for at least a year. So what could it hurt?"

"Her horse, for starters."

"It's her horse."

"Right."

Gemcie went back to the arena to find the woman in full leather chaps, hard hat and spurs. She was walking a regal bay with white sox and a blaze, on a loose rein.

"This is Dandy. He's beautiful, don't you think? He won a whole bunch of ribbons in the junior jump-offs," she boasted, beaming.

"Yeah, he's a beauty. You can start this lesson by taking your spurs off," Gemcie said.

"He's dull to the leg; I'll never get him going."

"Take the spurs off or *we'll* never get going."

The woman looked at Gemcie with an air of confusion.

"You wear spurs."

"I know what to do with them."

"Really!" she exclaimed, obviously offended.

"You have to build the muscle in your legs to hold your position and give cues through your body; the spurs are just a reminder."

"All right," she said, removing her spurs.

"Now you can take your feet out of the stirrups and raise them up. You won't be needing them for a while."

"I can't ride without stirrups!"

"You are going to learn how. It will help you find your balance, and save you if you lose your stirrup over a jump, or at a gallop."

The woman managed at a walk, so Gemcie called for a trot. A bit hefty in the beam, she bounced from side to side like a sack of russets. Her thighs had the consistency of Jell-o. Before Gemcie could call her to a halt, the woman slipped off the English saddle into a heap on the sandy bottom of the arena.

"I hope you are satisfied," she sputtered, hot tears rolling down her red cheeks.

"I'm so sorry. Are you okay?" Gemcie asked, as she hurried to help her up.

"No. I'm not okay, and if you think I'm going to pay you for systematic torture, you're mistaken," she snapped, rolling over onto her knees, not allowing Gemcie to help her up. She brushed off her back side and limped out of the arena with Dandy in tow.

Gemcie headed back to Kate's grooming table.

"How'd it go?" Kate asked.

"Not too good," Gemcie said, flopping down on a canvas chair, letting her legs go wide.

"She's a pretty tough customer, but I've got others who could use your help."

As Kate rubbed liniment on her filly's legs, Gemcie watched the tail of a white Hanoverian cock-up each time he went over a jump at the fancy barn next door. It was a full training facility with a hunt field, hot walker and top trainers. The Circle K was the dilapidated home of geriatric horses and green riders. Fly specks coated the table where Kate sat under the shade of her oak tree. Gemcie hadn't noticed the barn earlier because she was so busy tacking, grooming, mucking stalls, cleaning saddles, or riding. Without a horse to take care of she was extraneous to the activities at the barn and so saw it in a different light. After life at the Mariposa, working at the Circle K was an embarrassment.

"You know I used to jump for a living," Kate said, blowing smoke through her nose. She held a cigarette between thin fingers, capped with chipped nails with dirt under them. Once beautiful, she'd long ago turned herself over to the grit of the barn, letting the elements have their way with her. Her bronzed skin was etched with deep grooves from the drying sun. She kept her thick strawberry blonde hair, which went to her waist, contained in a heavy braid. Her doe-brown eyes were hidden in the shadows below a straw Stetson.

"You did?"

"That's right. I made about $500 a week from my riding. That was a lot then. I had three kids at the time that needed shoes."

"I didn't know that either!"

"My husband doesn't like me to talk about it. He didn't want me to ride. He was sure I would get hurt."

"Did you?"

"No, but I used to get sick before every event. I was so worried about cracking up, being left unable to take care of my kids; I finally let it go, Gemcie. My family meant more to me than riding, so I found another way to be with my horses."

Gemcie looked away from Kate distracted by the swish of the

white tail attached to the rump of the Hanoverian. Kate, sucking on her ever-present cigarette, seemed to be a poignant picture of loss to Gemcie.

"I can't do that, I'm a rider," she heard herself saying to Kate.

*****

"What are you day-dreaming about now?" Sue Ellen said, trying to bring her daughter to her senses. "Things don't always work out the way we want."

"All I know is I can't lay around here watching soap operas. I don't fit in at the barn anymore. Maybe I could go back to school. I'd be a senior on campus, but that's okay."

Sue Ellen plopped down in the chair beside the breakfast table, and looked her daughter in the eye.

"I spent my whole life scraping and sacrificing so you could rise to the top. One little setback and you are ready to throw it all away," she said.

"Mom, this isn't one little setback. I can't ride. Even if I could I don't have the money to compete. I don't even have a horse."

"You are going to get plenty of money from that spoiled little rich kid you married. You went to see the attorney, like I told you?"

"Yes, mom, I saw her, but I don't expect to get much from the settlement."

"Why not, he kicked you when you were down, didn't he?"

"Let's just say, I wasn't what he wanted after all," Gemcie returned, staring down at the eggs getting cold on her plate. She didn't know how to tell her mother she had signed a pre-nuptial that disavowed her of any monetary gain if the marriage failed.

"Look, mom, thanks for making me breakfast, but I wish you'd stop giving me these lumberjack portions. I've gained ten pounds."

Sue Ellen stood up, gathered the dishes with the half-eaten breakfast and scraped the plate in the sink.

"Okay, you looked downright scrawny for a while, but I guess I can ease off. I've got to get going. You want to come into the Smoker, you can. I think you should be thinking about getting that operation. I've talked to a lot of folks that have. They were fit as a fiddle in about six weeks."

"You can forget that idea. I'm not having an operation! That's

61

final!"

"You are one pig-headed girl, Gemcie. Of course, you come by it naturally.

"What do you mean?"

Sue Ellen turned back to the dishwater, rinsing off the breakfast plates and staring out the window.

"Oh, nothin'. I didn't mean nothin'. Forget I said it. Now hurry up. If you want to come with me to the Smoker, you've got to get dressed."

A long-time hangout for the studio set, the Smoker boasted walls covered with autographed black-and-whites of celebrities. Old-fashioned red leather-upholstered booths, frayed from fifty years of celebrity bottom-crossings, lined the walls. A massive wooden bar backed by a mirror stretched the length of the dance floor. The nocturnal creatures sitting in the dark cool bar sipped martinis and manhattans. Gemcie felt sad delivering more mind-numbing drinks to them, but it seemed to make them happy. The acrid smell of flat beer and stale cigarettes settled into her clothes and hair. She showered as soon as she got home to rid herself of the stench.

While setting up the dining room, spreading fresh white linens over the red cotton tablecloths, neatly folding napkins, strategically placing silver, snipping a rose for the bud vase at each table, she was surprised by a light tap on her shoulder. She turned to see Billy. She dropped the remaining roses in her hand, jumped up to reach his leathery neck, and gave him a fierce hug.

"Did you come for the prime rib? It's good tonight."

"No, I came to take you out. Your mama gave me the okay."

Gemcie looked over his shoulder to see Sue Ellen giving her the high sign. Gemcie ripped off her apron, slipped the crook of her arm into his, and marched past her mother, blowing her a kiss on the way out.

"Thank God you came. That place depresses me."

"Your mother asked me to come."

"I should've known. I don't suppose you think I should have a little operation?"

"No, I don't," he said, opening up the door on the passenger side of the truck for her. "Hop in."

"I don't remember this kind of service from you before, you must be after something," she sang out with a laugh.

"Where would you like to go?"

"How about the beach? The heat of the Valley is getting to me."

"Sure, we can make it by sunset if we hurry."

Billy was quiet while they shared a meal of ciopino, fresh bread, and salad. He seemed distracted by the gentle surf rolling in low-slung, cresting waves just outside the window. A crescent moon, shrouded in dark, fast-moving clouds, cast a luminous path to the black horizon. Finally, Billy broke the silence.

"Your mama called me. She wants me to talk to you about gettin' back into ridin'."

"Here it comes. She doesn't want me to throw away the years she spent paying for my lessons, boarding my horses, carting me around to shows. I think I've heard this before." Gemcie chuckled softly.

"That's right, Gemcie, that's what she wanted me to tell you, but that's not what I've got to say." Billy cleared his throat. "You were right; I should have told you about me workin' with Dominique."

"It's okay, Billy. You've got to make a living, I understand," she interrupted.

"No, it's not okay. I should have told you about that, and the fireworks that was goin' on between Jorge and that vixen. I may be old, but I'm not blind. It was the World Cup that kept my mouth shut. I could taste it." He stared out the window for a moment and then continued. "You and Marshal were my last bid. When you got hurt, I couldn't let it go. Now it's too late for that, but it ain't too late for me to tell you what I should have told you years ago." His rheumy eyes moistened with tears.

"What is it?" she asked, concerned.

"It's about your father."

"My father!"

"Yes, I knew your father. He never died in any automobile accident that I know about. Fact is, he could still be as alive as you and me. The last I seen him he was stuffin' his belongin's into his saddle bags headed out for the Pacific Crest Trail. Said he was goin' to take it all the way up to Canada."

Stunned by this revelation, Gemcie fell silent. She stared at the moon path sparkling across the rippling water, contemplating the illusion of what she once thought was true in her life. She wanted to evaporate. If only she could walk on that trail straight to the moon, away from her conflicted state of mind.

"Sue Ellen made me promise never to tell you," Billy continued. "Your mama's a good woman, but she wanted him dead in her heart. She couldn't live with the truth so she hid it from you."

"Why are you telling me now?"

"Because I think you're an awful lot like your dad. You got a right to know who he was. It might help you figure out the right thing to do for yourself. You ain't had much of a chance to do that."

"What was he like?" Gemcie asked, turning misty blue eyes on Billy once again.

"He was a ramblin' man. I met him up in Bishop when I was a packer in the High Sierras. He sort of appeared out of nowhere one day carryin' a guitar. He could play like nobody's business. It's no wonder your mama lost her heart sittin' under those stars listening to him howl at the moon."

"She told me he was a cowboy."

"That's right, he was, and a damned good one. Stuck to a horse like a tick on a dog. There wasn't a bronco born that could get rid of him. We did a couple of rodeos together, but we spent most of the summers haulin' folks in and out of the Muir Wilderness."

Gemcie stared into the black, grappling with the realization that her father had left her mother when she was an infant. She had never thought much about him. He was dead. Lots of kids didn't have dads. Besides, none of it could possibly matter now.

"I already called up Jed and Cindy. They own the lodge up there. They knew your dad. They got a horse waitin' for you just outside of Bishop at Rock Creek. They're aware that you might be comin'. You can stay with them as long as you want."

Gemcie was quiet for the rest of the meal as well as when Billy careened through Topanga Canyon on the way back to the San Fernando Valley. When they reached the crest overlooking the glittering lights blanketing the valley below, she was struck with the fact that she had never been anywhere else. Her entire life until now had been taken up by the horses, pre-arranged by her mother. Busy to the brim, it hadn't occurred to her that she might do anything except be a Grand Prix rider.

Her mother thought that it was "just a little operation" between her and continuing on her predetermined course, but Gemcie knew it was more than that. Fear had never been a part of the formula before. She had never feared getting hurt. That was why she could flow over the course, letting Marshal have his head, riding on his adrenaline, trusting his instincts. The last time she rode him, fear fluttered into her mind, interfering with her concentration. She saw disaster looming ahead, her dream played out in real life. She couldn't focus on her ride.

"Have you ever been hurt?" she asked Billy when they crested Mulholland, swerving around the bend that affords a view of the twinkling suburban sprawl.

"Yeah, I been hurt lots of times, but the most hurt I got was when I was ridin' as a jockey in quarter horse races. I was about thirty when it happened. My horse tripped. I went down in front of a pack of ten horses haulin' ass. Can't remember how many places I was stepped on. When I woke up I was in a world of pain. I had a broken pelvis, and a couple of crushed ribs."

"Did you race after that?"

"No, Gemcie, I didn't. It didn't seem worth it to me."

Chapter Eight

Gemcie lifted a corner of her sleeping mask. A bright line of sunlight shining below the drawn shade felt like a laser beam to her red-rimmed eyes. Sleep did not come easy these days. The two sleeping pills she took at midnight made her groggy. She often felt tired no matter how many hours of sleep she got the night before. She squinted to read the numbers of the alarm clock on the bed stand, not that she really cared what time it was. One day was just like the last. She didn't want to work at the Smoker anymore. She didn't even want to go to the barn. She had no reason to get up.

Sue Ellen knocked softly on the bedroom door. When she didn't get a response she poked her head into the darkened room. Gemcie pretended to be asleep.

"C'mon, sleeping beauty, rise and shine."

"Go away, mom. I don't feel good."

"How could you? Holed up in here like some kind of rodent. Now, get up, young lady. This is just stupid," her mother said, lifting the shade and letting the noonday sun spill into the darkened room. She pulled the sleeping mask from Gemcie's face, letting it snap back in place.

"Ow!" Gemcie squealed.

"This isn't going to cut it, kiddo. You don't have to work at the Smoker. I never did want you there, but you're not going to hide in your room all day either."

Gemcie sat up, covering her eyes with her hand, peering through the spread fingers.

"What do you want me to do?"

"I don't know. Go see Kate, ask her if you can help at the barn. There're lots of things you can do beside ride."

"Like what?"

"You can give lessons from the ground, braid manes for the shows, lots of things."

"I don't want to be there."

"Look, honey, this is just temporary. When you get your settlement you can have that operation, get a new horse and a new start."

Gemcie focused on her mother. Glaring into her gray-green eyes, she spoke slowly and deliberately, "There isn't going to be a settlement."

"Of course there is. How can there not be? He cheated on you. That's grounds in any court."

"I signed an agreement before we were married."

"What kind of agreement?"

"A pre-nuptial. I have no claim on any of the family assets. Jorge has nothing on his own. Nothing belongs to me, not even Marshal."

Sue Ellen slumped down in the white wicker chair beside the bed. It took her a moment to grasp that her daughter was as penniless today as when she entered the world twenty years ago.

"I can't believe you could do something so stupid! Why didn't you tell me?" she asked, incredulous at Gemcie's foolishness.

"I trusted Jorge's love for me."

"Yes, yes, he loved you, but he's so young and full of himself."

"Why didn't you tell me, if that's what you thought of him?"

"It was like a fairy tale. How could I ruin it for you?"

"For me?"

"Yes, for you! Everything I've ever done is for you!"

"Really? It's easier to live through someone else than to do it yourself, isn't it?" Gemcie stated coldly, glaring into her mother's smoldering eyes.

Outraged, Sue Ellen stood up and slapped her daughter's pale cheek solidly. Gemcie put her hand to her face to calm the stinging, but the ringing in her ears did not subside. The room spun in slow motion as Sue Ellen shook her finger in Gemcie's face, screaming.

"Is it easier to scrimp so someone else can own a pony, wear fine clothes, win ribbons, be invited to parties and end up living in a mansion? Oh yes! It's much easier to work twelve hours a day never taking time for yourself! It has all been for you, Gemcie, you little ingrate."

Gemcie looked squarely into her mother's face turgid with rage, and moved the trembling finger away from in front of her face.

"I'm leaving."

"Where do you think you're going?" Sue Ellen demanded, stepping back and placing her hands on her hips for ballast.

"To Bishop."

"Bishop! Why Bishop?"

"I think you know."

Sue Ellen turned away from her daughter. She saw her own reflection in the mirror of the dressing vanity. A tired, middle-aged, overweight woman who had spent her life running away from the truth stared back at her. She met her daughter's accusing eyes in the glass.

"You've been talking to Billy."

"You lied to me," Gemcie said. "My whole life is a lie. I can't stay here any longer."

Sue Ellen whirled around to face her daughter. She pleaded with weary eyes, "If you go, you'll be proving to me you are just like he was."

"And how is that, mom, 'just like he was'?"

"Selfish!" she growled. "Selfish to the bone, that's what. Doin' what he needed to do for himself, not caring about you, or me. He walked out on both of us, you know. You were just a month old when he turned his back on us."

Her mother crumpled to her knees beside the bed, lay her head down on folded arms and gave way to her years of tamped-down sorrow. Her body heaved with remorse. Gemcie put her hand on her mother's head, stroking her coarse dishwater-blonde mane.

"I've got to go," Gemcie said, softly.

Chapter Nine

Tears streamed down Gemcie's cheeks as she barreled north on the 395 to Bishop in the beat-up Toyota Billy gave her. She drove for three hours before the spider web of guilt over leaving her mother let loose its sticky grip. She saw herself as a marionette played by the strings held in her mother's hand; groomed, molded, trained from the age of two for a destiny she had no voice in. When she got to Independence she pulled into a rest stop. She needed to walk to alleviate the nagging needles of nerve pain shooting through her right leg up into her hip.

Bending into the warm wind, she tramped across a wooden bridge, traversing a stream. A lizard scurried along the sandy trail, leaving a tiny tread mark with his tail. She flushed out a covey of quail with cocky top knots and puffy black chests, calling sharply to one another, "Chicago, Chicago." Six of them rushed ahead of her on the path, in a feathery flutter, trying to get out of her way. The smell of pungent sage tickled her nose as she walked slowly through the chaparral. She felt a stirring in her body's muscles and blood as the fresh air laden with the perfume of spring flowers filled her lungs. To the west, Mount Whitney reigned supreme in the Sierras. She wondered how far one must trek up craggy peaks before reaching its summit. After a few stretches, she popped back into her truck and headed north.

She gassed up in Bishop, a lazy berg asleep in the noonday sun, and then forged up the grade to the cutoff for Rock Creek. She cast a glance over her shoulder for a last glimpse of the Owens Valley surrounded by jagged peaks. Shifting columns of light brightened a patchwork quilt of fields. Mares with foals grazing in emerald pastures faded from sight as she pressed higher into the Sierras.

Exiting at Tom's Place, she headed up a road that narrowed to a two-lane strip paralleling the path of Rock Creek. Clumps of yellow flowers topped sage nestled neatly between gray boulders. Purple spikes of pigmy lupine poked through the gray foliage hugging the ground. The sight of the silver thread snaking through the canyon enlivened her. With senses tingling, she wanted to walk along the water's edge, to lift its clear purity to her lips, to drink in its secret wisdom.

Rock Creek, a tranquil valley midway between Bishop and Mammoth, is protected by Bear Mountain, a gray granite, snow-capped spire poking into the heavens. The jade-green unblinking eye that is Rock Creek Lake feeds the river that tumbles through flower-infused meadows, forests of pine, and campgrounds where fishermen have flocked for one hundred years. At dusk brown, red, and golden trout tease tourists as they jump clear of the placid ponds for an insect tidbit, leaving rippling circles in their wake.

Seven miles into the canyon she spied Rock Creek Resort, with a cluster of tiny log cabins clinging to the hills behind the lodge. Jed and Cindy lived in the apartment below the general store of the rest stop for tourists and fishermen. Upstairs a tidy store with everything from T-shirts to fishing tackle shared an open-beam room with the restaurant. A breakfast counter with six stools faced the doorway opening to the cook's station. A sunny deck off the front of the A-framed building offered picnic tables for those waiting for the red sun to set behind Bear Mountain.

Gemcie slid onto a stool and spun to face the wall covered with photos of proud fishermen holding up the trout they had tricked from the clear waters into a frying pan. A duffer in a flannel shirt, crisp-clean blue jeans and suspenders poured coffee into the half-empty cups of a couple men getting ready to embark on a backpacking trek. He handed Gemcie a menu.

"What's your pleasure, miss? Care for some coffee?"

"Sure."

Gemcie surmised this was Jed, but didn't disclose her identity. While she was studying the menu, a refined gentleman, much too clean to be a fisherman, came in.

"I want to reserve a piece of lemon cream pie," he said.

The sign above the counter boasted the best homemade

boysenberry, peach, and apple pie in the county.

Jed yelled over his shoulder to Cindy, who was busy in the kitchen, "You got any lemon cream pie for this evening?"

"I'm workin' on it."

Jed turned to the gentleman who was obviously relieved to hear this satisfying news.

"Reckon there will be a piece set aside for you, Clive."

"Right, then. I'll be back."

Gemcie watched him leave, and convinced that the cooking here was not to be missed, she placed her order.

Moments later, Jed set a lumberjack breakfast of sausage, eggs, "taters" and toast before her."

"Will there be anything else?" he asked, with a half twinkle in his eyes.

"Just a little ketchup," she said.

Gemcie set to work on her meal, wanting, but not wanting, them to know who she was. She watched while Jed waited on a few customers, and listened to the register ding with regularity. Cindy, big-boned with wide hips, handled a rolling pin like it was an extension of her muscled arms. Gemcie watched her wade through mountains of soft dough, manicuring it into puffy pie crusts that she pinched with thumb and forefinger, as she spun pie tins around. She whistled through thin pink lips while she spooned blackberries into the pie crusts, topping them with a dough cover. The smell of earlier accomplishments wafted from the oven, filling the room with mouth-watering scents.

Jed came back to top off half-empty coffee cups. As he poured the steaming brew into Gemcie's cup, she announced, "I'm Gemcie McCauley."

Jed looked up from his work into her sparkling blue eyes.

"Why, dog if you ain't! Come on out here, Cindy. Tom and Sue Ellen's girl has come to see us."

Cindy came out of the kitchen wiping flour from her forearms with the tea towel stuffed in her apron. Flushed pink from the heat of the kitchen, she wiped small beads of perspiration from her tiny nose.

"Why, Jed, this is one time you are right," she exclaimed.

She took Gemcie's hand in her own and squeezed it firmly. "Honey, you sure do look like your papa. Gives me goose flesh."

"Billy told us you might be coming," Jed added. "You are

welcome to stay as long as you like."

"You can stay in the help's cabin," Cindy added.

"I want to help," Gemcie said. "What I can do?"

"No shortage of chores around here," Jed laughed. "Don't you worry none. You can earn your keep, if you've a mind to."

"But then again, you don't have to do a thing," interjected Cindy. "You can just take a rest here if you like."

"You got here just in time. I'm heading out with a pack crew on Friday up to Hilton Lakes. You can come along and ride shotgun with me, like your daddy did," Jed suggested.

Gemcie felt a lump rising in her chest, touched by their generosity. Jed carried her bags. Cindy led the way to her tiny red cabin behind the lodge. Jed pointed to the communal shower on the way. Crimson geraniums bulged out of the window boxes at the base of each window of the 12 x 12 cabin. Cindy shoved the bottom of the door with her foot, forcing it open.

"Hasn't been used since last season. Needs a little airin' out, but it should be fine. This was your mama's quarters when she was a cook with us."

"We used to take a lot of folks out, back then," Jed explained. "We was packin' in a couple sets of ten each week, but things have slowed down up here. Once you get settled, I'll help you pack a duffel bag for the trail."

Lifting a lace curtain, she cranked the window open and watched Jed and Cindy amble back down the flower-lined path to the lodge. The stern peaks with patches of snow pierced a blue dome. The warm sun shone down on her upturned face, while a tender breeze licked her throat. She decided not to tell them about her sciatica. They might decide she couldn't go on a ride that would take her out of the radius of a cell phone, far from medical help. Something was pulling her inexplicably up the canyons, extolled through the years for their ethereal beauty. Billy had told her, "Once you've been in the mountains they become a part of you, like the kiss of a lover."

Chapter Ten

It took two wranglers to pack the eight mules that would carry supplies into the base camp. Once strapped with leather harnesses, the mules' load was equally distributed in wooden boxes on each flank. More gear was stacked on top of the boxes. Then a white tarp bound with rope secured the rest of the supplies on the animals. Maxine, the more musical of the flop-eared mules, let out a long heaving melody, threatening to topple her share of camp gear as she sucked in air for the finale. A wiry wrangler wearing worn leather chaps put his frayed boot to her side for leverage as he pulled in mightily on the girth.

"Isn't that a little tight?" Gemcie ventured.

"If her eyes ain't bulging out, it ain't too tight," he answered.

Bronzed from hours in the sun, the cowboy flashed Gemcie a gleaming smile with a row of perfect white teeth. The sun glinted off his blue eyes buried in deep sockets shaded by a straw Stetson. Hard muscle girdled his middle. His legs were slightly bowed.

"Pete is saddling Mercedes for you. She's down in the lower corral," he told her.

Eager to meet her mount, Gemcie headed in the direction he was pointing.

"I can tack my own horse," she said as she approached Pete, who was busy wiping an appaloosa down with a soft brush.

"I bet you can, miss, but I got strict orders to see you are set before your ride out of here," he said.

Gemcie circled the mare looking for defects. She was an Indian pony, short from knee to hoof, with solid, full haunches. Her breed earned a reputation for being sure-footed on the trail, sturdy, dependable, but given to an attitude. Stubborn and hard-headed, they require a firm hand, but once convinced they are being ridden they do the job. Gemcie stroked her between her soft brown eyes, testing her guardedness toward the spot most vulnerable to any horse. Mercedes lowered her head like a puppy looking for a scratch on the ears. Gemcie rubbed her under her chin, and stroked her muscled chest while Pete tacked her up.

"Okay, climb aboard," Pete said.

In all her years of riding, Gemcie had never sat in a Western saddle. It felt cumbersome and bulky to her, and put a huge distance between her and her horse. She let her leg stretch down to meet the massive wooden stirrup, cringing inwardly at the thought of undoing a lifetime of riding discipline. In English, the knee is bent so you may rise out of the saddle with each stride, the toe held slightly in. In Western you must relax the leg to its full length, let your behind sink into the saddle, rock along with the movement, and let your toes fall out and away from the horse.

Soon a string of eight riders were mounted and formed a dutiful line behind Jed heading up the trail to Hilton Lakes. They clomped through altitude-stunted aspen, with round leaves spinning like silver dollars in the sun. Splotches of flame-red Indian brush dotted the mountains. Yellow and white daisies, blue aster, and clumps of pigmy lupine lined the trail. Soon they arrived at a summit overlooking Rock Creek Lake. Mist hovered where the sun struck the ice crusting the surface of the emerald eye below.

Gemcie rode with a loose rein, letting Mercedes pick her way through the smooth boulders in the time-worn trail. The pace allowed Gemcie to settle into a rocking chair motion, leaving her mind at liberty to wander and absorb the new sights and smells. Letting her bottom sink into the broad leather saddle, legs dropped to full extension, she felt blood rushing to forgotten muscles. Her nagging sciatica subsided.

Mercedes marched forward like a tank, swinging her head from side to side, ears pricked, excited to be out of her muddy stall. She forged through the rising waters of a spring-swelled creek that came to her belly. Gemcie lifted her feet back out of the stirrups to keep her boots dry while Mercedes sucked her fill of the sweet liquid. She watched the sun-spangled water charging down to white-foam pools, while the mare stretched her neck to drink. Once satiated, the mare pawed the waters, creating a great splash, looking for a nice place to roll herself and rider in the glacier runoff.

Quickly averting disaster, Gemcie pulled the mare's head up, pressed her forward, and got back into line with the other riders. They reached a sandy summit with an inviting canter trail, but the journey was to be made at an ambling walk. Gemcie chafed at the pace while spotting fallen logs perfect for the gentle spring over, but diverted her attention to the birds twittering in the trees. Yellow finches no bigger than a cat's mouthful, flitted in the underbrush still wet with morning dew. Their busy songs filled the air.

At the head of the band, Jed slumped into his saddle, back rounded at the shoulder, head buried under a wide sombrero, a siesta on the move. His pinto, Oriole, knew the trail, so Jed let him lead the way. Kathy, the young cook, pulled up the rear, making sure none of the group strayed off course. The string of less-than-perfect riders on a mix of mule and horse flesh, strolled single-file through the forest. One woman, given to incessant chatter, seemed to believe silence is something that must be broken. She rattled on about favorite recipes, relatives long dead, anything and everything, unable to be still. Gemcie likened her to a parakeet that had no choice but to twitter, and tried to incorporate her banal conversation into the sounds of the forest.

Several hours from civilization found the group making camp on the shore of a lake so clear the shadowy brown shapes of trout could be seen flitting through the water. The dull roar of a waterfall tumbling down through a chasm of boulders called Gemcie closer. She sat on a sandy beach staring intently at the amphitheater of peaks in jagged rows like shark's teeth: the result of violent trembling in the earth's crust millenniums ago. White patches of snow remained above the tree line even though it was the middle of June. After twenty minutes of trying to absorb the stark beauty of the peak across the way, it magically materialized before her. The reflection in the clear lake, like an image hidden in a dot picture, came to life at her feet. Her soul settled into the placid calm of the water, mirroring the deepening beauty before her.

In the hour that time stood still for Gemcie, thick gray clouds crowded into the sky to the east. A cold wind feathered the water to a yellow gray, whipping up tiny whitecaps. She smelled rain and felt a storm mounting. A clap of thunder reverberated through the canyon, signaling the flash of jagged lightning to come. In twenty seconds a wicked gash ripped the sky. Dime-sized drops splashed on the dry rocks. She scurried back to camp, hoping to outrun the storm.

"You need to pop your tent if you don't want to get good and wet," Jed said.

She pulled the tent from its pouch and a pile of poles fell to the ground that looked like a stack of pickup sticks. She laid the tent out trying to figure what side was up, but it seemed like a giant jigsaw puzzle to her. She fumbled around with the poles strung together by elastic bands that snapped into pretzel-like formations.

"Can I give you a hand?" came from a silver-domed rider named Fred.

"I think you'd better," Gemcie said, relieved to have help.

Fred snapped the poles into straight lines and laid the tent out ready to be popped into position. "Okay, now you hold these two cross-hatched in the center and I will stake them to the ground. Then you pull the tent up in the middle and snap it to the center poles. It's easy once you get the hang of it."

Gemcie felt stupid for needing help but grateful for the kind gentleman's rescue.

The main camp was already assembled under a blue tarp flapping in the wind. Kathy had camp coffee brewing and stew warming for dinner over an open flame. The other riders had raised their tents, staking them in the flattest spots. Gemcie hurried to get her tent up before the downpour. The rest gathered around the rock fire pit that served as the center of entertainment, warmth and sustenance, just as it had for the cave man at the dawn of time. Once her personal camp was organized, she went to join the group by the fire.

Pulling up a low lawn chair, she propped her feet up on a handy rock, warming the soles her feet on the glowing embers. She noticed she was the only one of the eight riders wearing fitted riding pants. The rest wore regulation denim, flannel shirts and cowboy boots. Talk shifted from when was the best time to plant tomatoes, to the President's sex life, to what was for dinner, while thick wet clouds gathered over the valley. Soon great globs of wet sleet plopped into the fire with a hiss. Jed and the rest of the riders continued to talk, ignoring the snow falling on their heads and shoulders. Gemcie remembered the miniature folding umbrella in the pocket of her windbreaker. She popped it open, like the James Bond of the camping world.

"Why, you do come prepared!" Fred observed.

The group laughed softly. It was clear they'd noticed her English riding habit. Maybe she could ride, but there was some question about her ability to rough it in the back of their minds. Gemcie detected their condescension. A headache was hovering around her consciousness. The stew that smelled so scrumptious tasted like aluminum foil to her. Not in the mood for small talk, she decided to turn in early.

The spring storm was in full swing when she curled into her nylon mummy bag. The steady thrumming of the raindrops on the tent made her glad she'd purchased a new sleeping bag before leaving Los Angeles. With air mattress firmly inflated, she looked forward to a good night's rest. She had a touch of altitude sickness that felt like a spike going through the middle of her forehead. She looked forward to waking up the next morning feeling fine.

But instead of sleeping, she shadow-boxed with her sleeping bag for about an hour. The mummy bag was so confining she had to wrap her arms across her chest like Houdini to fit inside. She couldn't turn over in the bag. If she moved, she had to take the bag with her like a caterpillar in its cocoon. When she did move, the nylon bag slipped down on the rubber air mattress. Soon she found herself in a shivering, scrunched pile at the bottom of the tent. She couldn't stop trembling. Afraid hypothermia would overtake her, she wrenched herself from the tent and found Jed.

"I can't make it through the night like this. You've got to do something."

"We'll put a tarp over your tent and give you a stack of horse pads, but that's all we got. If that don't work, and you find yourself shaking' in the night, you come and wake me up. We'll have to get you back down the mountain," he said soberly.

Gemcie went back to her tent, now swathed in a blue tarp. She remembered Jed had told her to bring a wool cap, but she'd forgotten it. It was ninety degrees when she left home in L.A. only three hours away. It was hard to believe she would actually need wool anything. She tied a T-shirt on her head to keep the heat from escaping. Jed opened the flap of her tent and stacked sweat-soaked pads, matted with horse hair, on top of her sleeping bag. The musky odor of the blankets was so overwhelming it made her queasy. Squirming back into her mummy bag, wearing two layers of clothing, she prayed this would be enough to keep her warm through the night.

Just as she was feeling toasty, she flipped over to her best sleeping side, bursting the bag's zipper open. A rush of arctic air went up her spine. The cold creeping up her back settled into a dull ache. She didn't actually sleep that night. She just lay there trying to collect energy through her pores. She dreaded the moment she knew was coming when she would have to uncurl herself, put on her slippers, and head for the makeshift outhouse under the stars. She unzipped her tent to see a creamy swath of stars covering the heavens. The air temp was a crystalline twenty degrees. She was shivering and could see her breath in a vapor, but at least there was no rain. No matter how majestic the firmament, she decided she would go back down to Rock Creek with one of the wranglers in the morning. Jed would understand.

The camp came alive before the sun crested purple mountains jutting through pink skies. Wisps of smoke from the morning fire unfurled into the chill air. The rest of the riders stood in a circle around the fire, warming their hands when Gemcie arrived.

"Don't ask me how I slept," Gemcie said to Kathy, while she poured herself a stiff belt of brew filled with coffee grounds.

"Pretty darn cold last night," the parakeet chirped. "Had to wear everything I had in my duffel to keep warm."

"Yes, I had to wear horse blankets to keep warm," Gemcie said.

"Well, I sure wish I'd known, I would have flipped you for one of those," came from a plucky woman about sixty-five.

"Were you able to sleep?" Gemcie asked.

"Not really, but it's a small price. Sort of comes with the territory. The first night in high altitude nobody sleeps that good," she said.

"That sure enough was a cold snap," Jed said. "But we're looking at bluebird skies today."

Gemcie turned her backside to the fire, clasping her hands behind her back. She looked up to cloudless skies, saw the light shimmering on the emerald-green lake through the trees, and heard the waterfall's roar rising from the distant canyon. She felt ashamed that she had thought about returning. She resolved to learn how to take better care of her creature comforts in this sublime wonderland of lakes, meadows and forests, and to know the heartbeat of its beauty.

By ten o'clock the sun was high, beating down on the shoulders of the riders making their way to a lake Jed promised to be a good fishing spot. The trail meandered through a shady forest of sugar pine and red fir. Gemcie spied dun-colored chipmunks with black stripes on their backs stirring the forest floor. Bold columns of light filtered through the tree canopy spotlighting the orange tiger lilies that grew at the base of the trees where ferns spread their frilly garments.

Jed instructed her to pull up the rear to make sure none of the riders fell too far behind. He glanced over his shoulder when he reached the base of the tough climb that would take the group to lake number three. There were so many lakes sprinkled through the high meadows, early explorers ran out of names. Jagged rocks gouging the trail made this a daunting ascent. Mercedes hopped a three-foot ledge without hesitation. Gemcie stood in her stirrups, keeping her weight off the mare's back, giving her the greatest freedom of movement possible as she lunged up the narrow, eroded path. Gemcie tried not to look into the gorge below, keeping her focus riveted on the blue slot at the top of the narrow canyon.

Emerging into the bright sun, the riders were greeted by a crisp breeze coming off the virgin snowmelt waters of the third lake. Jed stopped to let the animals catch their breath and sip the pure waters of the shallow stream. Tiny blue blooms nestled the cleft of dry boulders beside the murmuring spring. Great chunks of snow edged in brown survived the sun's intense rays under granite ledges lining the still lake.

"This'll be our lunch stop," Jed declared. "You can fish, hike or just wander around for a couple of hours. Then we'll head back."

Gemcie took her sack lunch and headed for a warm boulder beside the cheery stream where it embarked on its frothy journey to the valley floor. Sliding quietly from the placid glacier lake over the rock brow, it tumbled down a steep chasm. Energized by the descent, collecting noisy strength, it would soon join the dazzling blue-green water of the lake in the distance. Ravenous in the mountain air, Gemcie wolfed down her ham sandwich, while she scanned the vista with squinting blue eyes.

Light-headed from no sleep and the altitude, she lay back on the warm rock like a marmot in the sun. An intense relaxation set in, making her feel heavy, as though she were melting into her boulder bed. She pulled her visor over her eyes to shade them from the huge ball blazing above in an azure sky. She gave way, not to sleep, but to a mild tingling of energy flowing through her body. She felt a part of the postcard scenery. Her human separateness vanished for those seconds her eyes were closed. She imagined herself a particle intertwined in the constant ebb and flow of molecules at the center of all creation. She sat at the wellspring of divine healing waters, eternally rejuvenating, that bring life to the barren land below.

On the way back to the base camp, the mules maneuvered the treacherous rock-strewn descent with amazing agility. She marveled at their ability to navigate the chasm with staggering loads of camp supplies strapped to their backs. Mercedes held no fear as she stepped into narrow rock grooves, going down, down, down the canyon. Gemcie, now accustomed to the rocking chair motion of the march, simply leaned back and let the mare find her own way. Her faith in horse flesh grew with each precarious step.

It occurred to Gemcie as she listened to the others expound about Chinese politics, that she had never known silence. She had gone to sleep to the blare of late night talk shows all through childhood. Often, Sue Ellen fell asleep with the eerie glow of the TV bouncing shadows across her face. Gemcie would switch the set off, tuck an afghan under her mother's chin, then slip back to her own bed more nights than not. Her bold mother hated being alone. The radio was her constant companion in the kitchen, car, even the bathroom. The incessant yammering of commercials and announcers was never questioned by Gemcie, until now.

The din of the city with its cars brakes squealing to a stop, buses exhaling noxious fumes, and alarms going off in the night, worked together to create a blanket of noise. Jets flew over their house starting at seven in the morning. She was accustomed to the news helicopter circling for hours over the nearby freeway tracking the morning traffic. Often awakened by the rude clamor of leaf blowers, in unison with the buzz of chain saws used by neighborhood gardeners, she accepted the sounds as part of the collective cacophony that is the city. Now, she yearned to know silence and to be still with her own thoughts.

Even on the ride she felt distanced from the sounds and citizens of the natural world. Hearing the chattering riders on a string of horses made timid forest creatures take cover long before the group reached them. Naturally, they scrambled into burrows, or took to flight before the loud approach. Cooter Jay, Jed's dog, saw to it that any remaining creatures were flushed out in advance of the group. Yipping and snorting, he rousted creatures great and small. Twice Gemcie had mistaken him for a bear as she studied the underbrush trying to detect wildlife. His shaggy, mottled coat, boxy shoulders, and square dower face could have easily belonged to a cub. She yearned to know the forest without interference, in unsullied quietude, on its terms.

After this first foray into the wilderness, she became obsessed with this desire and was determined to learn how to fend for herself in the mountains. She went out every weekend with Jed and Kathy, packing in a group to Hilton Lakes. Gus taught her to load the mules by placing the heavy, solid items on the bottom of the wooden boxes, lighter bulky ones on top. She learned to pack small measured portions of each item required for the campout. Jed had an exact list that she duplicated on each outing, making certain not to forget anything critical like toilet paper.

She watched Kathy rub rainbow trout with olive oil, sprinkle on pepper, parsley and oregano, and then wrap it in foil to bake in the coals to succulent perfection. Ears of corn, potatoes, and other vegetables were also delectable prepared this way. With dried hummus, energy bars, and lentil mush to fill in, she knew she could survive a week or two nicely.

On a jaunt to Bishop for supplies, she spotted a used Australian stock saddle at the tack shop. It was the perfect compromise between the lightweight jump saddle she was familiar with and the bulky Western saddle she could barely lift. It had a sturdy seat that would keep her securely in place in rough terrain, but the stirrup leathers were narrow so she could get out of the saddle and post to the trot. It hadn't been used for years. The leather was dry and stiff and some of the stitching was frayed. She oiled it with leather balm and had the saddlery make the needed repairs.

Jed went with her to pick out a sleeping bag that would see her through the darkest winter night in the Sierras. She secretly planned to travel in July when the afternoon summer storms were expected, but not much more than that should happen. She bought synthetic short- and long-sleeved T-shirts and a pair of nylon all-weather pants that could convert to shorts with the trip of a zipper. She invested in a sturdy Gortex parka that was completely waterproof with matching pants. She bought a wool cap, and an all-purpose bandana just like cowboys wear.

Each day she felt stronger. She avoided heavy lifting, making certain she wasn't around when it was time to haul the water in buckets up from the lake to camp. She never volunteered to hoist the weighty saddles onto the backs of the animals. Instead, she kept busy grooming, feeding, and cleaning up after them. She stole off to a private spot to do her stretches and the back exercises she needed. She didn't want to increase the odds of Jed denying her request to ride alone by letting him know she had an injury. Her sciatica was at bay. It still lingered around the edges, but if she did her stretches it was tolerable.

It was the end of June before Gemcie felt ready to do a point-to-point on the Pacific Crest Trail by herself. On her map the route was also referred to as the John Muir Trail, because the 211-mile trek between Mount Whitney and Yosemite is actually both. The Pacific Crest Trail, however, extends all the way from Mexico to Canada, running along the ridge of the mountains that stretch the length of the United States. Few equestrians have ridden the entire length of the magnificent route. Gemcie didn't know how far she intended to go, but she knew she was going.

The Fourth of July ride was perfection. The weather was warm, with a profusion of wildflowers scenting the air. The last guest stood and yawned, announcing he was going to bed. The fading embers of the evening fire cast a warm glow on Jed's face, grizzled by two days of beard growth. He seemed at perfect peace staring into the dying flames. Gemcie poked the charred wood with a stick, whipping up sparks that danced like fireflies in the night. A bold big dipper hung in the velvet sky. This looked to be her moment to spring the question.

"What was he like?" she asked, looking steadily into Jed's eyes.

Jed cleared his throat and spit to the side through the gap in his front teeth.

"Your poppa? Well, he was long-legged and narrow at the hip like you. He didn't talk much. Didn't care much for people, but he loved to sing. It was funny, he'd be working all day, and not say nothin' to nobody, mindin' his own business; then come nightfall he'd drag out his guitar, sing for everybody's pleasure for as long as they liked. He took requests. Knew every tune ever sung by a cowboy. He was hard working. I never had to tell him what to do. He knew what to do. I reckon he was the best hand I ever had."

"Is that why you've been so kind to me?"

"Sorta. Fact is, I wouldn't be sittin' here if it wasn't for your daddy. He and I went out deer huntin' one spring. Those critters were as scarce up here then as they are now. They like it down in the lower valleys, but we was up here lookin' for 'em just the same. Sure enough we got a fine buck and his doe in our sights. I was chasin' 'em flat out on Navajo, my best mountain horse. There was a log down in between me and that buck. I was salivatin'. Navajo trusted me as much as I trusted him, so when I pressed him to jump over that stump about six-feet wide, he let fly. His front hoof caught on a limb and he went down in the gully hiding on the other side. I flew about ten feet into the air and slammed into a fir, got knocked silly. Navajo broke his leg on the landin'. Your daddy had to decide. He put poor Navajo out of his misery, but me he had to carry me all the way down the mountain, or go for help. He put me on his mount and walked me out. Otherwise, I wouldn't be here to tell you this story."

"When did he leave?"

"Was just after you was born. He stayed with your mama the whole time she was big with you. Then he lit out about a month after you come into the world."

"Billy told me he rode the Pacific Crest."

"That's right. He come in that way and that's the way he went out of here, too."

"Will you let me take Mercedes for a month? I want to do the trail. I'll be happy to do whatever chores you think she's worth."

"I'm too old to be doin' any month-long trips, Gemcie. You might be able to talk Gus into goin' with you, but I need him right now."

"I want to go alone."

"Now honey, you ain't nearly ready to ride off into them mountains by yourself. This here country seems like a cakewalk, but I just told you how things can go wrong. You'd have no way of gettin' help. Cell phones don't transmit through granite walls."

"Please, Jed. I need to go." Gemcie stirred the fire with a stick. "I may never have this chance again to know why my father loved

83

the mountains…more than me."

"Youngun, I owe your dad, but I don't know if this is the right way to repay him. What if something happens to your horse? Do you really think you could put an animal down if you had to? You'd have to shoot 'im and quarter 'im up. You can't leave a whole carcass just lying on the trail."

"I had to put down an old horse once. It was hard, but I knew it was for the best."

"Your mama would never forgive me if you got hurt or stuck on the mountain. Don't you care about her feelin's none?"

"I've been pleasing my mother all my life. I need to please myself right now."

Jed fell silent, staring into the fire.

"Cindy would be awful upset with me if I let you go alone and you got hurt. I got to talk this over with her."

She crossed over to him, lifted his straw Stetson and planted a soft kiss on his scalp, sprinkled with a few white wisps of hair.

"Thanks for bringing me this far," she said, before slipping into the black, leaving him to ponder her fate.

Chapter Eleven

When they got back to the lodge, Cindy greeted Gemcie with a bear hug, lifting her off the ground and squeezing her in a powerful clench until she choked for breath.

"Land sakes, you are no bigger than a minute." she said, dropping her back to earth.

Gemcie giggled. Being treated like a lightweight was a new experience for her. At five-eight, 135 pounds, she wasn't ballerina material.

"You got a bunch o' mail waiting for you in the cottage," she said, then went to give Jed a hand unloading the pickup.

The cottage sat on a knoll where the sun was shining down on it brightly. Gemcie opened the windows, letting the sweet air into the stale room. She grabbed the stack of mail on the mantle, settled into the wooden rocking chair by the window, and tore through the remnants of her past life.

An official manila envelope held the divorce papers, a response to the request she filed before leaving. She scanned them, not really understanding the legalese. Yellow marks indicated where she should sign and a return envelope accompanied the papers. She tossed them on the floor. There would be no argument from her, Jorge had nothing she wanted, except Marshal, but her attorney made her promise not to sign anything before discussing it with her.

A short note from Billy informed her that Marshal pulled a rail in the Cup qualifier. Talk was that Dominique was trying to convince Nelia to have him cut. "It would be a cryin' shame to end his bloodline just because that girl don't know how to ride him right," he'd told her. The thought of Marshal being manhandled by

Dominique sent a fresh quiver of anguish through her. He was the one thing she couldn't bear to lose. His trusting, intelligent black eyes often came to her in dreams. The image of him questioning, wondering why she left him when he had done nothing but what she had asked of him, filled her with damp dread.

A card came from Val. She was in Europe for the summer. Sue Ellen must have given her the address hoping Val could convince her to come back to the horse world. Another letter had no return address, but Gemcie recognized her mother's sprawling scrawl. She placed it on the mantle, unopened. She might read it one day, but not today. She didn't want her mind confused with whatever her mother's wishes might be. She just wanted to sit and rock, reveling in the sweet feeling of being home. The intense womblike sensation of sitting in the chair that her mother rocked in waiting for her father to return from the mountains brought her peace.

For a fleeting moment she imagined her mother entwined in her father's arms. She very likely had been conceived in the feather bed in this very room. She quickly blotted out the image of the two lovers clinging to one another like vines. Imagining her mother with auburn hair down to her cream-white waist, hot, sweating in an animal clench with a man Gemcie would never know, seemed a gross invasion. She took her thoughts to the face of brooding Bear Mountain that looked over this valley. The bluebirds kept her company with their enthusiast chatter. With the soft gurgle of the brook not ten feet from her window and the sun beaming down, the breeze her gentle lover, she was lulled into an afternoon nap.

Tired from three days on the trail, Gemcie skipped dinner and turned in early. The mattress that had felt lumpy before she became a packer now exceeded all her standards of luxury. She snuggled into the down stuffing, the soft pillow under her chin, and pulled the comforter up around her shoulders. Sinking into a dreamless sleep, she slept soundly until roused by a loud thud. She ran to the open window to see Cindy chasing a black bear cub down the drive in the faint dawn light. She had banged a soup ladle on a metal garbage can cover to send the cub flying.

Gemcie stuffed long legs in her jeans, hoping to get a closer look at the cub. She'd never seen a live bear, except the sad docile varieties that lived at the zoo. Cindy huffed back up the drive, breathless by the time she reached the top.

"No matter how many times I tell people to bag their garbage, someone forgets," Cindy said. "Bears don't become pests by themselves."

The excitement over, they went inside. Jed poured two steaming cups of coffee for them at the breakfast counter.

"Did you see him? He sure was cute," Gemcie said.

"Yea, I seen 'im. He's why I don't relish your goin' up on the mountain by yourself. He's got plenty of relatives up there. You don't see 'em much, but they can be trouble when you do."

"I know to keep my food and utensils in the bear bags, away from my camp. You taught me to put all my food scraps and fish guts in the fire. I won't touch my face, clothes, or any of my gear before washing my hands really good to get rid of the food scent. Besides, these are black bears, not grizzlies."

"Yeah, well, a black bear can do a lot o' damage to a human if he takes a mind to. I admit they don't do it unless somebody gets real stupid, but it worries me just the same," Jed said.

Gemcie's face, while Jed lectured her on bear etiquette, evidenced her father's eyes, square jaw and high cheekbones.

"We know you can handle yourself on a horse, but we're worried you won't be paying attention to the elements or where you are going. You could get lost," Cindy said.

"C'mon, hundreds of people hike the trail every year. I've got the map that shows where the best grazing pastures and campsites are, as well as streams, lakes, and rivers. Even if I get turned around, I know how to fish. I can take care of myself. You've got to believe in me," Gemcie pleaded.

Jed turned to Cindy for an answer.

"The truth has been hidden from you too long," Cindy stated, nodding her head to Jed for confirmation.

Jed turned to Gemcie. "All right, you can take Mercedes to ride and Maxine to stow your gear, but I want you back here by the next full moon, or I'm sendin' out the helicopter," Jed said, with stern severity.

Gemcie stretched across the counter to hug him.

"You won't be sorry! I promise."

She turned to Cindy. "You don't know what this means to me," she whispered into her soft pink ear.

"You are like your daddy. We know you need to know where

you come from, but you got to promise me you will turn back if the weather turns ugly."

"I will," Gemcie promised, eyes glistening with gratitude.

"Cooter Jay is goin' with you, or you ain't goin' at all," Jed said.

"Whatever you say," Gemcie said, trembling with anticipation.

*****

Gemcie could see the vapors of her breath rising in the crisp morning air as she weighed the essentials for the trek, a hundred and fifty pounds being optimum. She was at one hundred sixty-five. She lifted the single Bunsen burner stove from the pile with her bedroll and tent. Concentrating on the scale needle, she pretended not to notice a loud belch breaking the early calm coming from Gus, on the other side of the loading dock.

"Ain't you got any couth?" Pete asked Gus, as he lifted Maxine's harness onto her back.

"Where I come from that's the mating call for a good woman," Gus returned.

"I'm glad I'm not from wherever that is," Gemcie interjected.

"You sure you want to be doin' this alone?" Pete asked, cinching Maxine until she let the air out of her belly with a great sigh.

"You are the first one going over Mono and Silver Pass this season," he said.

"Virgin territory. Sounds exciting," Gemcie said.

"Could be some snow pack up there," Gus warned.

"You're goin' to need this hack saw for down wood on the trail," Pete said, laying it on top of her stack of essentials.

"You don't look like a trail blazer to me, miss, if you don't mind my saying so," Gus said, hefting the heavy leather pouch up to catch its straps on the wood mounts of Maxine's harness.

"You want to be paying strict attention out there. There will be patches of snow up in the pass that make for some slippery footing," he warned.

The sky glistened in Pete's blues eyes as he squinted, looking up to the top of the mountains.

"Weather can come up any time. Gets cold on the top. You sure you want to do this?" he asked.

"I've never been more certain about anything in my life,"

Gemcie answered, as she strapped the white tarp over the supplies piled high on Maxine's back.

"You'd better take this bullwhip with you then. You got to have some kind of weapon on you," he said, tying it onto Maxine's harness.

"Do I look like Indiana Jones?" Gemcie laughed.

"I don't like this," Pete said. "Maybe you could wait 'til the end of the season when I can go with you?"

Gemcie looked into Pete's piercing eyes that had darkened with genuine concern.

"I'll be fine. There're some things a person has to do on their own steam," Gemcie said, loosening Maxine's lead line from the hitching post.

She slipped her booted foot into the wooden stirrup, swinging her leg over Mercedes, standing at the ready.

Gus handed her the lead line for Maxine.

"Pete, there ain't no use in tryin' to tell a woman what to do," Gus said. "I learned that too late."

Excitement bubbled through Gemcie as she peered down at Gus and Pete, and squeezed Mercedes forward with strong calves.

"No, it ain't," she responded with a laugh, and waved her hat goodbye.

Chapter Twelve

The trail to Mono Pass took her quickly up the belly of the mountain. As the wind whipped the bluff, blood rushed to her cheeks. She could see a fresh blanket of white settled on the peaks in the distance. Cotton-candy clouds draped mountaintops poking through powder blue skies. Below a sparkling necklace of glacier lakes dotted the valley floor. Tufts of pink penstemon pushed through the gray boulders at the side of the trail. A quilt of yellow rabbit bush and splashy orange paintbrush covered the sun-filled clearings.

Mercedes snagged clumps of lupine and fresh green grass lining the trail. A very clever girl, she found the sandy footing between the boulders and foot-high water bars. When crossing a creek, she tapped the rocks with an educated hoof, testing for stability before marching briskly forward. The increasing altitude made Gemcie lightheaded, but Mercedes pressed ever upward on the switchback, traversing the mountainside undaunted.

Gemcie planned to reach Mono Pass and cross the summit before nightfall. She felt she was riding the stairway to heaven as Mercedes clambered up rock ladders to the crest of the uppermost peaks. The stern faces of the granite crags that had looked untouchable from the valley below were less formidable at close range. Soon, patches of snow were at her feet. Cooter Jay rolled in the white stuff, rooting it with his snout, giggling with excitement. He shoved his squat barrel-shaped body through the crust, using his nose like a plow. Rolling onto his back, he flailed his short legs in the air. He righted himself and then shook his compact body violently, spreading a white mist in the air. His coal-black eyes glistened, as a ragged grin spread across his mottled gray face.

Mercedes took notice of the change in footing, but did not hesitate to cross stretches of snow tinged with a pink hue. She lunged through, sinking a foot into the remnants of a light winter. Maxine let out a melodious bray that echoed through the canyon, announcing their arrival. Fat yellow-bellied marmots stood guard at the turquoise glacier lake nestled in the cirque. Standing erect on hind legs they chirped signals to relatives as the tiny procession trammeled through the remote summit. Gemcie thought about camping at the lake, but the gray clouds amassing above told her to ride on.

From this vantage the mountains peaked like cake frosting spread to the horizon. The wind blew through her mind, disengaging her thoughts from the cares of a world she left far below. The clatter of hooves over the flat boulders was hypnotic, but her musings ended abruptly when the trail stopped at a precipice overlooking the shady side of the pass. The slope covered with a slick snow patch crusted with ice presented a steep descent. Dismounting, she stepped gingerly on the surface, testing for depth, and sunk in up to her knees. She determined to hand-walk the animals down the slippery footing on the diagonal.

With reins in hand, getting as far ahead of her mare as she could, Gemcie launched over the side of the mountain. Mercedes lunged through the drift, sinking in up to her belly. A surge of muscle and bone brought her out of the deep pocket of snow. Bunching her haunches, she jumped clear of the snow, clattering to an unsteady stop on the loose shale at the bottom of the slope.

Gemcie clamored back up the incline to get Maxine. Mules spend a great deal of time thinking of ways to get out of work. Feigning defects, creating delays, simply sitting down on the job, are usual tactics. Maxine didn't like the looks of the hill. She stared down with her great long ears tipped, sniffing the air for a sign. Digging her fore-feet into the ledge at the top, she brayed pitifully while Gemcie pulled on her lead line. Knowing she couldn't win an arm wrestle with Maxine, Gemcie remembered the bull whip Gus stashed in her gear.

After a couple of practice snaps, the whip let out a loud pop that sounded like a six shooter. Maxine jumped forward, bounding over the cliff, before Gemcie could catch her lead line. She watched, with horror, as Maxine slogged through the snow with her heavy load swaying from side to side. The mule threatened to topple down the mountain, taking a month's worth of supplies with her to the bottom of the pass. Instead she bogged down in the hole Mercedes made before her. Maxine grunted to a dead stop, snow to her chest.

Gemcie scrambled down the slope in knee-high snow to dig out the mule. Maxine went still. Unlike a horse, mules don't thrash and flounder when they are in trouble, they simply quit. After Gemcie had dug the mule clear of the snow to her knobby knees, Maxine managed to stagger down to the plateau where Mercedes waited patiently for them. Cooter Jay slid down the mountain, using his body as a sled.

Gemcie's cheeks burned from the brisk wind coming in from the west. Her ears, exposed under her hard hat, ached from the cold blast whistling up the canyon in the late afternoon. Even though perspiring from exertion, she felt a chill moving up her spine. She leaned into the wind, pressing her band toward the protected valley below the ten-thousand-foot summit. Curled orange fists of shy poppies hiding from the blustery wind laced the path. Tall grass billowing on the side of the hill looked like a glistening swath of wildness. Gemcie placed her hand over her brow, blocking the sun to survey the swaying blasts of bright yellow dandelion peppering the meadow below.

A rill veined through the top of the world, trickling sweetly beneath a weathered wood foot bridge built by the mountaineers of long ago. She jammed numb hands into her pockets to warm them, as Maxine and Mercedes tromped across the wooden bridge. Cooter Jay chose to swim, splashing madly through the icy water. The trail narrowed to a boulder-strewn switchback that delivered her to the valley floor in half an hour.

She put the grazing bell on Mercedes, and turned the animals out in the meadow where Mono creek chuckles through the valley floor. Safe from the bluster of the summit, warmed by the afternoon sun, Gemcie peeled off layers of clothing down to cream-white flesh. The caress of the tender breeze excited her every cell. She lay down in the soothing green of the meadow ablaze with shooting stars. Inhaling deeply, she tried to embed the scent of God's great garden into her senses.

She quickly filtered her water and pitched her tent. She knew that even though the glacier run-off looked pristine, the risk of giardia in the Sierras is high. Trail mix and turkey jerky made a quick dinner. After an exhausting first day out, sleep came easily and she snoozed soundly through the star-studded night.

Jeffrey and lodge pole pines scented the crisp morning air on her march through Mono Valley. Sun filtering through the trees warmed the upturned faces of flowers. A grove of stately aspen with white bark trunks chattered to one another in the breeze. Patches of melting snow dampened the earth when the trail turned into a narrow switchback taking her upward to Silver Pass Meadow. Mercedes's nostrils flared pink, her neck went wet with sweat, and foam flecked between her legs. The sun melted the snowpack, creating a trickling runoff that darkened the trail with soggy patches of mud to be navigated with care. Deeply inhaling the scent of pine, and the rich moist soil, Gemcie's thoughts turned as soft as the snow melt.

For the first time since her accident, she felt totally relaxed. She was finally free from nagging outside influences and voices telling her what to do and how. Just feeling and breathing in the beauty around her kept her riveted in the present moment. Despite all the disappointments she had experienced recently, she felt grateful to be vitally alive again. Thoughts of Jorge flitted in and out of her mind. If it was just a dalliance, why had he bothered to ask her to marry him? Billy's betrayal was lessened by the gift of the mountains and the truth of her beginnings that he had given her. She felt sorry for her mother who had allowed regret to consume her life. Winning the Grand Prix didn't matter much now. It all seemed so far away and long ago. Just being here was all that mattered.

A flashing blue bird dove across the path, taking residence on a sturdy twig. Swaying back and forth on his perch, he chastised her loudly. The trail intersected a brassy creek swollen with rain that paralleled the excited water gushing over boulder jumbles. Gemcie spotted a protected sand bar where she could take a sun bath. She tied horse and mule to a generous old tree bent low to the ground from storms. In search of her own kind, Maxine belted out a melodic bray that echoed through the canyon. There was no reply. After lunch, Gemcie lay down on the warm gravel bed, resting her head in the crook of her arm, taking a sweet rest in the sun.

While she was napping, cloud cover crept over the horizon. Waking and taking note of the troubled sky, Gemcie pulled her map out of her jacket pocket to trace her route. The trail should take her to a glacier-fed lake. She hoped to reach it in time to pitch her tent and set up camp before the thick gray clouds massing in the west let loose their wet load. With boot to belly, she cinched Mercedes as tightly as she could while checking to make certain Maxine's load was secure. She moved quickly up the rock-strewn trail to beat the summer storm.

A cold wind greeted Gemcie as she crested the ridge, affording her a farewell view of the meadow she'd lingered in earlier. The trail at the crest was a wide, easy march with a sandy bottom. She yearned to canter, but with Maxine loaded behind, a brisk walk was all she could manage. Stray droplets splashed on the dry rocks let her know the afternoon storm was closing in. Happily, she saw the lake on the map before her.

Tall green grass framed the south edge of the fast-darkening pool. Here, they would find plenty of feed for the animals. Patches of snow remained in the shade of the stunted pine trees on the far shore. A rosy pink crag with a crest that resembled a saddle stood guard. She spied a flat, sandy space big enough for her tent about thirty yards from the water's edge that would make a perfect campsite. With a whistle and a kick, she spirited her team to the spot.

Quickly dismounting, she secured the animals then lifted her supplies from Maxine's back. She quickly inserted the tent poles into nylon ribs then planted them into the ground. Shelter, just in case the storm let loose, was the first order of business. Then she gathered dry wood for a fire. Lots of small boulders close at hand made a cook site easy. With her bedroll and gear stowed inside her tent, she was free to go fishing.

Late afternoon found her at water's edge casting her line into the glassy lake. She rested her foot on a down log that lay across a purling stream running over mossy rocks. *This must be where the world begins*, she thought. *This soft, yet strong water succeeds in carving the world, though yielding, always flowing to the lowest point. This is the feminine way. Women yield in order to get what they want.* To be passive, non-threatening yet strong like water is what she wanted to be.

She donned her plastic poncho just in case the clouds opened before she caught her dinner. She could see small trout flipping completely out of the water to snap up the natural feed of mosquitoes and fly larvae. Her spinning red-and-white dare-devil lure dancing just beneath the surface of the water had lots of competition in tempting the brookies. She let fly her line repeatedly, listening to the rhythmical click of her reel, as she wound the lure back in. The succulent prey plopped not ten feet away, creating hypnotic concentric patterns in the water.

She flicked mosquitoes from her face, while the thick moist clouds provided a free mountain facial. A sharp boom of thunder broke through the heavens in long, rolling, reverberating waves, which trembled with magnificent strength a full ten seconds before a ragged streak of electric energy cut across the sky, casting an eerie glow on the bald saddle-shaped peak. Energized by the sight, she allowed the awesome thrill of the elements to distract her from the task at hand. Then another tremulous crack of brooding thunder came closer. The mist turned to large splotches of thick wet snow settling on her hair and shoulders.

Just as she was about to accept defeat, she felt a tiny tug on her line. She responded with a quick snap of the wrist to set the hook in the mouth of whatever was on the end of her line. She quickly reeled a small, brown speckled lake trout into shore, and lifted it out of the water with her net. Overjoyed that she didn't have to settle for lentil mush, she hurried back to her camp.

Satisfied with her camp, she crawled into her tent for a nap. Soon the rain was coming in torrents, thrumming a somber tune. She listened in happy contentment, snoozing like a chipmunk curled in the duff of the forest floor, soothed by the rhythms of the summer storm. The drenching downpour dissipated to a gentle patter.

Gemcie unzipped her tent to a world awash in the drowsy color of dusk. Wet leaves drooped to the ground, looking weighted by diamonds. She built a fire with a solid log that would last at least an hour. Then she whittled a couple of twigs to sharp points to secure a tarp, creating a windbreak for the fire. She gutted her trout with one clean movement of her knife, from center belly to gill. She next sprinkled it with seasonings, wrapped it in foil and set it in the coals. And last, she filled her canteen with filtered water for tea and hot soup. While eating the sweet pink flesh of the fish, she watched the columns of light walking across the rugged white peaks. The gray mountains served as a palette for a playful creator, casting first pink then bronze then gold illuminations over their flat faces.

A crimson sun slipped quietly behind the peaks, leaving a cape of pink resting on the mountain shoulder. Violet shadows strode through the sky as the stars speckled the heavens. A silver strand of moon rode on the saddle crest. Staring into the hot embers, hypnotized by the blue licking flame, she felt the storm she carried in her heart stir. A swell of hot humiliation rose from her belly, settling in her chest as she saw Jorge's broad, wholesome, smile before her. *Had his love ever been real?* Life at the Mariposa was once everything she had ever wanted and now it was gone forever. Hugging her knees, she rocked back and forth sobbing until her tears went dry. In time the crushing weight lifted from her chest, the heavy fury that swirled in her brain subsided. Spent, she turned in early and slept peacefully, lulled by the hoot of an owl on the night shift.

She awoke to a world dazzling bright in the morning sun. Crystallized grass framed the lake sparkling like gems. Mist floated over the water as the sun melted the ice that crusted on it over the night. The water in her canteen had a layer of ice. By nine the chill was out of the air. Gemcie had her animals packed, tacked and was ready to mount Mercedes. She gave one last swipe at the campsite with her boot, making sure her tracks were covered. Her visit there would be no more noticeable than that of a raindrop.

Chapter Thirteen

Today she would climb still higher. She looked up to the austere faces of the jutting block columns of granite that are the sentinels overlooking Silver Pass Meadow. Gus told her Silver Pass Meadow, a protected fertile expanse of green fed by the gentle Silver Creek twining its way through the meadow, was Jed's personal favorite campsite. Looking up from the valley floor, the ascent seemed unthinkable, but her resolve to reach this meadow was unshaken.

The clamorous thunder of a waterfall obscured by trees grew louder when the trail started to climb. The din drowned out the twitter of the chickadee and complaints of the stellar jays. Her heart quickened as the trail took her step-by-step closer to the imposing sound of the cascade. She emerged from the shady tree tunnel into the sun to stand at the base of the waterfall, a torrent of water sliding in fans over flat boulders as big as boxcars. She held her hand up to protect her eyes from the iridescent spangle of the water in the sun. Silver Pass Creek spilled over a cleft in the rocks a thousand feet above her in clear white sheets. It crossed in an energetic rush over the boulder path at her feet then funneled into a narrow channel and a gorge another thousand feet below. It plunged down the ravine in a rage of foam, creating rainbows where spray shot twelve feet into the air.

The water was too swift for Cooter Jay to swim. His twelve-pound body would be scooped up and swept over the precipice to a sure and sudden death. Gemcie's stomach churned as she jumped down to grab him. He wriggled to free himself, but Gemcie held him firmly by the scruff of his neck. He twisted and mock-bit, but soon resigned himself to being slung, belly down, behind the saddle horn.

Gemcie clucked Mercedes forward. The mare tapped at the boulder path three feet under the swift flowing torrent with her hoof. It felt secure. She stepped into the rush, sinking in up to her belly. Gemcie lifted her feet back and up to keep from getting soaked, letting the mare find her way.

Maxine would have to come in before Mercedes reached the other side. The lead rope wasn't long enough to let her remain on the other side. The mule hesitated, blowing at the water with fretful snorts. With huge ears crooked to half mast, she gave Gemcie a forlorn look as she felt a pull on the lead. If Gemcie lost the line she would not be able to go back. There was no room to turn around on the trail.

"C'mon, Maxine, get up," she growled in the most guttural sound she could muster.

"Get up, mule!" she yelled, giving another quick tug on the line.

Maxine lurched into the water. If she so much as teetered to the left, she could tumble over the boulder-lined trail, never stopping until she reached the bottom of the gorge. Gemcie looked back long enough to see Maxine floundering. If she tripped, Gemcie would have to let loose of the lead and let her go. Maxine stood stock still in the middle of the bulging stream for a moment, righting herself, balancing her load, before marching steadily forward. Once the unflappable mule was safe on the other side, Gemcie squeezed Mercedes up strongly to achieve momentum for the climb. The mare surged ahead, climbing up the granite stairwell like a cat. The trail narrowed to a two-foot wide switchback lined with rocks on the down side of the trail. Gemcie couldn't look down at the twisting boulder death below, so she looked out to the upper regions of the canyon where the tree line stopped. Vertigo threatened to overtake her when she looked over her shoulder at the spreading fan of water shimmering over the immense boulders. No matter how much the postcard scenery tempted her attention, her equilibrium was lost if she took her eyes from the trail for more than a second. All the while, Cooter Jay whimpered for his freedom.

Mercedes panted heavily at the exertion. Gemcie could feel her sides heaving between her legs. Halfway up the ascent she called her band to a halt. Mercedes took no notice of the gaping gorge below, splaying her hind legs for balance, and took a breather on the curve of the switchback. The untroubled mule took to munching a clump of lupine in a cleft of the rocks. Gemcie weighted her stirrup on the mountain side of the trail and held her breath, hoping Maxine wouldn't take an unconscious step backwards and go rocketing to the bottom of the ravine. Five minutes seemed to become an hour for Gemcie, perched on the ledge.

"Get up, mule," she clucked, swatting Maxine gently with her reins.

She kept her eyes riveted on the baby blue skies with thin streams of white cirrus clouds rushing by overhead. Never looking back, she leaned into the lunging upward movement of the mare, keeping her weight out of the saddle until Mercedes crested the uppermost stretch of the trail and stood solidly on flat ground.

Eagles soared in circles overhead riding thermals in the midday sun. Eye level with the stony faces she had revered from below, her heart lifted as she watched the great birds playing in the wind. A gentle tromp on good footing brought her to Silver Pass Meadow, the most generous helping of God's great garden heaped in one spot she had ever seen. Quivering with excitement, she felt a rush of emotion rise in her chest. Her lip trembled. Soon tears flowed from a heart overwhelmed with beauty.

She set the animals to graze on the spring grass. Flush with newfound freedom, they charged across the meadow like colts, twisting, kicking, turning hooves to the air and letting loose great blasts of wind to accent their happiness. She picked a spot nestled in the shoulder of the mountain, backed by giant boulders with a view of the verdant pine-ringed meadow. Silver Creek, a quiet stream curling through the meadow, was so clear she could see its golden trout darting below the surface. The stairway to heaven was not for the faint hearted, but she had arrived.

The skies began to grumble. Repeated low complaints rumbled from the thunderheads massing to the south. Flashes of light whitewashed the tender evening sky as Gemcie made a quick meal. By the time she was cleaning up, jagged flashes of light seared the sky soon, followed by loud metallic cracks threatening to rip the heavens open. She loved the excitement of the summer storms and looked forward to a cozy drowse to the din of the rain on her tent.

Once in her warm, dry bedroll she curled up like a newborn rabbit in its furry nest. The storm mounted. Soon the rain came in stiff sheets, pummeling her tent with ferocious indifference. It only intensified her sense of achievement in enjoying this smug snuggle. The sheets of water turned to hail that sounded like popcorn popping on her head. She chuckled at the railing storm outside, drifting into sweet slumber. Hours passed and still the storm did not subside. A clanging crack of thunder, like two cymbals clashing in her ear, woke her. She fumbled in the dark to find her headlamp. As she ran her fingers along the tent floor she felt the bottom floating. Adrenaline shot through her body, waking her instantly when she realized her safe haven was resting on about an inch of water. Her sanctuary was about to be lifted like Noah's ark off its rock. Soon her tent would be flooded, all her gear soaked, and she would spend the rest of the night trying to find shelter.

Quickly pulling her plastic poncho over her head, she unzipped the tent door and crawled out into the eye of the storm. A flash of lighting illuminated the sky, allowing her to see solid sheets of water sliding down the boulders behind her camp, funneling into a fast-rising river threatening to overtake her tent in minutes. The boom, boom, boom of thunder arrived quickly; telling her the storm was directly overhead. She crawled back into the tent, grabbed her clothing and whatever gear was on the floor, and jammed it into two nylon stuff sacks. Surveying the site for higher ground with her headlamp, she spotted a space with a gentle slope protected by a tree. She kicked the pinecones from the spot, leveling the ground with her boot. The, she ran back to get the tent, pulled up the stakes holding it down, lifted it from the top where the poles intersected, and carried it twenty yards to the spot she hoped would stay dry.

Nervous about the livestock, she went to their picket line to see if they needed attention. Maxine and Mercedes stood stock still, heads low to the ground, enduring the onslaught. Gemcie went back to her tent, knowing sleep wouldn't come until the storm passed. She crawled back into her tent, clicked off her headlamp and stuck her feet deep into the downy warmth of her bag. She screamed, bolting upright, when her foot touched something wet, furry and foul. Panic made her try to stand. She bumped her head on the tent poles, almost lifting them from their reinstated stakes. She tried to back away from the intruder, nearly toppling the tent. She backed out of the tent on hands and knees. Rain dripped off the flap, onto her waist, soaking her long johns. She scrambled to find the headlamp on the tent floor. Tennis shoes, canteen, socks, headlamp! She clicked it on, lifted the sleeping bag liner, to find Cooter Jay coiled into a ball at the foot of her bedroll. He gave her a sleepy smile, blinking coal-black eyes in the lamplight.

"Cooter Jay, you sorry mutt!" Gemcie cried, grabbing him by the scruff of the neck, flinging him into the tent wall. She tried to cozy into the damp, funky smell of mongrel permeating her bag and tent, but couldn't. Sleep belonged to someone else that night. Gus and Pete wouldn't hear about this one, she thought, as she listened to the angry drum of the rain and waited for the weak light of dawn.

Chapter Fourteen

For two days she kept to the ridge trail, treasuring the silence. She found it jarring to just be alone. There was no one to blame if she made a mistake. No one to come to her aid if she stumbled. There was also no one to interfere with her personal destiny, her thoughts or machinations. It was thrilling to test her own boundaries, with her self-imposed limits, and it was quiet. Quiet enough to hear her own thoughts, to watch them crystallize, then dissolve like snowflakes in her imagination, uncensored by convention, or the expectations of others. No one chattering in her ear, or talking on their cell phone in some inane conversation with someone she didn't care to know. She reveled in this newfound freedom.

On her second afternoon on the crest, she met two young men backpacking.

"Where you headed?" Gemcie asked, leaning her forearm on the saddle horn.

"Mt. Whitney," a young man about twenty-five, weighted with a bulky pack and wearing bicycle shorts, said.

"How long have you been out?"

"About two weeks. We started in Yosemite," said his partner, wearing a cap with a flap down the back to protect his neck.

"Anything up ahead I should know about?" she asked, blocking the intense sun with her hand.

"There's a few down trees across the trail, but mostly you should be fine."

"We saw some bear scat," the second hiker added.

"Yeah, and some scratches on a tree that looked fresh."

They confirmed that, in fact, she was on the Pacific Crest where it parallels the John Muir Trail. Eager to return to the luxury of solitude, she wished them well. Many people hike the trail and she really didn't want to run into any others. She wanted her mind to become a blank canvas, free to receive and respond to the wilderness and its new images, her internal discourse allowed to ramble uncensored, professing no purpose, no direction, no judgment and no goals. She breathed the clear air deeply into smog-smudged lungs, exhaling audibly. Lost in her thoughts, she clomped along like an old gold miner, whistling a tune she'd never heard before.

Surveying her map after breakfast the next day, she spotted a less-traveled trail digressing from PCT just outside of her campsite. She headed for the narrow tributary, ponying Maxine close behind. A sharp descent took her into a gorge where she passed through a stand of tall sequoia. She tried to absorb the strength of the towering giants into her psyche. She felt safe in the shelter of the shady tree canopy that survived the ax of lumbermen long ago. The sun's rays filtered through the boughs in wide beams of light, spotlighting wildflowers on the pine-needle floor. Noisy stellar jays sporting iridescent blue jackets flashed by her. After two hours' travel, she spotted a tiny nameless lake neighbored by a meadow ablaze with magenta fireweed. Drawn by the babble of a brook tumbling on the far side of the lake, she found a perfect campsite.

Quickly unloading Maxine, she freed the animals to graze on the silver grass feathering the meadow. The sun shone brightly in a cloudless sky. Basking in the sunshine on a warm rock, she watched the butterflies wafting over the wildflowers, landing just long enough to fan their magical displays of intricate design and dazzling color. Sighing into the sun, yielding to its lazy temptations, she rested on the heated boulder. While watching the clouds drift by, she resolved that tomorrow would be the day to do what she had wanted to do ever since she entered the high country.

Soft pink skies melted to saffron by the time Gemcie had coffee steaming in her cup the next morning. Fluffy mountains of clouds hugged the top of the knife-like peaks. She tacked up Mercedes, but left Maxine grazing in the meadow powdered with pink blooms. Heart thumping at the prospect of a real hack through the virgin countryside, Gemcie set out for a day ride. Ambling along, ponying a pack mule was fine for looking at the scenery, but she yearned for a real ride!

Invigorated by the chill morning air, Mercedes trotted smartly on the soft cushion of pine needles. She snorted, flaring pink nostrils. Gemcie posted to the trot heading for the open meadow. Green grasses tickled Mercedes' belly as she trotted briskly through mule's ears and larkspur. Butterflies lifted from her path. Energized, the mare surged forward. Gemcie stood in the stirrups, shortened the reins and pressed her forward with her calves. The mare responded with a gentle lift off the ground into a soft rocking canter. Gemcie's heart sang as she floated across the sunlit meadow with a gentle, cool wind in her face.

She spied a trailhead that would take them upstream into the heart of the canyon, on the far side of the lake. A soft, sandy beach perfect for her purpose lay dead ahead. She leaned into the wind and clucked the go-ahead into Mercedes' ear. The mare charged forward, lowering herself into a flat-out gallop, giving way to adrenaline surging through her thousand-pound frame. Flush with excitement, Gemcie didn't feel the chill of wind causing tears to stream down her cheeks. Freedom raged, tingling through her body. Like the Centaur, she felt connected to the power surging between her thighs.

After a half-mile stretch, she pulled Mercedes up to cross a brash creek swollen with rain. The mare plopped into the icy water and splashed gaily through the big round boulders without hesitation. The water came to her girth. Gemcie lifted her feet from the stirrups, holding legs back and boots up. The mare floundered on a moss-slick boulder, nearly toppling backward into the drink. She righted herself in time, and lunged up the bank on the other side. Gemcie pressed the mare up the narrow path paralleling the agitated water. The summer storm the night before had filled the creek with branch clusters and brown silt. Mercedes trotted briskly up the steep ascent, happy to leave cumbersome packs and mules behind.

Ears alert, the mare surged steadily up the canyon propelled by her strong hindquarters. It was a perfect trail for a hack. Not too steep, wide enough for a fast pace with soft, sandy footing. A fat gray quail flapped wildly to get out of their path. Dun-colored sparrows in brown mottled jackets took flight. Gemcie ducked under low-hanging limbs, waving boughs in the trail away from her body. Catching the occasional sticky spider web in the face told her that no one had passed this way for a while.

She hoped to spy the shy deer hidden in the underbrush. Patches of crunchy snowpack lined the path in the shade of the pine boughs. The solid, wide trail was taking her into unknown upper regions. The intense sun melting the snow fast made the way slippery. A bold breeze whipped the snow-laden boughs, dropping the wet onto Gemcie's shoulders. The forest was a green blur as they flew through it until Mercedes' sides were heaving.

Letting the mare settle back into a walk, she allowed Mercedes to pick her own way up the trail following the river. Cooter Jay, running full tilt on spinning wheel legs, caught up and ran ahead of Mercedes. Gemcie closed her eyes, lifting her face to the sun's warmth. She was nearly asleep in the saddle when the mare suddenly stopped. She stood stalk still, flicking her ears. She sensed someone, or something, was near. She whinnied into the firmament, shaking Gemcie violently, asking who, or what, was there to show themselves. She pranced, lifting forefeet off the ground, attempting to rear. Gemcie leaned onto her neck to help her balance, squeezing her forward with strong legs.

Cooter Jay came tearing back down the trail. He barked madly and began spinning in a circle until his nose touched his tail. Mercedes wouldn't calm down. Instead, she tried to turn on her haunches, tossed her head, and tried to snatch the bit. A snort from the brush announced a hulking dark figure with orange-brown eyes. He stood on his hind legs pawing the air, trying to get a better look at the intruders. The mare froze in terror for a few endless seconds. The hair on the back of the bear's neck bristled, saliva dripped from yellow canines as he opened his mouth wide and let out a growl deep from his gut. Returning to all fours, he pawed the ground in front of him with four-inch claws, sizing up his enemy.

In a black flurry of force the bear charged. Gemcie screamed when the bear hit his mark with a solid thud, barreling his body weight into the mare's chest, swiping her neck with powerful claws. The mare reared, pawing the air with her front hooves in defense. Her rear hoof slipped on the edge of the boulder-strewn trail and she toppled backwards into the bulging creek. Gemcie got her feet out of the stirrups in time to jump clear of the thrashing mare, trying to right herself in the white foam tinged pink with blood.

The bear hunkered at the edge of the creek, deciding whether to attack again. The smell of his foul breath, like rotten fish, registered somewhere in the recesses of Gemcie's consciousness. She tasted the cold metal of fear in her mouth and felt a sharp twinge of pain in her back where she'd landed on a jagged rock. Her water-logged leather chaps weighted her to the creek bottom. She couldn't out-run the bear; he could do thirty miles an hour on the flat. She couldn't out-climb him, or out-swim him, and she couldn't leave Mercedes, whose neck was splayed open in four wide bands, exposing red muscle. Scrambling backwards up the eroded cliff of the creek, she clung to exposed roots of trees where the earth had washed away.

A shot echoed through the canyon like a rocket blast. The startled bear cringed, looking around to see the creature possessing such a roar. Another booming blast, this time closer, ricocheted through the canyon, convincing the bear to take cover. He spun around and waddled on bowed legs back into the brush. He stopped long enough to glance over his shoulder with blazing eyes at his lost prey before ducking out of sight.

A horse and rider emerged over the rise in the trail. The stranger swung off his mount, keeping his rifle in hand, and rushed to help. First he gathered Mercedes' reins then helped the mare right herself. He left her standing in the rushing creek, stepped on a dry rock in the middle of the stream, leaned across the water, and extended his hand to Gemcie.

"Can you move?" he asked.

"I think so," she said, afraid to let go of the tree root keeping her from floating downstream. Where did this man with deep-set violet eyes below dark brows and a mop of disheveled black hair come from? He wore a flannel shirt tucked into blue jeans, a water canteen strapped to his belt, full leather chaps, and a bandana around his sunburned neck.

"Time's a wastin', I can't stand here forever," he said. "Take my hand. I won't let you go swimming."

Gemcie loosed her clenched fingers from the root and slipped down the eroded creek wall. She held her breath until she touched the tips of his fingers, snatching them so strongly she nearly pulled him off balance. He teetered on the rock but was able to keep both of them from landing in the icy brew. Gemcie tried to leap across the torrent, but her right leg went out from under her. He picked her up and carried her to a level spot in the trail, laid her gently down on the dirt floor, and stripped the heavy wet chaps from her body.

"Tell me if this hurts," he said, moving strong hands up and

106

down her leg, looking for tenderness, or a broken bone.

"No, I'll be fine," she said, knowing it was her old injury acting up. "Just give me a few minutes and I'll be okay."

"Well, there's fools and then there's damn fools," he said in response.

Gemcie felt her face flush hot with anger. Realizing she was totally dependent on this arrogant man, she held herself in check. The blood pulsed in her temples as he continued.

"Every year some tourist goes off track and lands in Blue's territory. I knew someday somebody was going to get hurt," he said, as a matter of fact.

"Blue?" she asked.

"He's the five-hundred-pound black bear that lives in this thicket. You woke him up from his day bed. That's why he was cranky."

"You think this is my fault!"

"I sure do. I've been watching you for the last couple of days. You had no business being camped so far away from the main trail. Coming up here on your own was just plain stupid," he stated with certainty, looking straight at her.

Gemcie choked back her mounting rage.

"That'll be enough free examination, doctor; I'll be fine," she snapped, pulling his hand off her thigh.

His harsh demeanor softened into a brilliant smile. He laughed, as if feeling self-conscious at having been too familiar.

"Maybe so, but your horse sure isn't in any shape to travel. I'll take you both back to my place," he said. "By the way, my name is Brady. Looks like you're going to be my houseguest for a while."

Mercedes' neck, flayed where Blue's claws had found their mark, bled profusely. She let her head hang low to the ground to allow the muscles in her neck to go slack. Brady gathered leaf mold, combining it with mud to create a poultice to slow the bleeding.

"Are you okay to ride?" he asked.

"I think so," she said. "Where's Cooter Jay?"

"Cooter Who?"

"My bear dog," Gemcie said, calling out to him.

Cooter emerged from under a low pine bough wearing a sheepish grin.

"That's a bear dog? I bet he'll fit in my saddle bag." Brady laughed.

"What about my mule? She is back at my camp."

"I'll get her in the morning. Don't think she'll mind taking a vacation."

"What about Blue?"

"He wouldn't have bothered you none if you hadn't walked into his bedroom."

He gathered up Tucker, a seasoned, seventeen-hand, mountain horse with a tawny chestnut coat. He stuffed his rifle in the scabbard then gave Gemcie a leg up, letting her sit in the middle of the saddle. He popped Cooter into the saddle bag, the dog squirming until his head poked out the side. Brady swung up behind her, resting on the poncho he kept tied in a roll behind the saddle seat. With Mercedes in tow, he clucked to Tucker, who responded with an energetic surge toward home. An hour later, they were still climbing higher into the alpine forest. Nasty pangs of guilt flooded Gemcie's mind every time she looked back to see her mare struggling over the boulder-pocked path.

The pines thinned to scrub as they neared the timberline. Gemcie felt the warmth of Brady's muscled body wrapped around hers. There was something comforting about him. She wanted to remain angry, but his easy manner and soothing voice disarmed her. She held the reins loosely as the horse trucked home on the trail he knew by heart.

"What are you doing up here?" she asked. "I didn't think anyone lived in the park."

"I work for the BLM, if you want to call it work."

"What do you mean?

The Bureau of Land Management is a lot like the army. They teach you a lot of skills, like fight fires, be paramedics, and then send you to a place where, with any luck, you never use your training," he said and laughed. "They got a whole bunch of rules they wrote down in 'the book' that no lookout ever reads, once he gets his post."

"What does a lookout do?"

"The biggest part of the job is glassing the mountain, every twenty minutes or so, for smokes; rescuing a hiker now and again. There's no special skill involved, but it calls for a mentality that enjoys doing a whole bunch of nothin'."

"How long have you been doing nothing?"

"About five years. The first three I spent the summers during the fire season with pay, but for the last two years, I stayed in for the winter without pay."

Gemcie fell silent contemplating the man whose bronze arm rested lightly around her waist. *What odd misanthropic tendencies must he possess to want to live here alone? What does a vitally alive man do with his powerful urges?* Her anxious musings were sidetracked by an unfamiliar twinge of nerve current in her lower back that traveled into her hip. It wasn't painful, just a fluttery electric sensation, but she feared it signaled the onset of another bout of jagged sciatic pain. She rationalized that worry is interest paid on a loan not due and effectively blocked the oncoming fear from her mind.

Chapter Fifteen

The trail turned into a snaking narrow ledge hugging the canyon wall. She dared not look down into the gorge a thousand feet below. She spied the lookout station on a plateau jutting out over the canyon. It rested on metal piers with concrete footings. Guy wires from the catwalk to the ground held it in place. The catwalk with wooden railings went all around the 12 x 12 cabin lined with wood-framed rectangular windows. It had a flat roof and a little smokestack. A ladder resting on the ground went to the trap door in the center of the cabin floor.

A small red barn sat on the knoll nearby overlooking the valley, framed in snow-scattered peaks. As they neared the lookout, Gemcie had the sensation of riding on the roof of the world, as close to God as she could ever come. The view of green pines, purple peaks stacked in the distance, and the silver thread weaving through the valley far below, was uninterrupted by roads, telephone poles, power lines, or any other trappings of civilization.

When they arrived at the tie rack in front of the barn, Brady hopped off and gave her a hand down. She wobbled when she touched ground. He caught her from falling and carried her to his cabin. In no position to argue, she let him carry her up the wooden stairs on the side of the stable that led to a small porch. He kicked the door open to a musty-smelling room with rough-hewn wood floors made from wide planks that creaked under his weight, as he brought her to a narrow bed. An oval rag rug blocked the light coming through the cracks from the stable below. The smell of wet hay made Gemcie feel at home. He laid her gently down on a colorful patchwork quilt draped over a feather mattress.

"I'll take care of your mare; you get some rest," he assured her.

More exhausted, and weaker than she realized, Gemcie felt weighted to the bed.

"What about Maxine?" she muttered, just before drifting off.

He unfolded a down comforter at the foot of the bed, and pulled it over her.

"I'll fetch her first thing in the morning. She won't mind standing in knee-high grass for another day. Don't worry. She'll be fine"

Gemcie fell to sleep lulled by the sound of the horses below who were rustling in straw bedding, grinding square molars on fresh feed.

Gray morning light filtered in through a window that needed cleaning. Awakened by a nagging pain that ran from hip to calf, she rolled over gently and tried to get out of bed. When she put her weight on her right leg, it gave way under her. Collapsing to the floor, she reverted to the postures the physical therapist taught her, attempting to alleviate the fiery sciatic pain ripping through her leg. The past day's events came rushing back. The worry in Mercedes's tender, dark eyes haunted her. She was stranded at a remote outpost in the High Sierras with a hermit. Anxious dread mounted with the realization that she could not walk.

There was soft rap on the door. She scrambled to the bed, pulled herself up and managed to crawl back under the covers.

"Come in."

Brady entered holding a tray loaded with a breakfast of blueberry pancakes and bacon. He used an empty coke bottle as a vase for wildflowers he'd picked outside. He set the tray down on the small pine table beside the bed.

"My cooking's not fancy, but you're probably hungry enough it doesn't matter."

He pulled up the battered wood rocker with a worn leather seat and torn straw back then made himself comfortable.

"How you feeling?"

"I've been better," Gemcie said, pulling the cover down, trying to sit up in bed. The movement caused her to wince. She pretended to sneeze, trying to keep him from knowing how much pain she was in. She slid back to a flat position, pulling the cover to her chin.

"Sure is a cozy bed. Thanks for letting me have it."

"No problem. I usually sleep on the cot in the lookout. Do my cookin' up there too, so I don't have to worry about the scent of bacon bringing Blue, or his buddies, up the hill. I keep all the food in the locker in the lookout. You can have meals here by yourself if you like until you feel better."

"That's awfully kind. I don't know how I can repay you."

"Well, I do."

Startled by his bluntness, Gemcie hesitated before answering for a moment, looking intently into his sea-blue eyes, hoping to discern the true nature of her keeper.

"You do?"

"Yep. I got a deal for you to think about, while I go fetch your mule. You and your livestock can stay here as long as you need, but you can't tell anybody about a bear attack. You just want to say your horse slipped into the creek, or some other made-up story."

"Why not?

"If you tell people, I'll have to make a report. Blue is a friend of mine. It wasn't his fault you happened into his valley uninvited."

"I never said it was!"

"Other people will. The BLM will order me to kill any bear that attacks a human or livestock."

Gemcie knew she had to trust this man who apparently felt closer to animals than people.

"I can't walk. I have a herniated disc. I guess wrapping myself around that boulder didn't do it any good," she confessed.

Laughter was the last thing she expected by this revelation. He found her comment cause to slap his knee and chuckle.

"You're more stupid than I thought!" he roared. "I'm no doctor, but I do have some vet training. You got no business being out here on your own, lady."

Gemcie's cheeks flushed crimson with humiliation. That was the second time, in their short encounter, he had called her stupid. She vowed not to divulge anything more than what was necessary to him in the future.

He got up, adjusted his bandana, and smiled tenderly, as though being charged with the care of a mildly mad woman was just part of the "great nothingness" he had to do.

"Well, you let me know if you want me to call the helicopter, or if you want to stay until you and your mare are well enough to travel. My deal still sticks," he said, and left.

Gemcie wolfed down her pancakes. She tried to rest but the

springs in the old bed creaked loudly every time she shifted when trying to find a comfortable position. Lying back with hands behind her head, she gazed over at the jagged peaks, rising one behind another into the horizon as far as she could see. Taking a deep breath and exhaling slowly allowed her body to relax into the sagging mattress. The pollen from pine cones had settled into yellow dust on the window sill. There was a screen to keep out the burly bumblebees by day, and blood-thirsty mosquitoes at night. The place had no electricity or heat, except for the river-rock fireplace. It was a step above camping, but still pretty rough. It would do just fine.

It was dusk before Brady returned with Maxine, loaded with camp gear. The mule let out a lilting bray that reverberated through the canyon. Mercedes nickered softly back. Brady un-tacked the animals, brushed them down, and gave them some feed. Heavy-booted footsteps up the wooden stairs and a solid rap marked his arrival at her door.

"Please, come in," she said sweetly.

"Don't mind if I do, happy to take a load off," he said, settling into the rocker, letting lanky legs spread wide. He took off his Stetson and planted it on his knee.

"You must be hungry by now. I'll bring you something to fill that hole in your belly in a few minutes."

"Thanks for getting Maxine."

"No problem; it's a nice ride and a good meadow for Tucker to get some natural feed."

"I've made up my mind, but there's just one thing you've got to do for me," she said.

"Besides wait on you hand and foot?" he asked with a smile.

"I'll be able to do chores around here soon. I plan to earn my keep." She could feel her blood rising but held her temper in check.

"Wasn't much to do before you got here, but I suppose that could change," he said, in his eyes a mischievous twinkle.

"You get word to Jed and Cindy at Rock Creek. Let them know I'm here, but don't tell them I'm hurt. Just tell them Mercedes pulled a suspensory. If you can do that for me, I won't let anybody know what happened."

"Fair enough," he said, "I'll bring in some water, so you can wash up." He grabbed the rusty water carrier on his way out the door.

113

Chapter Sixteen

For the next week Brady brought her meals at regular intervals, staying just long enough to ensure that her needs were met. Each morning and evening she could hear him speaking in a low moderated voice to Tucker as he brushed him down before placing a saddle pad on his back. Then he ponied Maxine and Mercedes to a nearby lake where they could drink and enjoy natural feed for an hour or so. The caravan, eager for freedom, clamored out of the barn. Brady livened his band with the crack of a whip, and a high shrill whistle. She wanted to join them but was left to lie alone on the creaking bed, listening anxiously for their return.

Soon she was able to stand long enough to clean her window. She opened it wide to get a better view of the green sea of pine that filled the air with its pungent, wild scent. Sitting on the window sill, brushing her shoulder-length curls became her morning ritual. Below her the sparkling silver strand continued to carve the canyon wall with ceaseless motion. From here she could track the movement of bossy cumuli clouds swelling into shifting mountains of white. Lazy with sunshine, the long days of summer drifted by.

In the evenings Brady built a roaring flame in the river-rock fireplace. He filled the tea kettle and hung it from a wrought iron hook over the fire until it hissed and steamed. Steeping the tea until it was perfect he served it to her with honey in one of the mugs hanging from the hooks on the wood mantle. Three photos rested on the mantle in dust-covered frames. One of a middle-aged couple sitting on a split-rail fence, another a boy about ten with a cowboy bandana sitting on his pony, and finally a recognizable Brady kneeling with arms around the neck of a laughing black Labrador.

After serving tea, he plopped down on the overstuffed couch with frayed cushions covered by an Indian blanket and propped his feet up on the wood table. The deer-skin shade on the battery-powered lamp cast a yellow light over his journal as he made his daily entry. Brady let Cooter Jay curl into a contented ball beside him. Filled with curiosity, but not wanting him to think she cared to know his personal thoughts, she asked casually, "You writing the great American novel?"

"Nope, I'm not a writer. I just like to take notes of my stay. I've got books in the lookout if you are wanting something to read. I'd be happy to bring 'em down."

He didn't volunteer conversation. She didn't want to seem overly interested in him. Silence reigned over their evenings before he left her to the crystalline night. A bald-faced moon floated above the granite peaks outside her window. She stared at the black heavens, watching for shooting stars, wondering if they held any answers for her. Lulled by the horses snuffling as they pawed at their straw beds below, she slept soundly.

One night, she was awakened by a scrambling sound on the wooden stairwell. It had to be Brady, succumbing to the mad sexual fantasies that haunt hermits, she thought. She sat up, pulling the bed covers under her chin, holding her breath. There was a clomping sound on the door, like a heavy door knocker. Why didn't he just come in? A rousted Cooter Jay jumped from the couch and snarled, curling up blue-black lips to expose sharp canines. She heard light flighty steps going down the stairwell.

The next morning when he brought her breakfast tray, she eyed Brady suspiciously.

"Did you sleep well?" she asked.

"Sure did!" Brady answered. "How about yourself?"

"Fine," she said. "Did you hear anything moving around outside last night?"

"Nope. Nothin' out of the ordinary, but the woods can get your imagination workin' overtime."

"I guess so."

After two weeks of nothing but rest and back exercise, the nagging nerve pain subsided. Gemcie was able to maneuver the stairs without help. Brady whittled a walking stick for her, with a bear-head handle that felt solid in her hand. It allowed her to get unaided to the outhouse with no door, which sat on a promontory facing the sunset. It was a one-holer with a magazine rack containing a book on birds, an ancient National Geographic, a scratch pad with a pencil tied to it with a string, and a half-smoked cigar. The view from the outhouse rivaled any vista monks enjoy high in the Himalayas.

"Light up the stogie if the skeeters get too pesky," Brady had told her.

From the window sill of the cabin, she could see Brady, feet resting on the catwalk rail, scanning the horizon with his field glasses. She heard the squawk of a two-way radio now and again but couldn't make out what was being said. He spent endless hours watching over his realm. He seldom came down from the tower, but when he did he often went to the rock ledge to relieve himself beside the wood pile the chubby marmots called home. She chalked this distasteful habit up to some primordial yearning to mark his territory. Sexual assault did not seem to be on his mind. In fact, he paid no attention to her beyond making certain her basic needs were met each day.

Gemcie was not a vain person, but she was used to being fawned over most of her life. With a high, broad forehead, wide-spaced intelligent eyes framed in graceful arched brows, narrow nose and strong jaw, she easily could have been a model. Clothes draped well on her square shoulders and narrow hips. She looked elegant in blue jeans and a man's oversized shirt. Her looks, combined with her riding skills, kept her in the limelight. The fact that he had no interest in either of these assets gave her a jolt.

She decided his singularity was for the best. She was on the mend, but bending over was still impossible. Sitting aggravated her condition, but she could stand without discomfort for an hour or so. Cleaning tack, grooming the horses and some stall mucking was about all she could do. The stable was a rough affair, built from logs, with two stalls on each side of a dirt path. One stall was filled with food bags, alfalfa pellets and bales of hay. A bold field mouse with round pink ears sitting on the hay twitched his whiskers with more agitation when she came near. Staring at her with glittery eyes, he let her know that this was his home. The halters, bridles and spare leather parts lining the tack room walls on hooks made from food tins, were covered in a thick layer of dust. Several worn cracked saddles rested on wooden stands. She set up her work shop by the hitching post, where she could stand in the sun.

Stringing the bridle leathers from a horseshoe hook on the outside of the barn, she cleaned the dry parched bits with soap and water then nourished them with leather balm. It soothed her to replenish the leathers, feeling them soften in her hand. While she worked, a chatty jay scolded her from the catwalk. She heard the thunk, thunking of a redheaded woodpecker pounding an acorn into the trunk of a nearby tree. He flitted past her showing off bombardier patches of white on his shoulders. Flashy bluebirds traveling in pairs made bold beggars. She accommodated them with breadcrumb leftovers from breakfast.

Mercedes leaned out over the stall curious to know what Gemcie was up to. She rubbed her chest against the stall, swaying back and forth, leaning her great weight on the door to get to an itch. The gashes on her neck were healing. Luckily the bear had not hit the juggler, or any other major artery. The mare could hold her head up, but preferred to let it relax down. It was her way of letting her body direct its great strength to where it needed it the most when healing.

Her woeful look convinced Gemcie the mare needed to be groomed. She rubbed the big round rubber curry in the center of the graceful back, then working it up the strong crest of her neck, brushed her coarse snow-white mane to the right side. The mare stretched her neck, allowing Gemcie maximum coverage with her curry. The mare's pricked ears telegraphed her pleasure. She looked back at Gemcie with tender, pooling black eyes, to say, "Please don't stop."

Gemcie ran her hands up the crest of her powerful neck, through her thick warm hair, stopping at the top long enough to waggle her ears. The mare dropped her head to let Gemcie get closer to her work, chewing on imitation cud, a sign of pure pleasure. Gemcie scratched under her chin with one hand, placing her free hand on her hot belly. The mare fairly purred from these attentions. Suddenly, for no apparent reason, Mercedes started to fidget in her stall. She got prancy, arching her neck. She lashed out with her front hoof, kicking at her stall door, in an attempt to break it down.

"What is it, girl?" Gemcie tried to calm her. She grabbed her halter, but was afraid to attempt putting it on. The horse began to whinny in a shrieking soprano, shaking her entire body, sending an alarm to all her kind. The ground trembled beneath Gemcie's feet. A rolling pitching motion forced her to spread her legs, like she was riding a surfboard, to keep her balance. The lantern in the middle of the barn roof swung to and fro, until it flew off its hook, and crashed to the floor. Maxine delivered a long wheezing bellow, capped off with a rolling lament. Tucker did a mule kick to the back of his stall, nearly knocking the wall down. Brady flew around the corner at a dead run.

"Whoa, boy, whoa," he said, trying to talk Tucker down.

"Are you okay?" to Gemcie. "Don't worry, it's just a little trembler, we get 'em all the time up here. You'll get used to it," he said, patting Tucker solidly on the neck. "Horses can feel a shaker comin' in the ground a long time before it reaches us."

"That was wild! We get plenty of them in L.A., but I've always been in bed."

"Only about a three," he said, surveying the tack shed. "Looks like you been doing a bang up job cleaning tack," he said.

"I want to help."

"Maybe you're up to picking some berries then?"

"Yes. I'd love to!"

"Okay," he said, giving Tucker a clap on the rump. "You're okay now, aren't you, big guy?" All of the animals in the barn mellowed at the sound of his voice.

"Bring a jacket. The weather likes to come up in the afternoon," he said, pulling a straw basket from its hook on the wall. Excited at the prospect of seeing the meadow and lake she knew were nearby, Gemcie dropped the curry she was using into the open tack box. She grabbed her walking stick, windbreaker, and the basket to collect berries in. Brady pulled his rifle out of its leather scabbard, and placed it barrel-down over his forearm. He strolled leisurely down the worn path so Gemcie could keep up. She watched his blue-jeaned bottom rise and fall with each step, envying his free and easy movement. She hoped the walk would alleviate the stinging nerve pain in her calf. The trail took a dip and descended back into the lodge pole pines to a sun-splashed meadow.

Pointing to the abundant clumps of purple pigmy lupine, he said, "Down in the valley they say those plants are toxic to horses, but up here they eat it like its candy."

Patches of purple lupine and yellow mule's ears made a fine carpet on the sandy floor of nature's garden. Flame-red penstemon dripped from limbs heavy with the blooms. Orange sticky monkey climbed over other plants fighting for the sun. Busy burying precious nuts in his winter storehouse, a lively chipmunk rustled in the leaf mold. Animated, energetic, he frisked away at hearing their footsteps. Sitting up on curled tail, he chirped and dared the giants to chase him with playful eyes. Brave in his striking cape of bold black stripes, he didn't know he weighed no more than a field mouse.

The tree-shaded path opened to a fine flat meadow dressed in green knee-high grass rippling in the cool mountain breeze. Gray spires powdered with snow encircled the placid glacier lake just ahead. Sturdy shrubs clung to crevices in the gray rock bordering the water's edge. Gemcie was infatuated by the mirror image of the mountain in the waters, undisturbed by time. This mountain lake, wrapped at the waist by a belt of shaggy dwarf pines, needed nothing but itself to impress.

"There's a good berry patch over there," Brady said, pointing to a ridge about a hundred yards away. "Can you make it?" he asked, glancing over his shoulder.

"Sure, no problem," she said, realizing that for the first time in three weeks she felt no pain.

Cotton clouds kissed the peaks then floated quickly over the meadow, casting cool shadows. The sun ran a race with them, sometimes running behind their shifting mass. Gemcie welcomed the warmth of the sun on her shoulders. Soon they reached a blueberry patch covering a knoll overlooking the meadow. There was more than one path where the grass had been matted down next to the berries. Brady put his rifle down, freeing both hands to pick the succulent fruit.

"This is Blue's favorite dessert."

"Is that why you brought the rifle?"

"Yep. Normally, I don't bother," he said casually. "I've run into Blue and his relatives lots of times up here, but they've never bothered me none. I even picked berries here with Blue one time. It's amazing. He can pick a berry up between two tips of those claws as well as you or I can."

"You brought me to a place where you know bear might be?" she asked, feeling her stomach lurch.

"I saw Blue this morning down in the thicket where you met him. He can't be two places at once."

Gemcie allowed herself to relax in part with this knowledge.

"But, of course, he is not the only bear in these woods. If we do see a bear, just stand stock still and look down. Don't look 'im in the eye. It'll probably just turn tail and run," he said, continuing to pluck plump berries, popping some into his mouth as he went along. Gemcie decided to follow suit, but also to stay close to Brady and his rifle.

"The Indians got a story about a woman who met a bear while she was pickin' berries," he said. "Do you want to hear it?"

"Sure."

"Well, a good-looking warrior appeared before a young princess and asked her to go with him. He stood on his two feet and looked just like a human. She didn't know he was a bear who had taken off his hide just for her sake. His power was so great, he pierced her heart with his orange eyes, just like he'd shot an arrow right through it. When she looked into his eyes, she saw the soul of her father trying to reach out to her. He was a great hunter killed by a bear when she was a child."

"Did she go with him?" Gemcie asked, charmed by the tale.

"Yep. He placed her on his back and loped with her astride across the meadows, up the mountain ridges, long into the night, until he reached his den. There he made love to her for hours, 'til she was reelin'. She stayed with him all that winter, fallin' in love with his big heart. He was generous with all he possessed, and was at home in the world. He had no enemies, feared nothin' and no one. He liked humans, and decided long ago to let them join him at the salmon-running rivers and in the berry fields."

Gemcie listened mesmerized by the sound of Brady's slow, deliberate voice while she picked berries, being careful not to let their black purple juice stain her fingers.

"Then what happened?" she asked.

"When the first tip of the spring flowers broke through the crust of the snow, she was heavy with a baby. She broke all the rules of her tribe to be with him, and to know his ways. Now she had to return to her own kind to find shelter for her young."

"But why would she leave him?"

"Male bears are known to turn on their younguns. She feared for her baby. She tried to return to her tribe, but soon the hair was growing long and black on her back. Her canines grew long and sharp. The tribe leaders wanted her knowledge of the hunt and the ways of the bear but were afraid of her power. They decided to keep her child, but to kill her."

"But why?" Gemcie asked, horrified.

"She'd gone too far into the spirit world of the one the Indians call 'the old man,' and had become one with him."

"How cruel."

"Maybe so, but after she gave birth the old chief threw a bear hide over her shoulders, and ran her out of the village with a stick. He gave her a two-day head start to climb high into the mountains, letting her lead his warriors to her husband's den. He used his best trackers to stalk her, so she wouldn't hear them coming. When they found the den, the chief ordered the woman and the bear killed while they were sleeping in each other's arms."

Gemcie felt a cold shudder run through her chest at the thought of the woman murdered for following her heart.

"What happened to the child?"

"He grew up to be the best hunter and the greatest warrior in the tribe. He taught the others the ways of the wild," he said, gathering up his rifle. "I think I've got enough here to fix blueberry pancakes for a month."

"I think you like bears more than people."

"Guess I feel for 'em. They've been dealt a hard hand. A bear needs to wander in the wildness. He needs to be free. He's not like a bird that can lift himself off this earth to migrate; he's bound to the land. The grizz are gone from here. Got too close for them. It takes about 50,000 wild acres to support 2,000 bears. The parks are all they have left and those are becoming islands cut off from one another like wilderness ghettos. People move in on the bears' habitat then kill them off because they can't be tamed. Don't seem right to me. We should be heading back; I smell a storm brewing."

Wet gray clouds crowded to the ground in a dense fog by the time they got back to the barn. Gemcie gathered up the curry comb and brushes she'd used to groom Mercedes and finished the job. When she turned to place the items she had lovingly cleaned back in the tack chest she saw brown droppings covering the bottom of the box.

"What is this?" she asked, exasperated.

Brady picked up one of the round droppings, still warm to the touch and smeared over the tack, to examine it closely.

"That would be Bucky," he said and laughed.

"Another one of your friends?"

" 'Fraid so," he responded, chuckling.

"What's so funny? It took me two days to clean the mouse droppings, old straw and string where they made nests, and God knows what else out of this trunk.

"I'm sorry. It's just that I've read about how deer can become so love struck with humans they claim them as their territory. I knew Bucky cared, but I've never had anybody test his feelin's for me before. Your scent is all over that box. He just don't like you."

"You're telling me I'm a victim of love?"

"Kinda sweet, don't you think?"

"I'll keep this trunk locked from now on. I can live without the vengeance of a love-struck buck," Gemcie said, wiping out the bottom of the box with a rag.

"No problem. Speaking of doors, how about leaving yours unlocked tonight? I'm planning on going fishing early in the morning. I'll just slip your breakfast inside the door, without waking you up."

"You don't need to do that. I can fend for myself."

"I'll be doing it for myself, so why not for you, too, while I'm at it?"

"If you insist."

Tired from the outing, Gemcie went to bed early. Staring into the sacred night she saw the great bear crossing the ridges of the vanilla moon, a beautiful princess on his back, her hair floating in the shadows, her legs wrapped around his lumbering sides. Unnerved by the tale, and energized by the full moon, she could not drift into sleep. Instead, she lay silent on the lumpy feather mattress, listening to the sounds of the night…a hoot of victory from the owl, silently stalking the meadow; the munching of the livestock below. Hours passed before she heard the strange clatter on the stairwell again. Though it didn't sound like Brady's heavy boots on the creaking boards, who else could it be? That must be why he asked her to leave the door unlocked. She held her breath, listening hard into the night.

She heard a heavy thud on the stairwell. Whoever it was on the porch! She trembled, staring into the black velvet with wide eyes, straining to see if the handle on the door was turning. Instead, she heard a loud *thwank* on the door that sounded like someone pounding it with a claw hammer. Too frightened to scream, she sucked in her breath, hoping to evaporate into thin air before the door crashed open. A heavy thud sounded like he was throwing his entire body weight into the door. But why? The door was unlocked.

"Who is it?" she heard words coming from her mouth, but they sounded like they were coming from someone else talking far away.

No answer, just another heave on the door.

"What do you want?' she asked, biting her lip.

A frantic racket down the wooden stairs, then silence, was her answer. She continued to listen for many hours but heard nothing, save the hoot of the owl, full from a good night's work.

Chapter Seventeen

Sunbeams streamed through the window before Gemcie lifted her head from the pillow. Her night of terror flitted in and out of her consciousness, as she stirred from a deep sleep. She felt uneasy, shaky, but calmed herself with the thought that Brady was gone for the day. She enjoyed the granola with blueberries waiting for her on the wooden tray he'd left, as promised. He must have taken Cooter Jay with him. The dog preferred a romp through the woods to his docile days in the lazy sun.

Planting herself on her window sill, she brushed her hair, wrapping it around her slim fingers into ringlets. Her gaze traveled the line of the timber belt searching for wildlife. Startled by a sharp snort nearby, she dropped her brush to floor. Sitting perfectly still, she peered intensely in the direction the sound came from but saw nothing. She hoped the creature would show itself. A stag with a six-point rack covered in brown velvet emerged from the underbrush. Sierra black-tail deer are seldom seen by hunters, their vivid, eager alertness keeps them well out of their gun sights, but this deer was bold.

He stared back at her with coal-black defiant eyes, pawed the ground and lowered his glorious crown, challenging her to fight. A Douglas squirrel, excited by the show, brandished his busy gray tail back and forth then spiraled around the trunk of a lodge-pole pine, flaking bark with sharp toes. A doe with two white-speckled fawns in her wake followed close behind the stag. Their movements were agile and sprite as they bounced on long tapered legs across the boulders ringing the ridge. This must be Bucky. She hoped the stag could get over his teenage crush on Brady, and become her friend too. He sniffed the air anxiously, trying to decide whether to head into the grove of fir trees nearby, or to stay put. The doe watched from the sidelines, daintily browsing on brush.

The crack of a tree stump splintered by a bear looking for insects echoed through the canyon, signaling danger. Bucky communicated the threat to his doe in a secret language similar to the one birds use in flight. In unison, the family of deer leaped into springy light movements across the clearing in front of the cabin. The delicate fawns on spindly legs imitated the powerful leap of their father. Cream-white, heart-shaped bottoms, with a scruff of bushy tail, vanished into a storm-bent thicket.

Left alone, Gemcie's attention went to the lookout. This was her chance to find out what Brady did up there all day. Maybe she could find some clue about why he would haunt her at night, yet be so charitable by day. She hadn't told him she was well enough to climb the ladder to the trap door. That could mean the end of room service, and quite possibly her stay. Her curiosity drove her to chance entering the lookout while he was gone. She would see him coming up the trail and could get back to her cabin before he arrived.

She climbed the sixty-foot ladder to the lookout easily, but the trap door at the center of the bottom of the small cabin was heavy. She lifted it cautiously, peeking in before entering the glass room. Her stomach fluttered nervously as she scrambled in, leaving the trap door up for a quick exit. Once inside she saw an Osborne fire finder; an azimuth, an astronomy instrument that surveys distance clockwise in degrees from the north point; and a sighting device that looked like an altar. A portion of a forest map mounted on a large disk on a cabinet was in the middle of the room. A high swivel chair with glass insulators, like those on telephone poles, mounted on the lower tips of the four legs, was also among the items there.

She couldn't resist sliding onto the chair. She imagined herself at the helm of a great ghost ship heaving its way across the vast ocean of dumpling-shaped clouds below. She could sail from here to the ridges, each a deeper hue of purple melding to black, lined one behind another into the horizon. The open catwalk door let the wind blow through the cockpit of the lookout. It filled the sails of her vessel to billowing white shrouds. She held the kinetic energy, captured in the mizzen and mainsail, between her hands. Tears streamed from the blustery breath of the mountain on her face, but her eyes remained riveted on eternity.

She spied Brady's binoculars sitting on the table by his chair on the catwalk. Knowing that he could return at any moment, she scanned the canyon to see if she could spy him coming up the trail. Leaning on the three-planked rail that surrounded the cat walk, she glassed the mountain for twenty minutes, fascinated with her new eyes. She spotted an osprey nest resting easily on the top of a tall pine swaying in the wind. The huge bird of prey returning from a fishing trip landed with extended talons, neatly tucking six-foot wings close to its chest. Two pink tongues between yellow beaks poked above the nest line, awaiting the morning catch. The great bird turned piercing yellow, intelligent eyes upon Gemcie, before feeding her young.

Unnerved at being discovered, she put the glasses down. Obviously this bird could see her as well with her naked eye as she saw the bird using the high powered 7 x 50 lens. She remembered Billy saying, "Marshal has the look of the eagle in his eye. He looks beyond men to the sky." It meant more now that she shared the vantage of the great bird. She was taller than the world, looking down upon nature's ever-shifting patterns. As she listened to the swish of the wind whispering through pine boughs, lifting them in a sweet cantata, her heart seemed to float out of her chest, trying to follow.

Then she remembered the journal. What did he do with his journal? He must hide it in case someone nosy, like herself, should visit. She couldn't help being curious about her keeper but didn't want him to know she was interested in learning his secrets. She went back into the lookout, trying to think where he might have hidden it from her. She opened the tiny propane fridge next to a two-burner camp stove to find nothing but perishables. She popped the top of the camp chest where other foodstuffs were stored. There was a cot, a couple of folding chairs, shelves, and a cupboard in the 12 x 12 box house of light and wind, but no journal. He had a book on clouds, an ancient dictionary, a flower book and a star book stacked on a Scrabble game by his bed. There was an army surplus ammo can he must use when he didn't want to hike to the outhouse. *Wait a minute. This is it!* She dared tip the lid high enough to peek in. Sure enough there lay the stack of journals he had written. Knowing she was being wretched, committing an unconscionable invasion of privacy, she tore the lid off and pulled the whole stack of volumes out of the ammo can without a moment's hesitation. She sorted through to the earliest entry, wanting to start at the beginning.

May 15

Many hours of my youth in Montana were spent lying flat on my belly watching the moist, loose earth of a gopher mound forming, as the vermin bulldozed their way to the sun. Waiting patiently for my moment to strike, I watched the heat waves undulating over the yellow grass plains just outside of Bozeman. The bounty on gophers was 50 cents a head. They are wily critters. I had to wait for them to poke brown heads out of their burrows to survey the plains with blinking eyes before I could clobber them with my club. By the time I was twelve, I'd earned $200.

Being a gopher hunter gave me plenty of time to think. I lay waiting on the ground chin on hands, staring at the purple Bear Tooths stacked way off in the distance for countless hours. I thought about the gushing streams, clogged with snowmelt, coursing down rocky gorges. The thunder of the waterfalls kept my mind cool while I was waiting for one of those blink-eyed buggers to stick their head up. I couldn't wait to grow up and live in the mountains.

My father owned a small breeding and boarding ranch. Poisoning the gophers was out of the question; the horses would eat the bait themselves. I wanted to flush the gophers with a water hose, filling up their canals and forcing them to run for it, but this method undermined the pastures. The horses would step on the weakened areas that broke away, creating gaping holes where they could break a leg.

Each morning at sunup, I got up to water our horses before school. Mom gave me a breakfast that would stick to my ribs; homemade biscuits with molasses, bacon, grits, and eggs over medium and crisp around the edges. I had a system of watering that allowed me to fill four barrels at a time. I put four hoses in buckets, turned them on simultaneously, then got on my bike and raced around to each hose, rotating them into the next empty barrel, until all the barrels were full and spilling over. It took me exactly forty-five minutes to water all the animals each morning and night. For this I received $2.00-a-week allowance.

Suddenly conscious of the time, Gemcie stepped out on the catwalk and scanned the gorge to find Brady and Tucker about two-thirds of the way up the trail. Cooter Jay's grizzled face, with lolling tongue, stuck out of the saddle bag. She scurried around the cabin making sure everything was exactly as she had found it. Backing down the ladder, she pulled the heavy trap down behind her. When Brady arrived she was standing in the sun by the hitching post oiling a cracked saddle.

"Got some speckled brown trout for you," he said, stepping off Tucker. "They have pink flesh kind of like a salmon but don't taste as strong."

"Sounds delicious."

Cooter Jay yipped from the saddle bag, as if to say, "Don't forget me." Brady hoisted the squirming mutt out of the leather pocket and set him free. "Maybe you'd like to have a cookout this evening? I like to fix these in coals with some potatoes."

"Sure, if it's not too much trouble."

"No trouble. You can gather some down wood. Just light dry twigs, about the size of your pinkie. I'll take care of the rest," he said, lifting the saddle off Tucker's back, and placing it on the wooden saddle rack. "I need to get up to the crow's nest. See you later," he said, leaving her to enjoy the afternoon sun.

She picked up a soft cloth to wipe down his saddle. Then she gave Tucker a needed rubdown with liniment. The days were becoming longer and lonelier now that Gemcie felt better. She wanted to tell him she could climb the ladder and join him, but held herself in check. The sun high overhead smiled warmly on her head and shoulders. As she worked, she tried to figure a way to get to the journal again without him knowing. She couldn't help wanting to know more about him. Why did he want to live in isolation? What caused him to have these misanthropic tendencies? She could slip up there when he ponied the animals to the meadow in the morning. She would have enough time to read an entry or two. It would take her as long to read the journals as it did for him to write them with that plan, but it would work until she could think of something better.

She dutifully gathered wood for the fire then stretched out on a warm boulder to rest. The chirping sound of the marmots in the woodpile nearby sounded like a brisk symphony. One fat fellow with chubby cheeks sprawled out beside her, lying belly-up in the sun. She smiled, flattered to have a friend to share the day. Their snooze ended when fast-moving clouds rushed in, blocking the sun. The bone dry rocks were splashed with big droplets, signaling a summer storm.

Cracking thunder, threatening to blast everything in its path to oblivion, rolled away in low rumbling tones. Within seconds a jagged, electric bolt cut through the sky, Thor sending love notes to Diana.

128

With face and hair damp, Gemcie ran for cover. Her furry friend scurried down his tunnel in the rock pile.

Soon the heavens opened in earnest, spilling torrents of water and buckets of dime-size hail stones that drilled the tin roof of the cabin. She ran up the stairs to her room and curled up under her quilt, feeling as cozy as a gray squirrel with a bushy tail wrapped around his head, chin tucked under him. By now, she knew the fury would be short-lived. Soon clear white droplets clinging to the pines would be spangling in the sun. She rested sweetly, sleeping like a woodland creature, waiting for the storm to pass.

When the sun settled that evening behind the tallest ridge to the west, flashing a rush of crimson across the sky, Brady descended from the lookout, carrying a picnic basket. He split a couple of logs with an ax to build a fire in the rock pit on the knoll that jutted into the canyon. The flame cast a yellow glow on his bronze skin. She sat quietly on a nearby stump, watching him de-bone the trout with a quick flick of his hunting knife. Rolled-up sleeves exposed the hard, tan muscles of his arms. He squatted to get close to his work. The shock of wavy black hair fell into his eyes. He brushed it away with his hand, and smiled up at her with teasing violet eyes.

"I like lots of garlic; is that okay?" he asked.

"Sure. I'm not doing any public speaking tonight."

He pursed full lips and whistled softly as he pared carrots and potatoes. "I like lots of seasonings. Worked in a French restaurant for a spell. Got me started on that stuff," he said.

"Where?"

"In San Francisco. I went to school at Berkley for a while."

"What did you study?"

"Medicine. Thought I wanted to be a doctor."

"What changed your mind?"

"The business of being a doctor doesn't have much to do with medicine."

"Yeah, I love riding, but I hate the business of riding."

"Are you a rider by trade?"

"I used to be."

"What kind of ridin'?

"I was a Grand Prix jumper. Ever since I was two, I've been sitting on one horse or another. I never thought about being anything else until now."

"Why did you quit?"

"I didn't, really. I got fired."

"Why?"

She stared into the fire for a moment. She wasn't sure she could trust him, but needed to talk.

"There was an accident. In all my years of riding rogues, I never really got hurt. I broke my arm once, but that's nothing. Everybody on the circuit has stories about broken ribs, ankles, wrists…you name it."

"I did a little rodeo'n. Busted myself up pretty good once," he said.

"The pros have all been injured one way or another. They learn how to carry themselves so that they don't put pressure on their weak spots, and just keep going."

"Bones heal, but the memories stay," Brady said.

"I've always been able to ride out whatever came my way, but that day I didn't have a chance. It happened too fast." Gemcie's voice became weak as she lost herself in the memory.

"What happened?" Brady asked, trying to bring her back.

Gemcie stared into the fire for several moments before answering, "Marshal, my jump horse, is always a little spooky around water. The water element on the course that day was thirteen feet across. He has a twelve-foot stride. I knew I'd have to press him up to get him over. On the approach, I did just that, but my timing was off. I had a rough time sleeping the night before. Somebody had called in a false fire alarm to the hotel where I was staying."

Gemcie stopped in the middle of her story struck by a sudden realization. She remembered Dominique asking her how she had slept the morning before the event. *It was her! It was Dominique who called the hotel.* Jorge must have told her where she was staying and that she always had trouble sleeping before a show. She had asked about Jorge's whereabouts, but she knew all along where he was! Saddened by the thought of her husband's complicity in an act that had ruined her life she fell silent, looking intently into the flames for answers.

"Then what happened? You can't leave a guy hanging on tenterhooks like that," he said, shifting the logs on the fire with a metal poker. His eager curiosity brought her back to the present.

"I squeezed him up too hard, too fast. He jigged just before takeoff. I knew we were in trouble when he struck off. His hoof caught on the rim of the jump on the way out. Parting company with the saddle was the last thing I remember. I guess I was airborne for a full thirty feet. I landed flat on my back. It could have been a whole lot worse. I could have broken my neck or my back, but I couldn't heal in time to get back on for the finals, so Marshal's owner found another rider."

That stinks," he said, as he sprinkled the vegetables with garlic and rosemary, then wrapped them in tin foil and tucked them in the coals.

"I still love to jump. Every time I see a low-slung log on the ground, I want to canter on and go for it! I can't leave behind the feeling of being lifted from the earth, flesh with flesh, and heartbeat with heartbeat. It is in my blood now," Gemcie said, sadness reflected in her voice.

"Wasn't it always?"

"Yes, I guess it was. I don't know. That's the problem: I don't know any other way of being. Maybe I was molded this way. Maybe it's who I am."

"The potatoes are going to take a while, so I broke out the best bottle of wine in my cellar," he said, stabbing the cork with his Swiss army knife. "Would you like to give it the sniff test?"

"Sure."

He wrapped the neck with his bandana, popped the cork and handed it over for her approval.

"Yes, must be a very good year."

Assuming the stance of a French waiter, he draped the kerchief over his forearm, poured the wine glass into camp cups, and handed one to her with a quick bow.

"Madam."

She sipped the warm, wood-flavored wine, savoring the liquid velvet as it slid easily down her throat.

"Most mellow," she pronounced.

As he poured a generous glass, she questioned his intentions silently to herself.

"Will you ride again? Professionally, I mean?"

"I don't know. That's why I wanted to be alone. I needed to think about it all. I'm not sure about any of it anymore."

"Well, you sure have had plenty of time to think here. That's one of the reasons I like being here."

"I've been meaning to thank you for taking care of me and letting me take a breather from it all."

"Are you about ready to be heading back to Rock Creek?"

"Not yet. It's so peaceful here. None of the past seems to matter. I'd like to stay a bit longer if it is all right with you."

"It ain't every day someone like you stumbles into my camp. You can stay until the snow flies and then we both have to head back down the mountain."

Etchings of deepest purple streaked across the opalescent sky. The remains of a perfect day lingered, while the coals ripened to a caldron orange. By the time the fish had baked to juicy readiness, the stars had filled the stage. A quarter sliver of moon was halfway up the sky. Bats flitted dangerously close to the fire, daring to set their leathery capes ablaze. The distant echo of the tree owl announced the night.

By the time the food was ready they were both starving. They sloshed down the remains of the wine, picking every tiny morsel from their tin foil plates with greasy fingers. Brady leaned back when he'd finished eating, his hands resting on his belly. He crossed his long legs, warming his feet on a rock close to the flame.

"What did you do before you came here?" Gemcie asked, feigning ignorance of his beginnings.

"I used to make my living mustangin' in Montana. I spent the summers gathering up wild horses, and rogue range horses that hid out in the high country not good for grazin' cattle. I would take a string of my own to pack my gear and set up camp near a creek. Water blinds from other mustangers were there, so all I had to do was mend them and stay up all night waiting for the herds to come in for a drink. One time when I was on my way there I noticed some tracks from a shod horse that was going in the same direction I was. He had small feet like an Arab. Figured he was a runaway and I'd catch and bring him back to his rightful owner for a reward. It was pretty near a hundred miles to the high country and this horse's tracks were keeping me company. He was headed back to his herd of mares.

"There was a fast-moving river between me and where I was going with only two ways to cross it. One was a ferry that I planned on taking, and the other was a train trestle about 100 feet up. I was having my morning coffee when I got my first sight of that horse. He looked to be an appaloosa cross with an Arab face and crescent ears. He was deciding whether or not he was going to cross that river on the trestle.

"He started across tapping each board with his hoof before putting his weight down. Watching him made me break out in a cold sweat. I felt certain he was going catch a leg, or panic and try to turn around. Either way he was a goner. But he made it. He tapped his way all across that trestle and high-tailed it on. I never knew a horse that wanted to be free that bad.

"When I hit the high country I saw his tracks again. I set up my blind and waited. Sure enough, after a couple of weeks of patience he came to me with his herd of mares. It was a fine catch. But my victory tasted like vinegar. He was snorting and tearing around the enclosure causing a fuss. He'd been caught before, and he knew the end of the story. His eyes rolled white as he lashed out with kicks that could kill. It came to me that he had earned his freedom. Any horse brave enough to cross that trestle ought not to be pinned up. I opened the gate and let him rip but kept his mares for my reward. It was the last summer I spent mustangin'. Figured there was some other way I could make a living that would let me feel better about myself."

Brady's deep-set eyes glistened in the fire's glow.

"Do you mind if I sing? Times like this make me twittery," he said.

She laughed. "No, I think I can stand it."

He lapsed into strains of "Streets of Loredo" as though he were the lamenting cowboy singing.

"As I walked out in Laredo one day
I spied a young cowboy all wrapped in white linen,
all wrapped in white linen,
and cold as he lay."

She joined him in the chorus.

"So beat the drums slowly,
and play the fife lowly,
for I'm a young cowboy
who knows he's
done wrong."

Silence settled over them. Each was lost in their own separate thoughts, until the blue flame transformed the coals to embers.

"Think you might be up to helping in the tower?"

His question caught her off guard. Did he suspect she had been prolonging her stay?

"I don't know? What does that mean?"

"You see a smoke you chart it on the fire finder, then radio it into headquarters. It's not difficult. I can show you how in an hour or so. I'd like to take advantage of your being here, to take a day off, do a little hiking."

"Sure. If you think I can handle it."

"A well-oiled robot could do what I do, and will someday, but for now, I think you'll do just fine."

Thanks."

Chapter Eighteen

Next morning, Gemcie took pains not to climb the ladder too quickly, and let him lift the trap door for her. Not wanting him to know her recovery was complete, she gasped appropriately at the view, pretending she was seeing it for the first time. Thunderheads shifted from red, pink, and orange on the eastern horizon about forty miles away. She slid into the swivel chair, the helm of the 360-degree glass enclosure, and propped her feet up on the map stand.

"You look comfortable in the electric chair," he said.

"What!" she exclaimed, jumping up from the chair.

"Ninety percent of the fires up here are started by electrical storms. That chair is grounded so you can sit through them without getting fried."

"That's what the glass bottoms are about?"

"Yep."

"How does this work?" she asked, pointing to the chest-high Osborne fire-finder standing squarely in the middle of the room. It consisted of a rotating metal ring about two feet in diameter with a handle to turn it, and a pair of sights, like those on a rifle, mounted upright on opposite sides.

"When a lookout spots a fire, he aims this thing at the center of the smoke and gets an azimuth reading from the base marked in 360 degrees."

She looked closer at the instrument to see the Vernier scale attached to the rotating ring where a lookout gets a reading not only in degrees, but precisely to the nearest minute, or one sixtieth of a degree.

"Once you ascertain the compass direction of the fire, you locate it on the map and call it into headquarters," he said, demonstrating how to operate the two-way radio. "Your code is Snowbird."

"You told headquarters about me?"

"Sure, there's a lot of radio chat between lookouts. If you want to get in on it, just turn this thing up."

"What's your code?"

"Medicine Bear. Chances of you spotting anything are pretty slim. Even if a serious storm came in this afternoon, the rain usually puts out elemental fires. Just in case, though, you ought to know the names of a few of the landmarks." He pointed to the west.

"That's 'Almost a Turtle' mountain. You can see his grumpy face if you squint at that ridge for a while. That one over there is 'Billy Goat Haunt.' Stare at it long enough in the glasses and you might see some white dots. Those are goats. That one way off yonder is 'Mount Despair,' that's where 'Lone Man' lives. 'Course you won't find those names on the maps."

"What good are they then?"

"No good at all," he said, flashing a brilliant smile. "I'll be back before sundown. Do you think you can handle it?"

"It's a no brainer," she said, tamping down her excitement at manning the lookout. She watched him march due west with a small daypack on his back, Cooter Jay trailing behind, until they vanished behind a ridge. She studied the cloud map that showed in pictures and words the anatomy of an electric storm. Outside the great, white cumuli mushroomed above the peaks, swelling out of themselves into great mounds of white taffy. She surveyed her kingdom for over an hour before she remembered the journal. She rushed to the ammo can and pulled the stack of notebooks out of the metal bin.

June 23

Still feels like spring. So crisp in the mornings, I can see my breath while I'm fixing breakfast. Spotted a sow at the edge of the meadow. She stood up on her hind legs, sniffed the air then stepped over some down wood, heading towards the berry patch. The fireweed was so tall it almost covered the two cubs clamoring behind her, trying to keep up. They were the "first cubs of the year." One was distinctly smaller than the other, but they both appeared to be healthy, scrappy black bears. The larger one with a white blaze on his chest attacked the smaller one, rolling it over on its back, inviting it to wrestle. The downed cub flailed, giving strong cat kicks with powerful hind legs to get free. The shaggy black cub who wanted to fight found a rotting log to attack, tearing at it with sharp claws, looking for insects. He reared, pawing at moths he'd rooted, spinning so fast on his hind legs he fell backwards into the grass.

The sun was high in the sky before the sow had her fill of berries. It's hard to believe such a hulking beast could be satisfied eating those tiny plump morsels. Bears are quite nimble and dexterous with their paws, even though they have four-inch claws in their way. I've been told that when you skin a bear's paw, it looks so much like a human hand, it's scary. That's why bear paw soup is still so popular among some spooky circles. People who eat this dish believe they are absorbing the power and knowledge of the bear.

The sow lay down in the afternoon sun, spreading her legs for the cubs. They dived into her warm belly for lunch. The larger cub kneaded her so hard, sucking so furiously for milk, the sow cuffed him soundly. This allowed the smaller cub, pushed aside by the other brash youngster, to find a teat and settle in. After feeding time, the sow slept for an hour or so, with her cubs curled up beside her. I glassed the meadow just before sundown and saw her loping across the meadow with the cubs galloping clumsily behind. She headed for the timber where her rippling flanks disappeared into the shadows, with the cubs close behind.

I radioed headquarters. "Cubs of the Year" are big news. Reporting new wildlife in the area is part of what I like to call a job.

June 30

The Forest Service arrived in a chopper that looked like a huge green dragonfly. It circled over the lookout a couple of times then headed for the meadow where I reported seeing the sow and her two cubs. The wind from the whirling blades lifted dust and whipped the boughs of the pine trees back and forth. The squirrels ran for cover in favorite knotholes, the marmots ducked into their rock tunnels, and the jays jumped off the catwalk, all eager to escape the thwopping of the great rotating blades. The pilot waved an arm out the window. I saw two other men in the body of the helicopter.

The chopper swooped down the canyon, diving in and out of the terrain. The pilot hovered over the meadow until they caught sight of the sow. The side door of the chopper slid open. I saw the barrel of a rifle extend out the door about two feet. At first the sow was so stunned by the whirl of the propellers she stood, frozen like a deer in headlights. Suddenly, she came to her senses. Even though she couldn't identify the monster in the sky, she knew it meant danger. She swerved sharply, spinning on her hind legs, and led the cubs into the underbrush. Forests overprotected from fires are dense with shrubs, and make good cover. Once the cubs were safely stowed away, she emerged once again.

The chopper just kept circling. She loped across the meadow toward a ridge covered with pine. She looked over her shoulder and tripped on a log buried in the tall grass. She did a somersault, but kept scrambling for safety, trying to divert the monster from her cubs. She headed for the canyon, scrambling up the trail, trying to get to higher ground. She ducked into a grove of lodge pole pine. I thought she had made her escape, but the chopper just kept buzzing and circling the area until she emerged from the tree cover. The sow broke into a flat-out run across the glacier moraine. She was an easy target barreling across the polished rock above the tree line. White flecks of saliva flew from her mouth, wetting her massive shoulders and chest. Her tongue lolled from the side of her mouth. The rifle came out of the side door again. The sharpshooter hit his mark. I could see a dart dangling from her flank. Muscle, blood and bone pumped with adrenaline just kept moving. Another dart fired. The drug took hold. She shambled on for another hundred yards before crumpling to her knees and falling on her face into the scree, with rear legs splayed out behind.

There was plenty of open terrain for the helicopter to land nearby. One of the men pulled out a hypodermic and drew blood from her inner thigh. Another took out a pair of pliers and pulled a molar to get an accurate reading on her age. I judged her to be about six, weighing around 480 pounds; the average size of a full-grown black bear. When they were through poking, prodding, and measuring they put a white radio collar on her, and punched a yellow-and-white tag in each ear. Finally, a nasty-looking punch was used to tattoo a number on her lip, which they smeared with indelible, florescent green dye. They left her looking like a sad clown.

With the job complete the three men piled back into the helicopter. It lifted off, and the rifle barrel came out a last time from the side of the chopper. Another dart delivering the antidote to the powerful drug used to bring her to her knees shot into her body. The chopper wheeled off, blowing bits of gravel, dust, and leaves that stuck to her wet fur. Then it was silent once more.

The cubs hiding in the shrubs emerged when they were sure the beast in the air was gone. Their croaking caterwauling echoed up the canyon. They staggered about at first, temporarily blinded by the noonday sun. The larger cub with the white blaze on his chest, which I dubbed "Blue," picked up his mother's scent. He loped up the canyon wall she traversed, with the smaller cub struggling to keep up. The smaller cub hesitated to venture so far from the thicket. It stopped every twenty yards or so, standing up to sniff the air for danger, or signs of its mother. Blue just kept pressing forward on the scent like a bloodhound. Life alone was not an option for the smaller cub, so it trailed reluctantly behind.

It took Blue an hour or so to reach the sow. She still had not regained consciousness. The drugs should have kicked in by now, unless something went wrong. It did go wrong every once in a while. The drugs the rangers use are strong enough to down an elephant. Sometimes it actually kills the animals they are attempting to monitor. He charged across the open glacier field at a dead run once he saw her. He circled her inert body. Then he butted her, prodding her to wake. He asked her to roll over on her side to expose a teat for him to nurse. She wouldn't move. Befuddled, both of the cubs circled her tirelessly, calling to her in rasping low whines for two days. Blue finally turned away and waddled on bowlegs back to the meadow in search of grubs, mushrooms, berries or insects to fill the ache in his belly. The smaller club would not leave its decomposing mother.

July 1

The sow never did get up after the helicopter took off. She never opened her eyes, or rolled over on her side lifting a leg for her cubs to nurse. She didn't even raise a paw to cuff them for bothering her while she was sleeping. Flies buzzed around her eyes and nose. She was dead, but the littlest cub wouldn't leave her side. It couldn't grasp the fact that its mother was gone. It was thinner and not as frisky as Blue, right from the beginning. Whenever they were tussling Blue always overpowered the runt. Bears eat most anything, even carrion. They are built for survival, but this one didn't have the will.

The cub's relentless bawling traveled up the canyon. I wanted to go to them. After all, I was responsible. If I hadn't placed the call to headquarters letting the rangers know about the cubs this would not have happened, but I couldn't interfere. Making them dependent on me for feeding would turn them into pests that would eventually be shot for raiding a tourist campsite. They would have to fend for themselves. Bears have no natural enemies other than man. Boars have been known to kill their young, but I didn't see any sign of their father in the area. Chances of survival were good for them, if they could make it through the next couple of weeks alone.

I keep a strict pact with myself not to turn any of the animals here into pets. The only thing I do that might upset the delicate balance, evolved over the millenniums, is to pee on the rock pile. This one transgression provides a salt lick for the marmots and deer. I feel I'm making a contribution to the cycle of nature, without upsetting the natural apple cart. This act connects me to all I see around me.

We are all connected to one another, but some ways seem more direct than others. The people in the jet planes going overhead are connected to this world through the fuel stream they leave in their wake. Those emissions trickle into this natural world as surely as the urine I sprinkle on the dry boulders. I remind myself that those people filling the cloud field with noxious waste products have as much right to be looking down on me, as I do to be looking up at them while I take a leak. Is one better than another? Is it a matter of degree? These were my thoughts as I watched the smaller cub give up on life. No room for weaklings, sentimentalists, or cowards in the wild. The smaller cub died at its mother's side.

The horror of the bear attack was still fresh for Gemcie. The helpless terror of that moment would always be with her. It was hard for her to see the ferocious creature that charged for no apparent reason as a forlorn, motherless cub. Just as Marshal was imprinted with the scent of human beings, so was Blue. But, instead of subconscious memories of nurturing caresses, it brought back to him unspeakable evil that caused him to live utterly alone in the world. She saw the vulnerable cub, wandering like a drunk, bawling for his littermate. The smoldering orange eyes of her nightmare bear dissolved to tender pools of moist tears.

Chapter Nineteen

The sun dipped behind the mountain leaving a chill in the air, with still no sign of Brady. Gemcie was getting worried, but kept reading, not knowing when her next chance to be alone in the tower would come. She stopped long enough to scan the valley for smokes like a good lookout. Satisfied by no signs of trouble, and no Brady in sight, she went back to the journal.

July 4th

A wet mist hangs over the black mountains, hiding the stars. An uneventful Fourth of July, yet I revel in my Independence. How long can I breathe in this air unsullied by technology? How long can I not participate in government, family, duty? My thoughts cool as I watch the cold fog silently roll in, clinging to the mountains like a gauzy ballerina skirt. A clean, shiny utility vehicle, without a trace of sludge in the wheel well, is parked in the drive of each tidy suburban homestead. It is deemed the best transport for the average housewife searching for bargains at the mall, while the electric car sits cold and unheralded. Proof that supply and demand's ceaseless march towards systematic plundering of the planet is as strong a force as the great river that carved the Grand Canyon. Unrelenting, unyielding, uncaring of the outcome in its thoughtless flow to the sea.

I'm often asked, "Don't you get lonely up there?" I've never felt lonely here; rather, I am blissfully alone. Watching constantly shifting seasons; touching, feeling, and breathing in the movements of the universe thrills me. Encased in hermetically sealed rooms, how can people know the sensation of being part of the hum and throb of the world? I've grown strong in solitude. It has given me time to unfold the complications of my life and to listen. Now I hear the song of the robin and can understand that he is saying, "Rejoice! Rejoice!" Before, his voice was nervous noise in my ears.

I wonder if there will always be silent places left in the world in which people can discover themselves anew. I worry that there will not be enough. I used to try to share this with friends, describing in wild enthusiasm those places that struck me as insanely beautiful. Now, I keep those places a secret. Afraid to share, because then that spot won't be there for me when I need it, if I do. It is a smallness in me, one I don't like. It saddens me to feel this panic.

A pang of sorrow shot through Gemcie's heart like an arrow. She shared his need for the beauties of nature and feared the end of wild places as well. She tore through the journal skimming entries as fast as she could before he returned.

December 25

I am the missing link between man and nature. After standing on my head for twenty minutes looking at the inverted slopes scalloped in snow drifts, I tingle. It's just the blood running to my head, you say, but for me it's more. I see myself as a conduit for energy, not the vessel where it rests, but merrily a transformer. The pulse of Mother Nature's great heart is too powerful for me to receive straight on, so she delivers her love in the form of white sparkling molecules that whip around my head in tiny pinpricks of light. I often perform this morning ritual naked, hoping my reception will be more complete that way.

Light slides down the top of the frozen wall in the distance, as though someone were lifting the shade on heaven's glow. The gusts of wind outside carry the message of the mountain to me. Crystals form in the corner of my windows, shaped like tiny pine trees, fanning out in sparkling displays. Winter is harsh and savage but looks as harmless as a box of powdered sugar sprinkled on the peaks, when you live inside a snowflake.

After lunch I walk, listening to squeak of the snow under each step. I won't surprise any wary woodland creatures today. They've all headed down the mountain, or tucked themselves away in warm burrows. My lashes frost up. I blink to keep them from icing closed. There is frost on my eyebrows and neck gaiter. The air burns my lungs if I breathe too deeply. It takes an hour at a brisk march to reach the river. It is locked in ice, but I can see the shadow play formed by the moving water beneath the crystal dazzle. I fill my water container, kneeling at a hole where the hooves of a goat have chipped the edge of the ice hole.

I am struck by the silence. It's like being in a muffled tomb of cold, immaculate purity. I see myself walking within the glass ball children shake to watch the snow fall on tiny villages. I'm distanced from any sound of this century. Deadly, unpredictable currents prevent planes from flying overhead. No car alarms blaring, or other rude city sounds can interrupt my thoughts today. It is the snowy silence in this Christmas card I cherish.

May-Spring is here again

    I've been looking for Blue since I got here in May. I'm worried that he hasn't made it through the winter. He'd need to be smart enough to find the ancient bear trails that lead to the denning sites, or build a den of his own to survive. To make a new one he'd have to dig downward and then up, putting a chamber under a mat of alpine tree roots, or under a slab of rock. Bear chambers are usually eight to ten feet wide with a three-foot entrance passageway. The bears snap limbs from the trees, then bend them over one arm and break them off with the other, gathering bedding and placing it in a den like a human. When the snow starts falling hard, the bear goes into the den, using the falling snow to cover its tracks. Could Blue know all of this instinctually, without training from his mother? I wondered, anxiously searching the timber line to see his wet, brown snout and glistening dark eyes emerge into the sun.

    I decided to do a little berry picking, forgetting this is a very likely spot to run into a bear hungry from a long winter. It's amazing how their entire systems shutdown into a dream state. They cease to urinate or defecate. Their bodies somehow metabolize their own waste. Through losing fat they increase their lean body mass and conserve their bone volume as though they were awake and active. Maybe they dream about the gatherings in the Inner Mountains where Bear is Lord and host to great feasts for all of the animals. Maybe he hunts the deer in a slow motion chase, like a dog in his sleep.

    Picking berries takes patience. The bears draw over the shoots and delicately rake through the clusters with their claws. The Indians made wooden rakes that look like bear-claws to gather berries. When the best slopes for berries are ripe there can be more than one bear gathering the harvest. They don't travel in groups but tolerate one another at choice feeding spots. It shouldn't have been a surprise when I heard a profound rustling in the bushes not fifteen yards from me.

    A bear standing on hind legs stretched his head to the sky and sniffed the air, trying to identify the creature moving in on his berry patch. His fierce intelligent eyes fell upon me. I froze, remembering that running from a bear encourages a cat and mouse game I would lose. I could see a white blaze on his chest. He was thin, about 250 pounds, but he had survived the winter somehow by his wits alone. How he managed, I don't know, but I'm sure it was Blue.

    The scent of humans left on his mother was indelibly printed in his mind. He could charge, even if unprovoked, reacting to the old hurt buried deep in his heart. I looked away, avoiding challenging him with direct eye contact, standing my ground. It was up to him that day. I didn't bother to carry a rifle. I like to travel light, sometimes forgetting that even in such a sweet setting, things can go wrong. He let out a low guttural sound, dropping to all fours. The Indians say that all bears see other creatures as bears, and all humans see other creatures as human, but we are all interchangeable beings. He must have viewed me as another bear. He decided to tolerate me at the berry patch, as long as I didn't get too near to him. He went back to shoving luscious clusters of berries into his mouth. I didn't tempt fate by wearing out my welcome but felt something significant had happened to me that day. Was it my acceptance into the wild? Or was it forgiveness from Blue that made me feel connected to all living creatures in a way I'd never felt before?

July 15

I have a house guest for the first time. She's got that scrawny, peaked city look about her. Gaunt with sunken eyes, pale white skin, flat-chested, like a model in Vogue. She stumbled into Blue's thicket and woke him up from a two-day nap. She doesn't know how lucky she was that I got to her in time. I've tried to fatten her up with my cooking, but there seems to be more wrong with her than her diet. She spends a lot of time cleaning tack nobody has used in ten years. I guess it's therapeutic for her to be rubbing and polishing all day. I don't want to tell her no one will ever know or care about what she's doing. The lookout is probably going to be closed in a year or two. Airplanes have taken over fire surveillance in other areas. Planes have been slow to come here because of the unstable air that creates turbulence, and treacherous updrafts. But it's just a matter of time before new technology will displace manned lookouts. Sometimes I think I should pay the BLM to be here.

She has trouble on her mind she's not telling me about. A person has a right to their secrets. There's nothing worse than prying eyes that leave no room for your thoughts to form, for good or evil. We all have ugly thoughts now and again. Thoughts so awful we tremble at the images we conjure. Who hasn't awakened with a scream caught in their throat just in time to escape their demons? Everybody's got a right to their dark side, to fears, anxieties, and deserves time to work them out on their own. Some things are better left to dissolve in the light of day, like sugar in morning coffee.

Privacy is a scare commodity and getting harder to find. Like the bears that have been stripped of their wild: Analyzed, probed and dissected, we are being neutralized by technology. How busy we are documenting the demise of the bears, along with that of our own civilization.

Gemcie's cheeks flushed hot. Weighted with a lead jacket of

shame for having invaded his private thoughts, she put the journal back in the ammo can, careful to set it back just as she'd found it. She slipped onto the swivel hot seat, and slumped before the fire finder. How could she have violated the sanctity of someone who had entrusted his entire universe to her? Not only had he saved her life, cared for her and her stock, but he also let her stay here without interfering in her thoughts, giving her the precious, necessary time to unravel her own emotions.

It hurt her that he did not find her beautiful, but to think that he felt sorry for her, viewed her as pitiable, was more than she could bear. Tears trickled over the brim of blonde lashes. She had ruined this world too. Did he know she was reading his journal, or was it just coincidence that his most recent entry was about her? Maybe it wasn't too late to cover her tracks. Meanwhile, the sky was darkening to a deep indigo, and he was still not back.

Chapter Twenty

A mass of fast-moving black-bottomed clouds coming in at eye level churned towards Gemcie. By dusk, the ominous cumuli ballooned out of itself threatening to let loose its heavy load. White, licking, snake tongues of electricity sought the ground from hot pink mouths. Five seconds later the crack of clanging metallic thunder vibrated the windows. The low rumbling that followed bounced off the walls of the canyon, trying to find its way home. Gemcie ventured onto the catwalk to get a better view. Huge droplets splashed on her cheeks, signaling the torrent to come. She scanned the ridge with the field glasses, looking for Brady. She spotted him, marching into the wind about a mile away.

The chicks in the osprey nest, two weeks away from flight, swayed in the wild wind. Their mother hovered over them, not knowing how to protect them from the savage storm. Even the scrappy stellar jays that bullied all other creatures off the catwalk were in hiding. Fat-cheeked marmots whistled alarms to their brothers before scurrying into snug burrows. Tangerine poppies curled their petals into tight fists, bracing against the onslaught. Golden grasses, bending in the wind, rippled up the canyon across the meadow, like a torrent rushing to the sea. It was a summer storm come to cool, come to soothe, come to kill. Brady broke into a jog, rushing to get back before the storm set in. About a hundred yards out, he started waving his arms and yelling, "Get off the catwalk! Get back inside!"

The wind drowned out his voice. She couldn't make out what he was trying to tell her. She lingered on the catwalk, drinking in the smell of the wet evergreens and moist earth. Soon the rain was coming in heavy gray sheets, so she went back inside. Huge droplets

146

ran down the flat glass in solid streams. She heard Brady climbing up the wooden ladder, and rushed to open the trap door for him.

"You silly little fool!" he said, his face purple with anger. "The catwalk is the most dangerous place you can stand in a storm. Get on the stool and stay on it."

"I'm sorry," she murmured.

"You are not supposed to get between the fire finder and any of the metal fixtures. They aren't grounded. Lighting could arc. You could get fried!" he shouted.

She winced back tears of frustration and did as she was told. Safe on the stool with the glass insulators she faced the anvil-shaped, rumbling, thunderhead, hiding her humiliation from him. A twin set of vertical electric fangs searching for the ground lit up the sky. For a split second she could see the shadowy outline of the granite peaks on the western horizon. Twenty seconds later roared a blasting boom, boom, boom! One of the shutters to the lookout banging in the wind ripped from its hinges. It landed on the whistling guy wires securing the lookout to the boulders below. The entire structure trembled.

"This is a real 'big-ugly,'" Brady said, sliding muscular legs around her as he hopped up on the swivel seat behind her. "It's about five miles away from us now. When it gets over us, just sit tight. Don't even think about moving off this chair. I'm not trying to get friendly, but I'd like to live through this too. The glass insulators on this chair are all we've got between us and about 1.5 million volts."

Afraid to say anything that would make him angrier with her, she kept silent. He reached around her to turn on the radio, brushing the side of her breast with his arm. The musky odor of his body, still damp from his hike, held an intoxicating animal appeal she couldn't ignore.

The two-way was going bonkers with frantic messages coming from other lookouts to Headquarters. A pillar of fire was sighted five miles away. Headquarters called for a cross reading. Brady checked his azimuth and called it in. Within fifteen minutes of his return, all was black outside. Strikes came down more rapidly, enormous bursts of light ripped branches across the heavens. Though frightened, Gemcie was awed by the sheer force of the storm. She'd never known anything so powerful, so overwhelming. Relaxing into the curve of Brady's flat belly, enveloped in his calm center, she felt snug and secure despite the ferocious winds threatening to topple the lookout.

"Hope it doesn't rip the roof off," Brady said as a matter of fact.

"Could it?"

"It did once before, but I wasn't here then."

"How do you know that happened?"

"I read it in the last lookout's journal."

"Isn't that kind of personal?"

"I reckon it is, but all lookouts are supposed take notes of their stay. I never did it before I came here, but after a while you enjoy talking to yourself."

The intensity of the storm mounted. Wind screaming through the guy lines sounded like the whine of a jet engine. It would die down and then build again like the sea swelling into crushing waves. It whistled around the window frames, shaking the glass. The old tower felt alive, pulsing with wild energy. Gemcie jumped when she heard the resounding crack of a dry limb peeling off the trunk of a nearby tree. It crashed to the ground. The pelt of the heavy droplets on the corrugated roof intensified to a pounding din when the droplets turned to dime-sized pellets of hail. Lightning again flashed, illuminating the sky, this time so close it burned her eyes with its brightness. When her eyes adjusted to the darkness once more, she could see a fire. A tree ignited by a direct hit had burst into flame on the ridge to the east. Brady took a reading.

"This is Medicine Bear. Flame at 280. Do you copy?"

The radio cracked and sputtered back. "Copy?"

"The storm is over us now. Copy?"

The reply from headquarters never came. Instead, the radio hissed and crackled, wild with static. A buzzing sound, a shocking light, a popping sound; and then the pungent smell of ozone filled the room. Gemcie broke out in a clammy sweat. The hair on her arms stood up from the goose flesh. The ensuing terrible blast of thunder punished the fragile tower until the guy wires creaked and groaned, threatening to snap from their sockets. Dazed at first, it took some time before she realized they had just taken a direct hit. Like waking up from a deep sleep, reality was blurred through the prism of the dream-state. Her ears rang as she stared into the dark, straining to see. She fell into a fit of giggling.

"I don't know what's so funny," Brady noted. "Every lookout knows lightning wants to strike in the same place twice."

It was more hysteria than genuine laughter that overtook Gemcie. She couldn't explain why she was doubled over in uncontrollable laughter. Her emotion was contagious. Soon Brady was laughing with her in the face of the ferocious storm. The stink of the burning copper antenna on the top of the tower that melted into a puddle permeated the air. The hard winds continued to blow, tugging on the cables anchored to the rock. They laughed until they were weak.

The heart of the tumultuous force passed over them, leaving a reminder of the puny mortality of the human condition in its wake. Gemcie and Brady remained melded in the moment, as though the electrical field had mutated and altered their differences. For an instant they were one body, one breath, one spirit, clinging to that tiny grounded stool, frozen in time. Brady wrapped his arms around her slender waist. She let him rest his chin on her head, as they watched fast-moving, ominous clouds give way to crystalline night sky. Neither of them dared to break the sacred silence they shared. The storm left as fast as it came.

Overcome with a mixture of strange emotions, a shuddering sob rose from deep in Gemcie's belly. First and foremost she felt gratitude for being alive. Secondly, the sheer power of the cosmic energy engendered a sense of awe and wonder, but it was the physical connection she felt with Brady that overwhelmed and frightened her the most. He could feel her crying softly to herself, even though he couldn't see her tears.

"I guess you'd be missing your world back home right about now," he said softly.

She choked and sputtered, crying in earnest, not able to explain why she was weeping. She managed to wipe her eyes with the corner of her shirt.

"I don't have anything to go back to, if you want to know the truth."

"You must be thinking, 'How did I get myself in this fix?'" he said. "Don't worry; I've got a feeling you are going to be just fine. Fact is I can see you in your red hunt coat wearing your spit-polished boots, riding Marshal. Yep, your nose in his mane, muscle melted to hot muscle, heartbeat to heartbeat, listening to the rhythm of his hooves as he approaches the takeoff. Then I see you flying. Yep, flying up high in the sky, as high as the moon slipping behind those clouds. I see you sailing so high you just go right over that moon, never looking back."

Gemcie looked up at the luminous sphere smeared with dark streaks. She could see herself on Marshal, arcing the vanilla moon in a perfect bascule. Resting in the concave of Brady's flat belly, she drifted into sweet sleep, cradled in his arms.

Chapter Twenty-One

Daybreak saw the sky a pink camisole, streaked with golden cream. The yellow sunbeams streamed through the clouds in bold columns, warming the up-turned faces of flowers plump with new life. Steam rose from the ground as Gemcie strolled through the flattened grass surveying the casualties of the storm. Pine cones littered the ground. Their yellow pollen load turned the rivulets trickling into the sandy loam to gold. Branches of lodgepole pine and fir glistened with a million diamond droplets. The air was livened with the pungent scent of evergreens.

Then she saw the osprey's nest of twigs and feathers down, scattered on the ground. The fish eagle's chicks, dashed to their death, lay twenty feet away. She kneeled to examine them. Ants crawled in streams through their eye sockets and down their yellow beaks. On her knees, she could hear the hum of the insect population, stirring to life in the wet grass. High above, the confused mother circled in her airy domain. Brady walked up quietly behind her.

"Mother Nature is not always kind."

Startled, she fell back on her haunches. She was so preoccupied with her examination of the chicks, she didn't hear him approach.

"You could have knocked," she said, brushing bits of gravel from her wet bottom as she smiled up at him.

Extending a hand to help her up, he said, "Sorry. I just thought today would be a great day to take a bath."

"What?"

"I found a thermal pool on my hike. Thought you might be tired of the water pressure in my solar shower. Besides, it would be good

151

for the horses to exercise."

It was now four weeks since her run-in with Blue. Her sciatic pain seemed to be gone.

"That would be wonderful!" She grew excited at the thought.

By the time the animals were tacked up the sun was high in the azure sky. Brady packed a lunch he stowed on Maxine, along with a couple of towels and a picnic blanket. Mercedes had four ten-inch scabs, an inch apart, on her neck. She looked like she'd been raked by a pitchfork, but other than that she was fine. Cooter Jay yipped, letting Brady know he'd like taxi service today. Brady picked up the scruffy dog, and popped him in the saddle bag. Cooter squirmed into position, wet black nose to the wind. Brady shoved his rifle into the scabbard, just in case.

The animals snorted hot breath, excited to get out on such a glorious day. The crisp air brought pent-up energy to the fore. Even Maxine strutted stiffly through the belly-high wet grass as Brady led the way. Thrilled to be outside, Mercedes marched briskly behind Tucker. Gemcie watched Brady's slim hips rock from side to side. Legs shoved into his stirrups, he sat a horse like a cowboy. He led them off-trail, through the trees, trotting on soft pine-needle footing. Posting lightly out of the saddle, Gemcie felt herself floating, in tune with her mare's springy step. Maxine broke out in a melodious song.

Brady stopped at a steep ravine, gazed over the side for a moment, then popped over the precipice, traversing the mountain from side to side in switchback fashion. Once at the bottom, he gave the animals a breather then pressed forward up the opposing steep incline. They traveled for a couple of hours up one basin, then down another through the water-laden forest. More than once Gemcie lifted a soggy bough just in time to keep it from slapping her in the face as Brady charged ahead through the underbrush. Her jacket was soaked when they reached a rock plateau high in alpine wilderness, warmed by the sun.

Stark, like a lunarscape, the flat rock was pocked with round indentations. Clumps of crimson Indian brush flourished in the clefts, giving bright relief to the barren landscape. A stand of dwarf pine fringed the edge of a flat river coursing across the plain. Mist rose twenty feet above a churning pool as if staged with dry ice. About a hundred yards beyond the pool, a thunderous waterfall plunged over a rock ledge, pushing out any other sound.

Brady pulled up Tucker. "That would be your bath tub," he said, pointing to the steaming pool. "I'll picket the horses down canyon then hike back up."

He stopped long enough to unload Maxine before heading for the meadow, ponying the mule and mare behind. Gemcie found a sunny, flat spot on the glassy granite rock to spread the blanket. She went to the water's edge, knelt down and gave the water the pinkie test. It was perfect spa temperature. She tore off her wet jacket, peeled off her riding pants and gingerly made her way into the roiling bubble bath. An underground thermal spring fed the pool. She could feel the water becoming too hot when she ventured near the source. So she stayed near the edge of the pool, resting her head on a rock ledge, letting her body drift in the soothing water. Bubbles snapped around her face, tickling her nose. The water lifted her aching body. She let her toes float to the surface. The fatigue in her muscles melted away as the sun shone brightly on her face. She grabbed her visor from the pile of discarded clothes, pulled it over her eyes, and slipped into a trance.

Afloat in the embryonic soup, she pondered the liquid lifeline of evolution. *Our bodies are eighty percent water. It is from water that the first creatures crawled, trading fins for legs. It is water that first sculpted the world. What begins as a drop from a glacier melting in these high airy regions joins hands with other drops to form the trickling tributaries, clasping hands joyfully with other streams, to finally form great rivers. Rivers that carve the canyons erode cliffs and mold meadows while giving life. It is the most essential character on Earth.* She felt blessed to be intimate with the world-shaping beginnings that lay in this lofty region.

When Brady returned, he settled onto the blanket, cross-legged Indian style, and then pulled a bottle of wine out of the picnic basket. He tore off a hunk of sour dough bread, and sliced a piece of cheese. He took a hearty bite of both and washed it down with a slug of wine.

"Would you like some?" he asked, holding up the bottle.

She rolled over in the water to face him, putting her chin on her forearms, resting her arms on the ledge to meet his flashing blue eyes.

"Sure," she answered.

"This is Nature's Best. I got it in Glen Ellen. Been saving it for something special," he said.

The woody liquid slid down her throat warming her inside.

Euphoric with pleasure, she undressed him mentally. Black curly hair tumbled from his denim shirt, open to the sternum. She imagined a flat belly, strong arms, lean muscular legs capped with tight, white buns, and private property nestled in a black bush of hair. Was it true he didn't find her attractive? Inspired by the wine, warm water, and the sun beaming down, she decided to find out. She lifted her steaming body out the water, and stood before him with the sun behind her, framing her head in a solar halo.

He looked up at her, dumbstruck at first, and then rose to the challenge. Standing up, he slipped a towel around her shoulders. He pulled her into his arms and kissed her deeply with a warm soft tongue searching to know if she meant for him to love her. He felt her trembling. He took her by the hand, guiding her down to the blanket. He dried her, rubbing her with strong flat palms, gazing intently at each area of her body as he lovingly toweled her dry. He gazed at the firm mounds of white flesh that were her breasts then looked into the depth of her heather-blue eyes to see if she approved. Her lips parted in a wistful smile. He leaned over her, planting sweet sucking kisses on each pale pink nipple. She clung to his thick mop of black hair, pulling him into her body. He moved the towel over the swell of her belly. He licked her navel then followed the trail of blonde hairs that lead to her center. He blew lightly on the patch of wet curly hair then turned her over to rub her backside with the towel.

With long fingers he massaged her firm buttocks, running his hands up and down her strong legs. Sitting lightly on her behind, he spread his palms wide, massaging along the base of her spine with strong fingers. He worked his way up from the small of her back to the top of her head. When he placed his thumbs in the cleft of her skull, white light burst from the top of her head. Her heart leaped with anticipation when he finally moved to take off his own clothes. Remembering the goat-like thrusts of Jorge, she expected a brief moment of blinding fury then stillness, but he was in no hurry. He melted into her, blazing her mind with searing eyes gone soft with pleasure. They made love for hours, taking turns giving one another pleasure, cooled by the silky breeze, beneath the taut blue canopy.

Once satiated, they dressed and walked hand and hand to view the thunderous waterfall that had kept them company all afternoon. They sat on the edge of black rocks jutting over the cascade and watched the smooth bottle-green water approach the precipice. It looked still and silent, but was, in fact, moving slowly, steadily to a violent destiny. When it reached the sharp brow of the rock it fanned over the top, forming an arcing spray of flat streams. Gemcie imagined herself standing on the rock ledge behind the falling water looking through the prism of clear wet. Spumes of white spray shot up thirty feet where the water met the boulder jumble below. Eddies swirled viciously, awaiting the unsuspecting traveler, pulling leaves and twigs into sink holes, spitting them out far downstream. A rainbow of yellow, green, and blue arched over the spray.

"There's one thing I want to know," she said.

"Just one?" He smiled, pulling her close to him with his arm resting on her shoulders.

"What was the idea of pounding on my door late at night? Were you trying to scare me into coming to you?"

He pulled back and looked at her incredulously. "I don't know what you're talking about."

"You mean it wasn't you about a week ago coming up the stairs, threatening to shove the door open?"

"Wait a minute!" He started laughing uncontrollably, pounding his thigh with his free hand.

"What's so funny?" she demanded. "Scaring the wits out of me isn't funny."

He sobered enough to stutter, "I'm devious, but I'm not that smart."

"If it wasn't you, then I want a rifle in my room at night."

"You mean you could pull the trigger on whoever is on the other side of the door without knowing who it is?"

"If it's me or it, I sure would."

"Even if it was Bucky?"

"Bucky!"

"Yeah, I spoiled that deer when he was a fawn, used to let him come up and have the run of the place when I was living in the cabin. He must think you're trespassing."

"How do you know it's him?"

"I don't. Next time it happens we'll check for prints. I'm not sure about giving you my gun, though. You might shoot me instead."

"I couldn't do that now."

"It's comforting to know you could have before," he said with a sly smile.

The ride back to the lookout was slow and thoughtful. Neither of them spoke, lost in their own wanderings and the soft thud of the horses' hooves in the forest duff. She watched his denim-clad bottom rock to and fro in the saddle as he tapped Tucker rhythmically with the tip of the reins, humming a cowboy tune. Suddenly, he put his right hand up, signaling a stop. He pointed to some mushrooms that popped up overnight.

"Chanterelles," he said. "They make for some good eatin'."

She saw the yellow trumpet-shaped mushrooms bulging through the leaf mold. Their thick, firm, wavy-edged stalks make a good meal when plucked soon after a storm. Brady took off his bandana, exposing a white line on his sun-tanned neck, lined his Stetson with it and used his hat for a bucket to collect the delectable fungus. It was hazy dusk by the time they got back. They groomed the animals quickly, giving them a onceover with a fat brush. After picking their hooves clean of any rocks collected that day, they left the livestock munching placidly on alfalfa pellets. Once in the lookout, Brady struck a match to the fire he had pre-laid that morning in the pot-bellied stove.

"I've got garlic, shallots, butter, and wine. I guess we can live without the limes," he said, pulling the ingredients out of the tiny propane refrigerator. He rummaged another bottle of wine from a hiding spot under the cot and popped Debussy into a cheap plastic boom box. The strains of a tinny Clare de Lune filled the lookout while he cleaned, chopped, then sautéed the wild mushrooms in butter. While he cooked, Gemcie spun around on the swivel chair, glassing the 360-degree view for leftover flames. She saw no signs of fire, not even a smoky vapor rising from a downed tree. All was calm and serene, as though the storm had been a dream. After eating their fill they snuggled on the narrow bed made for one, and gazed at the blanket of stars wrapping the lookout.

"The Indians say the Big Dipper was formed when a boy turned into a bear and chased seven maidens up a tree stump," Brady said. "In order to get away from him they had to jump to the sky." Gemcie fell asleep listening to his soft voice, sheltered in the crook of his arm.

Chapter Twenty-Two

For the rest of the summer Brady and Gemcie took turns manning the lookout and ponying the livestock to the meadow each evening and morning for a drink. Sometimes she made the ride to the river with him to catch a fish dinner. He liked to hunt quail, which were legal this time of year. He rolled the tender dark meat of the birds in batter, dipped them in flour and fried them in a cast iron skillet. One day drifted into another. She never felt the need to pry into his journal again. If she wanted to know something she would just ask.

"What are you going to do when you leave here?" she asked, flipping skillet potatoes for breakfast.

"Do I have to think about that now?" he answered with a laugh as he doctored powdered eggs with herbs.

"You have to think about it eventually."

"I don't like to think much beyond today."

"Seems simplistic."

"Try it sometime," Brady said. "Most people are busy making money for the first half of their life, then worrying how about how they're going to keep it for the last half. Don't leave much time in between to enjoy what they got."

Brady stopped stirring the eggs cooking on the Bunsen when static from the radio broke through the morning silence.

"Medicine Bear, come in," sputtered a crackling voice from headquarters.

"This is Medicine Bear. Copy?"

"Is Snowbird still with you? Copy?"

"Yes. Copy?"

"Good. Can she handle the lookout on her own? Copy?"

Brady glanced at Gemcie before responding. She nodded a hearty affirmative from the swivel chair.

"Sure, why? Copy?"

"There's been a mauling on PCT camp twelve. A couple tried to defend themselves from a rogue black bear."

Brady's face went ashen.

"How bad was it? Copy?"

"The woman is still in the hospital. If she lives she will be disfigured. Her husband is suing the park. Says the camp wasn't posted properly. Copy?"

Brady looked away, his eyes cast down, avoiding Gemcie's incredulous stare.

"Were they careless?" he asked.

"I don't know, but you've got to track the bear. It's not wearing a collar. It has to be disposed of immediately."

"What if it was their fault?" Gemcie blurted.

"It doesn't matter. Headquarters wants that bear dead, pronto."

"I'll take care of it," Brady said, still staring at the tips of his boots.

"Let us know when the job's done. Copy?"

"Right. Copy?"

"They're sending you out to murder the bear without knowing what happened?"

"It doesn't matter what happened. The park doesn't want bad press. It's easier to kill the bears. Once they become habituated to tourist garbage they hang around the campers and can be dangerous. Can you manage the lookout for a couple of days?"

"Sure."

After a breakfast eaten in silence, Brady pulled his rifle out from under his cot. He polished the silver-blue metal of the barrel, wiping down the molasses-colored wood stock with oil. He stood on the catwalk, put the rifle in position at his shoulder, squinted through the crosshairs of the sights, aimed at a limb on a tree a hundred yards away, and squeezed the trigger. A rude bellowing roar ricocheted down the canyon walls, putting any wildlife within twenty miles on notice that "man" was in the neighborhood. The limb splintered and broke away from the tree trunk where the bullet found its mark. Then he tacked up Tucker, packed a duffel and left without another word.

From the catwalk she followed the side-to-side movement of his denim jacket as Tucker picked his way down the steep trail. Brady tucked his chin in, pulled his Stetson down, and pulled his bandana over his face to protect himself from the bone-chilling wind. Summer ends abruptly in the Sierras. A cold snap turns the spinning silver aspen leaves to gold. The brisk air is filled with the fecund smell of moist earth and dead leaves. He slipped from her view, swallowed up by the gray, wet fog hovering in the basin.

Indians say bears actually like human beings. They even enjoy being near them and learning about their funny ways. They like to be seen by people, to surprise them sometimes, even though they might be caught or killed by them. They might go inside their houses and hear their music. Brady wondered if Blue was just trying to know humans better. He knew it was Blue. The summer his mother was killed, there was a report of a cub on the Pacific Crest Trail pillaging the garbage of campers that didn't secure their foodstuff high in a tree away from their tents. He hoped it wasn't Blue, but he suspected that was how the cub managed to survive the first lonely year of his life.

Brady chose not to tell headquarters about Blue. He allowed the bear to live outside the law of the park. If he wasn't collared, they couldn't find him with telemetry. Maybe he could live to a ripe old age, confident, roaming free in the land of his ancestors. Bears can lope a hundred miles overnight. They make love for hours, have no enemies, can be silly, and are big-hearted. Indians consider bears the closest of all animals to humans. Brady knew that, like humans, they remember. He wondered if Blue remembered the stench of human permeating his mother's fur. When they had met at the berry patch, it seemed the cub had forgiven even the death of his mother, allowing Brady to share the berry fields with him.

The Indians believe rules and manners exist shared by all, having to do with knowledge and power, with life and death, because they deal with taking life as well as eating and dying. Human beings, in their ignorance, are apt to give offense. "There's a world behind the world we see that is the same, but more open, more transparent, without blocks. Like inside a big mind, the animals and humans all can talk and those who awaken to that reality get power to heal and help. They learn how to behave, and how not to give offense. To

159

touch this inner world, no matter how briefly, is to help in life." These were the lessons the woman who married a bear brought back to her village after a season with her husband in his snug den, or so the story told.

He wondered how much of this was true and how much was legend as he navigated the squishy, wet meadow. Tucker was sinking into the dry, collapsed plants and grasses up to his hocks. The southern end of the meadow was a marshy wetland, perfect for birdlife but not much good for a man on a horse. He guided Tucker to a deer trail that traversed the steep slope. He rode for a couple hours through the thick underbrush with soft footing. This route eventually connected with the main trail to the Crest. He arrived at campsite twelve by dusk.

Daybreak found him searching the campsite for tracks. The black bear print has a flat pad and four-inch claw marks that are pretty easy to spot. It hadn't rained since the incident, but the ground was packed hard from a summer of tourists. He searched the perimeter for over two hours before he found a deer trail that looked to have been traveled recently. He followed it for a half mile on foot before he saw a tree stump pulverized by a bear in search of termites. This was a good lead. He returned to fetch Tucker and break camp.

The deer trail led him deep into the far western side of the canyon and a section of forest he'd never before traveled. A thick tree canopy gave it good shade and protected it from helicopter sightings. He figured Blue felt safe in this cover, as it gave the bear the advantage. Brady could not penetrate the thicket without announcing his arrival. If Blue were here he would hear the branches cracking and twigs snapping as Brady and Tucker made their way down the narrow trail into the heart of his territory. Brady stepped off Tucker to examine a pile of scat. He stuck his finger into the still-warm pile with the texture of dog dung. Brady kept a third eye open while he stirred the scat with a twig, examining the window to Blues whereabouts. Purple patches told him that the bear had been feeding at berry fields recently.

Brady dared move farther into the dense underbrush, knowing he could accidentally step into a sleeping bear's day bed. Startling a bear can be fatal. They don't usually attack unless provoked, but even the sweetest bruin is grouchy when awakened. Another wider trail intersected the one Brady was following. Brady dismounted to get a closer look. It was an ancient bear trail, probably leading to denning sites above the timberline. He had heard about the trails that haunt these hills but had never seen one. The bears take care to step exactly in the same footprints offered by these paths. Over the centuries the paths that take the bears to their winter's rest become human-like footprints embedded in time.

Tucker reared back, jerking sharply on the reins, pulling Brady off balance and onto the ground. The horse's eyes rolled white, his nostrils flared red, and he whinnied sharply. Brady tried to calm him long enough to grab his rifle from the scabbard, but before he could, he heard a log snap under the weight of a large bear. He spun around on his heel to face what had made the sound. The bear, standing on all fours, peered intently with orange, intelligent eyes at the stranger invading his domain. He pawed and scratched at the ground, trying to decide whether or not to charge. Brady was careful to look away, not wanting to challenge the animal. Standing his ground, he spoke softly to the bear while backing slowly towards the rifle.

He knew it was Blue. It was a full-grown black bear in his prime with a blaze on his chest.

"It's time, Old Man, for you and me to talk. I've been watching you for the last three years. You don't know me, but I know you," he spoke in a low, soft voice hoping to calm the animal. At first Blue seemed to be listening. Then he rose on his hind legs and pawed the air, woofing. The hair rose on the back of his neck as the scent of human filled his nostrils. His eyes rolled back in his head and he roared, exposing dripping yellow canines.

"I can understand your not liking me," Brady continued, edging towards Tucker and the rifle still in the scabbard on the side of the saddle. "I wouldn't like me either, if I was you. I know you haven't done anything except be the beautiful beast you were born to be with God-given powers to survive and the will to do it. I know you were here first." Brady maintained a monotone voice, moving imperceptibly towards the weapon. Tucker, trembling with fear, threatened to bolt at any moment, taking the rifle with him. The bear went back down to all fours, swaying his head from side to side. He seemed to be accepting the presence of the stranger.

"It is you, isn't it, Blue? "Brady said, finally grasping the butt of the loaded rifle, pulling it slowly out of the scabbard.

"It is you, old friend," Brady confirmed, as he lowered the rifle, squinting through the sights, finding Blue's forehead in the cross hairs. He saw the vibrant, vital animal looking inquisitively at the barrel. He felt an electric shock of energy arc between them, as he squeezed gently but surely on the trigger. Blue crumpled to the ground, bawling in pain. Brady stepped closer and took aim, this time at close range into Blue's brain. When he fired his jacket was splattered with the brains and blood of a beast that had done him no harm.

He knelt down, feeling the thick fur, rubbing it flat with his palm, exposing warm flesh. He lifted his hand to his nose, sending the pungent scent spiraling in his brain, branding his own mind with the scent of Blue. He heard the smell of bear was foul, but it seemed to him no more powerful than the smell of a dog too long in the house. Heat radiated from the leather pads of the paws with claws as long as his little finger. He put his hand flat against the paw, matching it up to his own hand. He clasped it in a handshake, letting the curved ebony claws wrap around his wrist. Tears welled, rolled down his cheeks and fell onto the deep mat of lifeless black hair that was Blue.

The power of nature brings the animal to the hunter, not the power of the hunter bringing the animal to him, echoed in Brady's mind. *Man operates as if all of life is subordinate to him. We declare ourselves "top of the food chain" and therefore superior to all other life forms.* He didn't feel superior. He felt small and ashamed. Remembering the ways of the Nez Perce, the stories he had heard as a child around the campfire in Montana, he took his hunting knife from its leather case. He held it up to see it glisten silver in the shadows. Slowly, meticulously, with careful intent, he removed Blue's tail and severed his mutilated head at the neck. Gathering twigs, moss and down wood, he built a bonfire that could easily spark a flame in the thick tree canopy. He placed Blue's skull and tail on the flame, filling the air with the stink of burning hair. He watched the black fur curl, popping and snapping into oblivion, and sang the song of safe journey for Blue through the halfway world of bear and human, into the spirit world of ancient hunters.

Chapter Twenty-Three

Gemcie scoured the mountains with the field glasses looking for signs of Brady's return. She had spotted a plume of smoke on the western ridge the day before. She assumed it was the work of careless campers. It died of its own accord. Sitting on the hot seat for hours at a stretch gave Gemcie time to think about what was most important to her. Like all lookouts, she put pen to paper and started talking to herself.

September

A chill wind is blowing up the canyon stirring the crowns of the pines. No sign of Brady. I know going after Blue is hurtful for him, but it is something he has to do. I can't stop thinking about Marshal and how I let him down. He trusted me completely. His eyes, dark tender pools of emotion questioning me, are all I can think about. He needs me. I know he is doing his utmost to please his rider, but he is not able to comply without resistance to such confining methods. Dominque, for all her duplicity, is a wonderful athlete and tremendous rider. I admire her classical form: erect, controlled, brave in the saddle. But she is not the right rider for Marshal.

I feel guilty about leaving him to her devices, but I don't know how I can get him back. Without money to buy him—let alone pay for his board, the visits from the vet, his shots, entry fees, his blacksmith—it's impossible. I'm happy here where time has kindly stood still for me. I don't want to go back. I want to stay here with Brady forever.

Her heart leapt wildly when she finally saw the tip of Brady's Stetson bobbing through the scrub pine. She clamored backwards down the ladder and ran to the boulder jutting over the canyon where she waved to get his attention. It had only been three days, but it seemed an eternity since she nestled in the sweet strength of his arms.

He didn't respond to her yahoos. He just kept his head tucked, chin to chest. When he arrived at the lookout, he walked straight past her in sullen silence to the stable. Dazed and confused by his mood, she put her hands in her pockets and followed him to the tie rack. He lifted Tucker's saddle off the horse's wet back, unbridled him and rubbed him down with a towel, without acknowledging her presence.

"What happened?" she ventured.

"What was always going to happen,' he said, nudging Tucker to lift his front hoof for inspection.

"You found him?"

Brady picked Tucker's hoof in thoughtful silence then placed it to the ground. He stood to face Gemcie.

"It's time for you to go," he said with flat, metal-blue eyes.

"What do you mean?" she sputtered. "I'm not ready."

"It doesn't matter whether you're ready. The season has turned. Snowbirds fly before the snow flies."

Gemcie was stunned. An involuntary rage took hold. She slapped his face with all her might. He turned his head with the blow and responded with a steady vacant stare. Receding into his own mental interior he did not retaliate. He simply left her behind. "Have your stuff ready in the morning. I'm taking you down the mountain," he ordered, putting Tucker away then heading for the lookout.

She lay in bed in the cabin that night unable to sleep, trying to reconcile the change in Brady. He had turned to water, slipping through her fingers. It frightened her that he could be so detached, not just from her, but from the rest of the world as well. When he made love to her it was like being enveloped in a womb of embryonic water. She felt safe, protected and calm in his arms. She could feel his energy trickling through her brain, reaching each cell. He was so strong, yet soft. How could he have changed this way? What had happened?

Daybreak found Brady pounding on her door with one hand, holding a breakfast tray in the other.

"Get yourself together while I take the livestock to the meadow. I'll be back in a half-hour," he dictated.

She did as she was told, stopping long enough to look out her window one last time, trying to memorize each detail of the vista before her. Wet fog drifted through the jagged rows of shark's teeth thrusting to the sky. Mist clung to the shoulders of Lone Man like a cape. She saw the mountains as the bridge between heaven and earth, and wanted to climb them to a place far away. The yellow marmot stood upright from his boulder pile, chirping to her through two sharp front teeth. He twitched his wet, black nose at her as though saying goodbye, then quickly turned and ducked into his tunnel.

Brady was back sooner than she wanted. He quickly trussed up Maxine, loading her with supplies.

"We need to get moving," he said in a monotone voice. "The weather comes up in a hurry this time of year."

Gemcie gathered the rest of her meager possessions, stuffed them into her saddle bag, and fell into line. Brady led the tiny procession down the ravine for the last time. She pulled the hood of her jacket up over her head, breathing into the wool scarf at her chin to stay warm. The wet mist, threatening to become snow, was as heavy as her mood. Silent tears trickled down her cheeks as she watched his behind weaving from side to side down the narrow canyon trail. Cold fear clutched at her throat when they passed the spot where Blue attacked. The stream that was once colored red with Mercedes' rich blood, was restored to pure, sparkling waters bubbling with vitality over the clefts and hollows of the rocks. There was no trace of the day Blue had brought Brady to her.

They crossed the magenta meadow, turned to golden dry grass bending to the ground in the stiff wind. A flock of Canada geese flew overhead in formation, rushing to summer quarters. Their cackles warned of the harsh weather to come. He pressed forward, leaning into the wind that turned into a biting blast of air when they reached the crest of the ridge. Wanting to get her back to Rock Creek in two days, he struck into a brisk trot across the flat terrain. Maxine trailed behind in her stiff-legged strut with her load threatening to topple if he went any faster.

Recoiling at the thought of returning to civilization, she wished he would slow down. *What's his hurry? What have I done? Why is he in such a rush to get rid of me?* He needed to be alone—that was clear; but did he have to boot her off the mountain and out of his life? She felt the mountains belonged to her as much as him now. Feeling her spirit unleashed in the vastness, free to wander the heavens, her senses were livened by the visceral experience of nature. She dreaded the confines of society. Her heart stirred with unchained emotion when she imagined her father's slender frame sitting in the saddle ahead of her instead of Brady's. His long legs jutted forward with frayed boots shoved into wooden stirrups and a guitar tied to his saddle. It was his spirit in her that was raging inside, struggling to be free. Though she'd never seen a picture of him, she imagined this was her father, leading her back to civilization and away from him. She bubbled over with a hiccupping sob, sensing the finality of his goodbye.

They were making good time. Tucker marched crisply over a bridge of gray log slats. Gemcie came behind with Maxine in tow. She was halfway across the weathered bridge that had seen one too many winters when it gave way beneath the mule's weight. Maxine's front leg slipped through the splintered slat now coming up to her chest. The mule reared back, trying to pull her leg free.

Gemcie screamed.

Brady turned to see Maxine bawling in pain, falling over onto her side. The weight of her load pulled her into the icy creek. She tumbled backwards, off the bridge, into the rushing water. Pinned between three enormous boulders, she was trapped with her hooves in the air, head just above water.

"We've got to get the pack off her back!" Brady yelled.

He ran to the mule, tried to un-strap her load from the shore, but couldn't reach the buckles to her harness. He jumped in beside her.

"Steady, mule. Steady, girl," he said. Maxine looked back at him with eyes as helpless as a child's.

He found the harness strap and loosened it, freeing boxes of kitchen supplies. Gemcie grabbed the boxes from him, and hoisted them onto the slick, grassy edge of the creek.

"Don't quit, mule," Brady growled. "Get up."

Gemcie couldn't believe the cruel, menacing tone he'd used on an animal obviously stunned by her circumstance. Gemcie, as flustered as the mule, paced back and forth on the bank not knowing what to do.

"Don't just stand there; get hold of her lead. You pull and I'll push," he shouted.

Brady positioned himself between the mule's rump and a rock. He put his boot on her bottom where her weight rested on a boulder.

"All right, get up, mule. Don't give up," he growled with all the ferocity he could muster, shoving her rump with all his strength. The mule floundered, sprawling her legs in opposite directions, finding no ground to regain her balance. She threatened to crush Brady with her body as she lurched about, trying to right herself. Maxine couldn't find footing to scramble up out of the slick boulder bed. Brady couldn't tell if her leg was broken or whether she was simply resigned to her fate. They were at a stalemate, meaning he would have to shoot Maxine and cut up her body for predators to enjoy. He couldn't leave the mule in the creek. Gemcie remembered the bullwhip Gus stowed in her gear. She dropped the mule's lead and ran to get it.

"Where the hell do you think you're going?" Brady shouted after her.

She returned with the whip and cracked it smartly. The crack that sounded like a six-shooter in her ear got Maxine's attention. Her eyes rolled white and she lurched, almost managing to get upright. Brady scrambled to get out of the way of her powerful hindquarters. Gemcie gave the mule a stinging snap of the whip on her rump. Maxine rolled over, found purchase with her hind feet and surged up the side of the creek with a great snort and the clatter of metal shoes on wet boulders. Once ashore, she shook her body violently, letting loose six feet of spray, and brayed pitifully.

Maxine trembled as Gemcie felt up and down her front legs for injury.

"Nothing feels broken," she determined.

"That was a close one," Brady said, tending to the gashes on the mule's hind leg.

"Do you think she'll be okay?"

"Yeah, but we have to keep her moving, or she'll get so sore she won't be able to walk."

"I've got some painkillers in my saddle bag."

"Good. Looks like you saved both of us," he said, smiling for the first time in days.

Her heart flooded with relief when she saw a flicker of tenderness return to his eyes.

"We're going to have to hustle," he said. "Let's walk her out and load her up before she gets as stiff as a poker."

Brady didn't stop to make camp until well after dusk. They pitched the tent in the dark avoiding eye contact. She gathered wood for the fire while he built a nest of twigs and moss for kindling. Colder here on the crest than in the valleys, the wind whipped the sparks into a wild, fire dance. She removed her gloves for the first time that day and held her hands close to the flames. Brady produced a quick camp meal of power bars and jerky. Knowing they would soon be back at Rock Creek and that this was her last chance to reach him, she dared to speak.

"I thought we had something special."

The fire cast a bronze glow on Brady's chiseled features. He stared into the fire with eyes buried in the shadow of deep sockets beneath bushy black brows.

"I tricked you into loving me," he finally replied.

"What do you mean? I'm a big girl." She attempted a laugh.

"When I was a boy in Montana, my dad used to take me out once a year to round up mustangs. I watched those herds for days on end trying to figure out their ways. It became clear that the lead mare was in charge, even though the stallion was full of flash. If a foal got too rambunctious, kicking and biting his brother and sisters, she would turn him out and run him away from the herd with savage bites. Pretty soon he'd get so lonely he'd be beggin' her for her attention and mercy. That's what I did to you."

"What are you talking about?"

"I don't know much about women, but I do know they're curious. I propped my feet up in front of the fire, writing in my journal each night, knowing it would rouse your interest. I left my journal in the unlocked ammo can, with a hair across the spine so I'd know when you opened it. Then I left you in the lookout for a day so you'd have plenty of time to find it. Of course, I culled entries I thought might offend, and left in the ones I hoped would make you love me. Then I put one in that would make you want to push your way into my heart, just like that foal trying to get back into the herd."

"You conniving bastard!" Gemcie said, flushing with fresh anger.

"That's about accurate." he said. "So you aren't losing anything as special as you think. You can have the tent, I like to sleep under the stars," he finished, reaching for his saddle bag.

Flustered by conflicting emotions, Gemcie fell silent in her confusion.

"There's something I didn't tell you."

"What's that?"

"I'm married."

A glint of cynicism sparked in Brady's response.

"Well, well. Looks like I'm not the only one hiding behind the truth."

His smile was so disarming, she couldn't' believe he could be capable of such calculating cruelty. The days of working hand in hand at simple projects, the quiet care, how could it have been a sham? Was he that tender, his embrace that gentle with every woman? She felt transformed into a powerful being in the glowing light of his love. She was stunned that he did not share her conviction that something wonderful had happened; something that might not come again.

"Won't you tell me about Blue?" she asked, pleading with soft eyes for him to open up to her.

"Nothing to tell," he said, settling down with his saddle as a pillow. "It's time for you to get back to your world. That's all," he concluded, pulling a thin blanket over his shoulder and curling up with his backside to her.

"My world!" she said, trembling with rage. "You think you aren't part of the real world because you hole up here like a mole?" she continued, grabbing the blanket from his shoulder. "It's easier for you to hide out, not to deal, isn't it?"

He turned back to face her, this time tenderly. "We've all got to deal. We're all connected, whether we want to be or not. Now go to sleep, Gemcie. This isn't going to change anything."

Confronted with the brick wall of his resolve, she held her tears back until she was snug in her sleeping bag, where she cried herself to sleep.

Daybreak found smoke curling from the campfire through the sweet-scented dwarf pines. There was a nip in the air, and a brisk wind tossing leaves high, but the wet clouds had passed in the night. Brady broke camp quickly, wanting to get her to the trailhead that would take her back to Rock Creek by noon. It was an easy tramp across the top of the world on the same trail that John Muir traveled a hundred years ago. He rhapsodized about it with such lively detail that no one, before or since, has ever matched his ardor in words, though many have loved it and tried.

Gemcie said goodbye to the spinster-gray faces of the snow-sprinkled peaks as Mercedes splashed through the teeth-chattering creek. She wanted to take with her the lessons of water. Nothing in the world is weaker than water, yet nothing is better at overcoming the strong. She would be like water. She would be soft and yielding, yet strong in relentless motion. She would not be beaten by this disappointment or any other. There would be no resistance from her. She would flow ceaselessly from one moment to the next. For the first time, she felt ready to go home.

The horses clattered across a worn wooden bridge. Brady held up his hand on the other side of the roiling water and dismounted. He knelt down to a pool formed in a rock cleft, cupped the clear water in his hands and took it to his lips. Gemcie followed suit, discarding fear of contamination from civilization. She leaned out over the rock pool and sipped the lucid water, bright as light itself, absorbing its beauty with her mind, not just her body. Like a fawn she sucked the water daintily, watching the muscles in the horses' throats ripple as they sucked their fill together.

"Your trail is about a hundred yards up," Brady said. "If you stay on it, you can get to Rock Creek by nightfall. If you want to take your time and camp a night, there are lots of good places. This is as far as I go."

Wiping the water from her mouth, Gemcie rose, meeting his gaze. "I remember this bridge. I know how to get home from here," she said. "Thanks for everything."

Brady wasn't ready for her Gandiesque approach.

"Look, I'm sorry, but I need to be alone right now," he said.

She leaned up and kissed him fully and deeply, asking for no more than the moment. His arms slipped around her slim shoulders and pulled her near.

"I'll always remember you," she said, gently pushing herself away from him. He released his embrace and let his arms slide from her arms, stopping to clasp her fingertips. She looked one last time into the depth of his fathomless eyes, now soft with tenderness, and said, "Goodbye."

"C'mon, Cooter," Gemcie called to the mutt tucked into Brady's saddle bag.

Brady lifted Cooter out of the bag and dropped him lightly to the ground. Cooter stretched each hind leg out behind himself until it trembled. Then he laid his head on Brady's boot. Brady gave Gemcie a leg up onto Mercedes and gave the mare a last swipe over the scabbed streaks on her neck, which were almost covered in new hair.

"By Thanksgiving, her scars will be gone."

Gemcie cued the mare to turn on her haunches, squeezing Mercedes up to a brisk trot, ponying Maxine behind. Cooter Jay didn't budge. He sat on splayed haunches, looking up to Brady aboard Tucker, wondering why he was still on the ground.

"Git, Cooter," Brady said, waving his hat to let him know he meant business.

"C'mon, Cooter, it's time to go home," Gemcie called to him.

"Git, you sorry mutt," Brady growled.

A confused Cooter gave way to his fate and barreled after Gemcie on low-flying legs.

171

Chapter Twenty-Four

In the weeks spent laconically at the lookout, Gemcie had forgotten the danger in the daunting descent from the crest to Rock Creek Canyon. The treacherous trail wrapped the canyon wall, overlooking a gorge carved by a brash creek foaming over bridges of down wood. She let Mercedes pick her way down the granite stairway gouged into the boulder-strewn trail. Sections of trail were eroded so badly that all the topsoil had washed away, leaving slippery bald rock for footing. The mare sat back on her haunches to traverse this terrain without tipping forward. She tripped and toppled onto her knees. Gemcie leaned as far back in the saddle as she could, keeping her weight shifted to the horse's rump, remaining perfectly still to help the mare right herself. She dared not look back at Maxine, who curled up her lip and let go a long, heaving complaint that reverberated down the canyon. Thoughts of the mule stepping into a gully and being pulled over by the weight of an unbalanced load filled her with anxious dread. She imagined Maxine's body belly-up, legs floundering, weighted to the floor of the creek far below.

Once on the valley floor, the flat, wide trail led them through a canopy of sun-washed leaves. The dead leaves crunching beneath the animals' hooves smelled of fall. A silvery stream snaked through the tapestry of tall amber-colored grass with splotches of silver sage. Orange-leaved sycamores ribboned the stream's edge. The gray-and-white mottled trunks of the trees held firm as strong winds buffeted the top boughs, lifting brown curled leaves from outstretched limbs, setting them free to drift airily to the ground. A gust of wind whipped a pile of leaves to a river of gold crackling across the valley floor.

In no hurry to follow the stream chugging down to the 395

HWY where the world zoomed on, Gemcie stopped for lunch. She found a view seat in Nature's restaurant on a warm rock overlooking the sun-washed meadow. She spotted finches, thrushes, and a blue heron standing stock still trying to disguise himself as a water reed. The great bird spread his five-foot wings and wafted away once certain of detection. Blue asters, white daisies, and clumps of yellow sage, a surprise in mid-September, dotted cinnamon-colored grasses. Maxine and Mercedes tanked up on the sweet, clean water in a slow-moving stream that tumbled over boulder ledges to swirling pools. She dreamed of never leaving this serene meadow that, as far as she knew, had no name.

The water seemed alive, busy sculpting the world anew while she watched, gnawing on beef jerky. She wondered at the strength of the water, its illusiveness, its ability to stay low and devoid of ego. The gurgle of the water flowed through her brain, cleansing it of memories. Thoughts of Jorge's deception and childishness, anger with her mother's manipulations, and confusion over Brady's mixed messages flowed through her, out of her, and down to the primal sea. She contemplated how water is supportive, how it nourishes without expecting reward. It simply provides all that is needed. She prayed to possess the strength of water.

She gathered herself in time to reach the summit that overlooks Rock Creek before sundown. When she reached the summit overlooking Rock Creek Lake, the jade-green window to the soul of Bear Mountain, she resolved to make her world right. The inverted reflection of the harsh peak resting in the calm of the lake seemed different to her now. It stood on the edge of two realms. The world was divided by a warm sash of rust that wrapped the lake at the waist. A joyous breeze tossed her hair, spinning the metallic-colored leaves of aspens to fool's gold. Maxine curled her upper lip, exposing yellow teeth, and belted out a heehawing bray to her stable mates. It was the first time the mule smiled since she had left home. Mercedes joined the mule in a long plaintive whinny, heaving her sides with an effort that nearly shook Gemcie from her perch.

Jed was visibly relieved to see Gemcie and his livestock come home in one piece. He rushed from the coffee shop to the barn to help Gemcie unload Maxine. Gemcie lifted a leg over the saddle and jumped to the ground, pushing herself away from her mount and into Jed's waiting arms. After a warm welcome, Jeb took note of the fading scars where Blue left his mark on the mare's neck.

"I knew there was more to this holiday than we were told," he said, running his fingers along the four gashes nearly concealed by Mercedes's winter coat. "You want to tell me about this?" he asked in a stern, paternal tone.

"Not much to tell. A black bear did attack us, but it was my fault."

"Oh really? Did you whisper in his ear?"

"Does it matter? He's dead now."

"Are you sure? I take folks up in those mountains. I don't like the thought of a tourist-hungry black bear roamin' around."

Gemcie looked down at her dust-covered boots, away from Jed's stern stare.

"Yes, I'm sure."

"Well, come along," he said, linking his elbow with hers. "Pete will put the animals up. Cindy's been worried sick about you. Let's show her you're okay. You can tell us all about it."

The aroma of fresh peach pie emanated from the tiny kitchen in the Lodge cafe. Cindy, up to her elbows in pie dough, dusted the flour from her forearms, wiped her hands on the apron tied to her waist and rushed to Gemcie, giving her a hug that lifted her from the floor.

"My goodness, we were getting good and worried over you. The snow comes quick and hard up here. You could've been caught out," she said, wiping wisps of white hair from her pink forehead.

"I'm sorry; I thought you were notified that I was okay."

"Yes, we were, but that was near two months ago. If something happened to you, it would be our fault, that's for sure."

Gemcie flushed hot with guilt. She hadn't considered their feelings. Totally absorbed in the moment, she'd forgotten about them.

"I'm sorry; I didn't mean to scare you."

"It's okay, honey. You're back now," Jed said. "No harm, no foul."

Cindy gave her another huge hug. "Yes," she said, picking up Jed's lead. "You must be awful tired. You want some supper before you turn in?"

Relieved at seeing they forgave her so easily, she smiled brightly.

"What do you have?"

Cindy quickly materialized a plate full of pot roast, vegetables, and gravy with homemade buttermilk biscuits on the side. Suddenly ravenous, Gemcie shoveled in the robust beef, so tender she could cut it with a fork. Stuffed to shameful satisfaction, she turned in soon after the meal.

The tiny cabin smelled musky after being shut up all summer. She struck a match to the kindling Jed had set in the river-rock hearth for her. It cast a warm glow on the rocks and filled the room with the aroma of dry pine boughs that crackled to smoky wisps rising up the chimney. She spotted the unopened letter from her mother resting on the mantle. She picked it up, settled into the rocker at the window with a view of a crescent moon resting on the shoulder of Bear Mountain, and read her mail.

Dear Gemcie;

Your father gave you that name. He thought you were such a gem, like one of the glacier lakes in the high country he so loved. He said there was magic in those lakes that he couldn't capture. He had to go to them, to the world of emerald meadows, aquamarine lakes and snowy peaks to keep their wonder close to his heart. It wasn't that he didn't love me. It was that he never belonged to this world.

He was a power unto himself. He had no need for society or anyone in it. He didn't want houses, fancy cars, cruises to the Caribbean, or anything else a person might want. He didn't have much money and didn't want or need it. A saddlebag full of rations and a fishing pole were enough for him. He sang like a nightingale, as though the angels were coming through him. He never had a music lesson, but he could play the guitar by ear and sing any song he'd heard even once.

He was a natural cowboy, hooked to the moon and the stars. He tried to tell me that he was meant to be a rambling man, and that he couldn't settle into a family life. He'd run away from home, hopping freight trains until he got out West. He couldn't support a family and wasn't interested in having one. I didn't want to believe him. When we made love we became intertwined so tight we were like grape vines wrapped on an arbor.

Soon stirrings in my belly announced you were on the way. I think I wanted your father so badly, I allowed myself to be careless. I've never said it out loud, or even to myself, but I used you to keep him. I couldn't believe that with you in the world he could leave me. When I told him about you, he cried. It was so wrong of me to have placed us all in this double bind. He never asked me to change the way things stood, but he told me he couldn't stay.

"Do you want to be a saddle bum the rest of your life?" I'd cried.

He was not unkind, but he was cruel, like nature is cruel. There was no sentimentality in him. He would kill the runt of a litter knowing it would only drain strength from the mother and make it harder for the healthy pups to survive. He wanted you to have everything and me to have a man who would give us a home. He waited for a month after you were born to make sure I was okay; then he left. I watched his backside as he rode up the trail to the crest, cursing him for deserting us.

I kept watch for his return for a full season. I told Jed and Cindy to find me if he ever showed up, but they never had a reason to call. He was more at home on a horse than anywhere else. I saw you inherited this from him, and I wanted you to know the joy of growing in his gift. I saw to it that you had riding lessons from the time you could walk. Billy agreed to be your trainer. He loved your father, the way a man loves another man for being himself, but he also loved me. For years he tried to fill in the painful, empty spots, but he just couldn't do it. I wouldn't let him. So he became a father to you as much as he could and kept his feelings for me to himself.

I'm not saying that the way I raised you was right. I'm not saying the way I've lived my life is right. What I am saying is that I loved you more than myself. I tried to give you the opportunity to express your God-given talents. I think your father would be proud to see his Gemcie girl riding like the wind, stuck to horseflesh like it was a part of her. But I'll never know; he never came again.

Love, Your Mother

Gemcie folded the letter slowly, holding it in her lap for a long time. She looked to the sliver of moon, hoping for an answer to her deep sadness. Her heart flooded with fresh anguish for her mother and for herself. They were both condemned to love men who would never come home. It was clear that without forgiveness in her heart, she had no future. She rummaged through the stack of mail that had accumulated while she was away and pulled out a letter addressed to her in Billy's wobbly scrawl.

"Dominique convinced Nelia to cut Marshal. He'd come up studdy on her and she couldn't control him for nothin'. Too bad, she could have made a small fortune in stud fees from him alone. He's entered in the qualifier on September twenty-first. I tried to get my colt in, but he just wasn't ready."

Gemcie culled out the big manila envelopes with Heinrich's

lawyer's address in the corner. She'd missed the hearing for her divorce. Jorge's father wanted to settle with her quietly. He felt she deserved financial acknowledgment, and was sorry for his son's actions. He considered her a part of his family. There were no letters from Jorge.

Her thoughts drifted to Marshal. She could see his tender black eyes shaded by dark lashes, the stiff wiry mane, and his muscular arched neck. She saw the graceful slope of his back meeting the perfect swell of his rump. Remembering the coiled strength in his haunches, she saw herself bounding across uncharted countryside, uphill, down valley, lifting over rail fences, charging up banks of green that ramped over channels of deep clear water, landing on soft footing. Rocking gently back and forth in the same chair her mother had once rested in waiting for her father's return, she resolved that she would ride again.

Chapter Twenty-Five

Gemcie rapped hesitantly on the door of her mother's cottage. Flame-red geraniums tumbled from flower boxes beneath leaded glass windows on either side of the oak door. She heard the latch of the metal peep-hole snap open and saw her mother, still in her housecoat, peering out to see who might be calling at this hour. She had closed the Smoker at three o'clock the night before, but was instantly awake when she saw her daughter standing on her doorstep.

"Come on in, honey. What are you doing out there? Why didn't you use your key?" she asked, swinging the door open wide.

"I wasn't sure how you felt about me being here."

"What do you mean? This is your home and always will be."

Gemcie faltered for words and managed a wobbly, "I'm sorry."

"Don't be sorry, darlin'. There're some things we just can't change."

"I'm not sure I would if I could," Gemcie said, looking squarely into her mother's glistening green eyes.

"It don't matter, honey," Sue Ellen said, wrapping muscular arms around her daughter's shoulders and squeezing the girl into the sweet, white cleft of her breasts. Gemcie lingered longer there than an acceptable moment, breathing in the scent of her mother's rose perfume. At 5'8" Gemcie was much taller than her mother, but Sue Ellen was standing on the porch so she could rest her chin on her daughter's head to inhale the freshness of her champagne hair once again. Great heaving sobs took hold as she clasped close to her heart the dear little girl she'd almost lost.

"C'mon inside. I'll fix you some breakfast," Sue Ellen said, wiping her eyes with her sleeve. "Tell me all about your stay with Jed and Cindy."

Gemcie wolfed down eggs sunny side up with four strips of bacon, while her mother sipped coffee. "They were wonderful. Being there gave me time to think. They let me stay in your old cabin."

"I loved it there. I'm glad you got to know the mountains," Sue Ellen said, gazing out the window.

"I'm going to see Kate today. When I get Marshal back, I can offer her a percentage of our winnings in exchange for board."

"Takes more than board. You got to have money for entry fees. They don't call it the sport of kings for nothing. I'm afraid you're dreaming."

"Val told me she's got a couple of new foals that need training. I can work them from the ground. Plus, I can go to the barn next door. Lots of trust-fund babies come there that need a trainer. I don't have to be riding right away to make money."

"Yeah, but you need training yourself. You haven't ridden for almost a year now."

"I'm going to talk to Billy about that. He would work for a percentage of Marshal. He loves him almost as much as I do."

"What about shoes, vet bills, all the stuff that comes up?"

"Remember Bobcat, my old boyfriend? He's a shoer, and Val's a vet now. I know they'd want a piece of the action."

"Ain't going to be much action left for you when this is over, even if you do get everybody to join in," Sue Ellen quietly observed.

"I don't care! It's getting Marshal away from Dominique and riding him again that matters. I can't bear the thought of him trussed up like a turkey in all that hardware. I've got to get him back."

"All right, honey, but I've never heard of a profitable horse co-op."

"I can make it work," Gemcie affirmed, eating the last mouthful of egg, swabbing her plate with toast.

Gemcie forded the creek to Circle K to find Kate. She found her smoking her tenth cigarette of the day sitting at her table in the shade of an oak, littered with flyspecked bottles of ointment and creams for the horses. An ashtray piled high with butts rested in the middle of leg wraps, hair clippers, and fly masks. When Gemcie approached, she stubbed out her cigarette and lit another.

"How's it goin', Kate?"

"It's goin'; my mares givin' me fits, but what's new with you?"

"Not much. I was wondering if you could use a hand around here."

"Can always use a hand, but don't have the money to pay for it, that's why the fences need mending and the sprinklers don't work."

Gemcie outlined her idea to Kate then sat back and waited, hopeful for the right answer. Kate stared at her with vacant brown eyes. Her face, etched with deep grooves from her life outdoors, reminded Gemcie of the stoic expressions of plains Indians she'd seen in history books.

"Gemcie, I'm not running a charity here. I can give you one season with this idea. After that, you're a paying customer."

"I can't ask for more than that!"

"You should know that if you can't pay his board that horse will go to me in the end. I'll sell him for what I can get, and that will be that."

"I understand!" Gemcie exclaimed, jumping up to give Kate a hug.

"You can start working my filly as soon as you are ready. She's got a good mind. I know you can bring her around in no time."

That Sunday Dominique was slated to ride Marshal in the Cup qualifier. Gemcie leaned over the white rail fence assessing the field. She hadn't been back to the Mariposa yet, and didn't want anyone to know she was in the crowd. Adrenalin raced through her body, charging her with excitement as she studied the daunting test for horse and rider before her. A chill wind ripped through the stadium, snapping the banners high on flag poles around the course. The noise could impair the horses' performance, plus the wind blowing in their ears was like a maddening tickle. Marshal wasn't normally troubled by wind, but he picked up on the wildness in the air generated by the other mounts.

The first rider entered the arena on a big warm-blood gelding. He seemed heavy to be doing a jumper course; in fact, the breed is preferred for dressage, but this guy was doing a nice job. He was steady on course, untroubled by the crowds, wind or degree of difficulty. Great strength launched him and rider through the triple jump without incident, but he lacked maneuverability. He couldn't navigate the tight turns required to put him in position for the last three obstacles without slowing down and losing time. He jumped a clear round, but was given a time fault that would keep them out of the jump-off.

Six more riders attempted the course before Dominique entered on Marshal. She had a martingale on him and held him in a tight frame as they trotted through the warm-up. His nose nearly touched his chest and his neck was over-arched in a studdy pose. Dominique sat perfectly erect, in textbook position, making a striking picture on Marshal, whose glossy coat gleamed in the noonday sun.

She touched him lightly on the side with her spur, striking off a canter, and he responded by dipping his head down and bucking. She pulled in even more tightly on him and sat deep in the saddle to correct his behavior. Gemcie could see his energy was blocked. He was like a time bomb ticking to readiness. Dominique gave him no room to release the pent-up frustration building in him. He tossed his head wildly, trying to free himself of the pint-sized tyrant on his back. Lowering his head, he broke into the rolling buck of a bronco with his genitals strapped. Dominique, furious with this outbreak, rode out his outburst while exhibiting expert technique, and then cracked him smartly with her crop. He responding by rearing, pawing the air with his hooves. She leaned forward to keep from falling over backwards, managing to press him forward into a choppy canter. The whistle blew, signaling elimination if Dominique couldn't get her mount onto the course within seconds.

Even though he was breaking his stride, fighting her authority, she turned Marshal and headed for the first jump. He went over and seemed to be freed mentally for the moment with the release over the jump. He went nicely to the second ramped-oxer, meeting it straight on, easily sailing over to the other side. His masterful arc and form with knees snapped up to chin, demonstrated optimum form. She bullied him around the course. He seemed bent on doing the job at hand, until she turned him towards the triple jump. He bolted, losing his rhythm, holding his head high, choking up before he took off, and lurching over the first jump, he pulled a rail on the second, just as in the dream she'd had a thousand times.

Gemcie's heart froze, filled with black dread, as she saw her reoccurring nightmare unfold. He lost his balance on the second landing, crashed into the third fence, pulling the entire obstacle to the ground with him. He lay in a heap of rails and standards, flailing his legs, unable to get up. Dominique flew over his head, landing a good twenty feet away, rolling with her fall, instantly rebounded and was on her feet in seconds. Gemcie jumped over the white rail fence surrounding the arena and ran to Marshal.

In the dream she was riding, but she always had the sensation of being outside of herself watching the incident, and now she understood why. It was Dominique, not her that was in the saddle. The canvas was raised as the doctor examined the fallen animal. Marshal's eyes rolled white as he groaned, his great strength draining fast. He tried to rise, but he floundered. His right leg, bowed under him, would not support his weight. The vet gave him a shot of butte to ease the pain. Jorge rushed onto the field. He went to Dominique first to make sure she was all right, then on to the vet kneeling over Marshal.

"How is he?" Jorge asked the vet, not seeing Gemcie standing behind him.

"I won't know for sure until we x-ray, but it could be a torn suspensory or a stress fracture.

"You're telling me he'll never jump again?" Jorge asked sharply.

"I'm not telling you anything yet," the vet snapped back, obviously cross with Jorge's impatience. "He'll need to have a thorough examination. Right now he has to get up. I've given him enough painkiller for you to haul him home."

Gemcie stepped out from behind the vet. "He's going with me."

"Gemcie, what are you doing here?" Jorge exclaimed.

"He belongs to me," she said to the vet.

"Since when?" Jorge demanded.

"Since now. If you want me to sign the papers your father sent me."

Dominique, shaken but not hurt, was standing beside Jorge.

"Let her have him. He's a pig."

"Are you sure?" Jorge looked to Dominique for confirmation.

"I don't want to ride him, you can't breed him, what good is he?" she said, with a cold, defiant glare directed at Gemcie.

Jorge looked back to Gemcie. "He's yours," he said, placing his arm around Dominique's thin shoulders.

"There is not much hope he will ever be sound enough to jump Grand Prix again," the vet admitted to Gemcie, as two field hands managed to get Marshal to his feet.

"I'm the one to worry about that. Just help me get him in the trailer."

"Okay. I guess you know what you're doing," the vet conceded, as he gave Marshal a sedative so he could be transported. Billy was waiting for them with the trailer ramp down.

"I'm sorry, Gemcie," Billy said. "The plan was to get Marshal back whole, but looks like we're too late."

Marshal hobbled up the ramp of Billy's slant rig. He balanced on three legs the entire trip to Circle K. Gemcie feared he would tumble over as the trailer bounced across the rutted creek. Kate puffed on a cigarette, with smoke curling into her eyes, as she watched them pull in. She rose to help unload Marshal. Her mouth dropped when she saw the once majestic stallion, head drooping down to the floor of the trailer, standing on three legs.

"He looks one step away from the killing lot," she stated. "You can put him in the covered stall by my trailer. I've got fresh shavings there for him."

Kate believed problems with horses always stemmed from the conscious, or unconscious, abuse of their owners. Her ranch was mostly populated by geriatric horses that had outlived their usefulness. Like old people in a rest home, they were forgotten for the most part, visited occasionally on holidays by owners now busy with other pursuits. With no money for a vet to care for them, Kate tended to their maladies with homespun remedies. Once Marshal was safe in the confines of his stall, she ran knowing fingers down the injured leg, careful not to apply pressure. It was hot and swelling fast.

"He's got a bowed tendon at least, and probably a stress fracture on top of that. He needs x-rays, but we can put a poultice on until the vet gets here. Heat up a bucket of water on the hot plate, and get me some of the feed bags behind the trailer," she barked the orders to Gemcie, who did as she was told.

Kate ducked into her trailer, emerging with a clay-based poultice mixture of glycerin and skin emollient that would produce warm, damp heat. As well, she held a eucalyptus and peppermint oil brace that would work as an antiseptic and skin-tightener. She cut the brown paper bags into wraps about eighteen inches high then put on surgical gloves. She dipped her gloved hands into the water repeatedly to keep them wet while wrapping Marshal's leg. She spread the sticky mixture evenly on the tender wound then wrapped it with the wet paper to keep it moist. She applied the cotton wrap on top to secure the poultice. With the immediate problem addressed, she took a closer look at the rest of Marshal. She pulled his lips up, exposing lesions in the corners of his mouth and along his gums.

"They've been pumping him full of butte."

Billy, who held Marshal by the halter line and was rubbing his neck to soothe him during the procedure, peered under the lip to see three large lesions lining the inside of his upper lip.

"He must've been showin' signs of lameness before Dominique entered the ring. They got him numbed to his own pain. Surest way to cripple a horse I know," Billy said.

"It takes about six months for this size lesion to come on from taking anti-inflammatories," Kate observed. "He could have ulcers in his stomach by now. If he gets dehydrated his kidneys will fail. We can't give him any more butte. He's going to have come off the stuff, or it could kill him."

Kate continued to run her fingers along Marshal's limbs looking for lesions or hot spots. When she ran her hand with light pressure along his spine in the middle of the back where the saddle rests, his back sank down until he was almost swayed. She poked him with her forefinger, testing for more soreness. He couldn't step away, so he looked over his shoulder with baleful eyes. His back muscles in spasm were tense and painful to the touch.

"Well, that explains why he was a bucking bronco today," Billy said. "I told that girl she needed to warm him up better, but she was so impatient she would just hop on and yank him into the frame of a Grand Prix dressage horse, then muscle him around the course."

"It's going to take some doing to bring him back. I just hope it's not too late," Kate said. "This money maker of yours could be ruined, Gemcie. If he doesn't come together, I'm going to end up owning him," Kate sighed as she stated the unavoidable truth.

"I should never have left him with them," Gemcie said, eyes moist with tears.

"Don't think you had much choice," Billy said.

"It's my fault he's the way he is."

"Don't blame yourself."

Gemcie knew Marshal could be permanently damaged because she didn't fight for him. He trusted her. She'd failed him completely. Seeing his magnificent body twisted in pain, she vowed that if nothing else, he would have his freedom.

"Take care of him, Kate. I'll be back," she said. Can I borrow your truck?"

"I reckon so. We are partners now."

Gemcie bounced through the creek so fast her head nearly hit the cab liner. She wheeled around the corner and headed for the Mariposa. The guard recognized her and let the wrought iron grill gates open. She stomped up the stone steps and pounded on the massive door until the maid answered.

"Senior Heinrich is in his office. I will tell him you are here," she said. Gemcie brushed past the servant, marching through the arches into the living room with its stenciled beams and milky leaded glass windows. The cold, silent room held no hint of the champagne and laughter of her forgotten wedding day. Heinrich was making an entry in his ledger, sitting at his massive mahogany desk, when she entered unannounced. At first he seemed not to recognize her. Then, he removed the wire glasses from his thin nose and smiled at her with piercing blue eyes, seemingly pleased to see her.

"Have a seat, my dear," he said, indicating with a wave the chair nearby to make her comfortable.

She settled into the red leather chair, sinking below eye level. She felt small, weak and childlike before him. The room smelled of books and sickly sweet cigars. A half-smoked stogie rested in a marble ashtray on his desk.

"You are well?" he asked with courteous interest.

"Yes, I'm great."

"No more pain in your leg?"

"No." Gemcie's courage suddenly shriveled. She was an anemone in his tide pool. He had just stuck his finger into her solar plexus. It was nothing he said, or even did, yet she felt his abiding confidence and control over all situations.

"You received my attorney's letters?" he asked, lighting his cigar and settling back into his chair.

"Yes, but I don't want money."

"What then? My son has told me he wants his freedom. I don't agree with his decision, but he is still my son."

"I want Marshal," Gemcie said, mustering the strength to meet his gaze.

Heinrich, unaware of the day's events, stared at Gemcie with intense blue eyes.

"Marshal has a home here where he can live to fulfill his

185

promise. Not to be cruel, my dear, but can you do that for him?"

"I have to try."

"I see. We all have our destinies."

"Yes."

He leaned back, drawing on his cigar, filling the room with coils of aromatic smoke. "When I was a young man my parents were killed in the war. I went to South America from Germany. I had not one penny, not one friend. I was hated for the color of my skin, and told that I had eyes that could not be trusted, and yet I survived. It was my destiny to struggle, to claw, and grasp my way up. No matter how I railed against my station, or how often I was beaten down, I grew stronger. Sometimes we don't choose our destiny, sometimes it chooses us."

"Yes," was all Gemcie could stammer.

"My son is a silly boy who doesn't know what it is to struggle. Can I ever know him?" he asked rhetorically. His eyes softened as though he might be on the verge of revealing something painful, but his mood quickly flashed into twinkling inner amusement. He turned the key in a lock to the secretary by his desk and pulled out a leather-bound journal. Scribbling his signature on the back of the papers he pulled out, he then handed them to Gemcie.

"My wife will be upset with me for not asking her first, but Marshal belongs with you."

Snatching Marshal's papers from him, she examined the print to make certain they were authentic. "I think I belong to him," she said smiling at her own joke.

He then handed her a stack of papers finalizing her divorce. She signed them all, without reading a word.

Chapter Twenty-Six

The next day Val arrived in her shiny, new vet truck. Still in her twenties, with curly auburn hair that blew out on both sides of her thin face, she was wearing blue jeans and a skin-tight tee shirt that made her look like a kid playing doctor.

"You look good," Val said, giving Gemcie a hug.

"Thanks for coming. He's over here," she said, leading Val to Marshal's stall.

He nickered softly as she examined the troubled leg, removing the poultice to get a better look. To check his temperature, she poked a thermometer in his rear, with a yard-long piece of yarn tied to it. She pinched his nose to test his breath, and listened with her stethoscope to his four-chambered heart, then thumped him on his knees to check his reflexes.

"He's got a bowed tendon for sure, but I think it's more than that," she finally pronounced. "I think the x-rays will show calcium deposits that've been causing him pain for a while."

"That's why they gave him all that medicine. The pain wasn't bad enough to make him lame, but it was enough to make him not want to work," Kate said.

"That's right. Now he could be injured for good," Val said.

"Should I give him Vitamin C?" Kate asked.

"Yes, 4.5 to 20 grams a day will help the tendons and ligaments heal, but that's not going to do anything for the calcium deposits. If that's what the problem is, he'll need surgery."

"I'll do whatever you say needs to be done," Gemcie said, knowing she didn't have the money for an operation and no idea where she would get it.

"Put him on a supplement for now that will give him extra protein, copper, and manganese in his grass hay, along with the C; that will help him mend quicker. Put a new poultice on him every other day, and let him rest. I'll be back when I get the test results in a couple of days. I don't want him on steroids or butte until I get a clean drug test out of him."

Gemcie watched Val's vehicle bounce back across the creek, her aluminum medicine trunk sparkling in the sun behind the cab. Gemcie was determined to find a way to make the money for whatever Marshal needed before she returned. Every barn owner from Griffith Park to Malibu knew her reputation as a rider, but she'd never approached them to train horses, or students at their facilities. She would go to each one of them, ask if they had boarders who needed a trainer or horses that needed to be worked. She didn't care if they were kids on ponies, or middle-aged women over their heads with mounts they couldn't handle; she would train them.

Two days later, Val was back with the test results.

"He's got calcium deposits that have to be planed or he'll be dead lame. There is no guarantee he'll be sound enough to jump, or that they won't come back again, but it's not a serious operation. I can do it here, with local anesthetic."

"When?"

"I'd like him to get two weeks of rest and supplements to strengthen his ligaments and tendons before I operate. Plus, I want him to have a clean drug test, so I'm working at ground zero on that score. He'll need a painkiller after the operation, but I don't want to add to an already dangerous level of toxicity in his system."

"Whatever you say, Doc. You're the boss," Gemcie said.

For the next two weeks Gemcie worked around the clock acquiring clients. She culled a few from the fancy barn next door. One trim fifty-year-old woman with platinum blonde hair the same color as her gray horse's tail bounced a foot out of the saddle with each stride. It had to be rough on her kidneys, but she swore she loved the sport. Gemcie got her lower in the saddle, out of the pain zone, and made her a safer rider. She found there was joy to be had in training amateurs if she kept an open mind. Riding rogues was too risky, so she thought of ways she could make a living from the ground. She worked Kate's filly, too young to be ridden, on the lunge line. Plus she added to her daily lunge list a few old timers that only needed a little exercise.

Kate tended to Marshal's leg, changing his poultice every other day, rinsing his leg with warm water. She also saw to it that he received the right vitamin supplements, administering them with regularity. She brushed him daily with a stiff brush to stimulate his skin, and she put heat compresses on his back to ease the spasms in his back muscles. Gemcie helped her when it was time to give him a serious massage. Together they went over his entire body toning, relaxing, and loosening muscles.

When Val returned to perform the surgery the swelling in the leg was reduced substantially, the lesions in his mouth receded. The dull, lackluster color of his black coat was restored to its original glorious shine. His nervous, furtive look was gone, replaced with an intelligent, inquisitive soft eye. Val lifted his hoof to examine the injured leg. Kate had removed his shoes to make it easier for the farrier to trim his hooves during his recovery.

"He looks good. I'll draw some blood today to make certain his system is clean and if it is, I'll be back Thursday. He'll want a clean bed of fresh shavings for the procedure," she said.

Gemcie held the door open for Val as she slid behind the steering wheel. Gemcie placed a mud-crusted paddock boot on the running board, resting her arm on the open window ledge.

"I can pay you at the end of the month, but how much will I need?" Gemcie asked.

"More than you got. Besides, I want a percentage, and I'm not settling for anything less."

"You said he might not be able to jump, even with the operation. That's not a good bet."

"Wouldn't be much of a doc if I didn't believe in my own talent. Wouldn't be much of a friend if I didn't believe in yours."

Gemcie looked down, unable to meet Val's eyes.

"The co-op now includes Kate, Billy, Bobcat, and Sue-Ellen. The purse is already pretty thin," Gemcie said.

"So, am I in?" Val asked.

Gemcie laughed. "Yes, you're in!"

The sky hung low and gray when Val pulled into the barn on Thursday. It wasn't cold, just dreary, with a fog rolling in over the crest of the ridge that blocked the sun to the valley. Gemcie felt the old ferret in her stomach doing flip flops for the first time since she'd returned from the mountains. She trusted Val, but scalpels and knives put her on edge. Val unrolled a packet of gleaming instruments in a flannel jacket and hung them carefully on the stall door.

"Kate, hand me these as I call for them," Val ordered, knowing Gemcie was squeamish, but that Kate could be counted on.

"Gemcie, you hold his head still so he doesn't try to reach down and rub his leg. Just keep talking to him in a soft tone. He won't feel anything, but he could get curious about what I'm up to."

Unable to watch, Gemcie kept her gaze riveted on Marshal's trusting eyes. She rubbed his forehead, curling his forelock over her finger, while Val made a small incision in his right pastern. Gemcie remembered the story about the oldest horse on record. He belonged to a farmer in Wales, who used him to pull his wagon of milk from village to village. The horse was fifty-seven when the old man died. They worked and shared their life together all those years. Within a month after the farmer's passing, the horse was found dead in his stall. His job was finally done.

Marshal jerked his head up.

"It's okay, big fella," Gemcie soothed, holding him firm.

"Make him stand still, damn it," Val said, holding up for a moment.

Gemcie rubbed him under the chin, pulled his nose down into her chest and rubbed the white blaze on his forehead. He nickered softly, remaining calm for the next half hour until Val was finished.

"You don't want his wraps to be so tight you cut off the circulation."

"I'll keep them loose, and change them every day," Kate promised.

"He won't be able to walk for at least three weeks. After the first week you can start some passive manipulation to help loosen up the joint, but until then he needs lots of rest. I'll stop back in a couple of days to see how he's doing."

Kate took Marshal under her wing, insisting on taking care of him alone. Gemcie decided to repay her by slapping some white paint on the decrepit fences surrounding the arena and turn-out pasture. Kate's husband had passed away five years ago. Her two daughters had married and left the state, and her only son was off at college. She had one hand, a Mexican named Jose, to help her feed all the animals and do the endless chores at the barn. The tired fences with sections threatening to topple over, never quite reached the top of the work list.

In between training sessions, Gemcie shored fence posts and replaced sections of rails nearly chewed through the center. While painting in bold sloppy strokes, she listened to the woodpeckers knocking on the oak trees shading the pasture. The music of the blue-green leaves of the eucalyptus towering hundreds of feet overhead and swaying in the brisk breeze kept her company. The screech of the red-tailed hawk, circling over the empty field next door while looking for ground squirrels, took her back to the wildflower meadows of the high country. She saw Brady's welcoming broad smile and teasing indigo eyes. She imagined him sitting on the swivel hot seat, his boots on the fire-finder, looking over the white blanket of snow softening the jagged ridges to puffy faces.

Each morning the crisp November air inspired Gemcie to get more done. She rushed to the barn, worked a couple of horses, drove to a nearby facility where she taught a few students, giving them their lessons, and then returned to the Circle K, and her painting projects. Soon the arena and turnout pasture were done. She moved to the jumps rotting in the field next door. Jose helped her carry the standards, poles, barrels, and saw horses back to the arena. She mended the broken wooden feet of the standards, sanded the poles free of six-inch splinters, and gave them all a fresh coat of white paint. Then she slapped on bold bands of hunter green in the center of the jump poles so the horses could see them better on the approach.

Inspired by the facelift the barn was getting, Kate bought some blood-red roses and stuck them in the weathered half barrels placed around the barn for just this purpose. Gemcie slapped a coat of fresh white paint with a green ring around the middle on the barrels. She painted the trellises on the stalls for the bower vines that froze in last year's killing frost. Heartened by Gemcie's enthusiasm, Kate planted fresh bower vines, casting a vote for a brighter future.

Val stopped by to see how Marshal was doing. Kate wouldn't let anyone else administer his medicine or change his wraps. Val showed her how to stretch the muscles in his leg each day by lifting his foot slowly back and down twenty times.

"Do it once in the morning and once at night. Work both sides of his body. He needs exercise now, but he can't be turned out. He's liable to become too rambunctious and do himself harm."

"Can I hand-walk him?"

"Sure," she said, as she snipped the remains of the stitches from his incision. "Hydrotherapy would be good, too, if you have the equipment."

"What about the creek?" Kate asked.

"That will work. You can take him down to the creek a couple of times a day and let him stand in the cold water. It'll act as a brace and bring him back quicker, but sterilize the wound after you're done," Val instructed.

Kate's days were devoted to Marshal. First she manually manipulated the stiff joint then hand-walked him for twenty minutes. Donning her rain poncho, she led him to the creek where he pawed the water, making giant splashes. Energized by the brisk water, and the wild smells floating on the scent-laden breeze, he brightened after three dull weeks in his stall. He snuffled his nose in the water, shaking his head like a colt discovering the world for the first time. Kate wore her rubber waders so she could stand with him in water deep enough for him to roll. He did, creating great waves. He drenched her with spray when he rose to all fours, shaking his tremendous body violently to get rid of the wet.

Gemcie ended each full day with laps at an indoor pool. She needed to build up her own body, as well as Marshal's. She especially needed to strengthen her upper body. Laps were the best way to keep her muscles limber and lithe. Each time she entered the water she felt the thousand tiny fingers of her secret lover caressing her body, reaching every hidden dark place of hers. The gym pool was kept at a tepid, therapeutic temperature to please older women with maladies.

She looked forward to floating in it at the end of the day. Cushioned in the turquoise water, she looked up at the steam-covered skylights. Stroking the water slowly, methodically, rhythmically, she let her thoughts rise like fish bubbles from the bottom of a rock pool. She was safe here, out of harm's way, troubling no one. Remembering the quiet strength of water, she stretched her arms overhead, cupping her palms, collecting the power of water into her own body. After an hour of swimming, she went home to a hearty meal via the efforts of Sue Ellen, an hour of TV, and bed.

"How's Marshal coming along?" Sue Ellen asked, scooping

another helping of mashed potatoes onto Gemcie's plate.

"He's doing great! He has no sign of a limp. Of course, he hasn't been turned out yet, but he looks good on a lead."

"How long to do think it will be before you can ride him?"

"I'd say about a month, but Kate may have other ideas about that."

"Yeah, she's not going to be in a hurry for you to undo all the good work she's done."

"Can't blame her for that. It's her call."

"This came for you today," Sue Ellen said, casually handing her daughter an envelope. "Looks like it's from your mountain man, by the return address."

Gemcie snatched it from her hand. Bureau of Land Management Headquarters, Bishop, California was printed on the left top corner. Her name was written on the envelope in Brady's scrawl. She laid it quietly down beside her plate, covering it with her hand, trying not to show her excitement, but then excused herself to her room to read her letter in private.

Dear Gemcie:

I couldn't talk about how I feel until now. I've always known that the life of a lookout is precarious. It's not something a person does forever, but I belong on this mountain more than anywhere else. I don't fit well into small places. I come alive here, energized by the great thumping heartbeat of Mother Nature. If I put my ear to the ground, I hear the churning and clenching of her heart, pushing life to her surface. Witnessing these turnings was all I needed. I never felt bored, or complacent. I never felt lonely, but now I know the dull ache of feeling alone.

It isn't that the sun smearing purple, fiery orange and magenta across the heavens at day's end is less beautiful without you, but that it is more beautiful with you. It's not that the muffled stillness of the snow-covered mountains is less of a cocoon for my thoughts; it's just that I want you to be wrapped inside that solitude with me. I never thought I could share my world with anyone. It was an accident that you came to me, and I know you have your own world, and you belong there. But I want you to know that you are still here in my dreams of sun-dappled days and thermal streams.

I want to explain what happened the day I killed Blue. It was as though I pulled the trigger on a part of myself. When life left his innocent eyes, a door slammed shut in my own mind that was too painful to reopen. It is still not clear

193

to me why the connection between me and Blue was so visceral, so real. I felt an electric shock of energy flow between us just before I fired and hit him squarely between his trusting eyes. He had already decided that he was not going to charge. I could feel his acceptance of me, and yet I fired. The remorse I feel is intolerable. I destroyed the essence of wildness; killed the best part in all of us. Shame doesn't share well. Shame wants to be alone.

I hope you can understand.
Love, Brady

Gemcie folded the letter, placing it under the velvet liner of her jewelry box for safe keeping. He was talking, but she didn't know how to answer. She had to ruminate over how she felt, before she finally wrote back to him.

Dear Brady:

I know how bad I felt when I saw Marshal crash into a fence, nearly crippling himself for life. I felt responsible. I'd seen it happen so many times in my dream it was as though I had willed it upon him. Could I have that power? I don't know. I just know I have to make it up to Marshal. He's mine now. I met with Jorge's father and signed the divorce papers. It felt good to sink into the red leather chair across from his desk, realizing I would have my way. He agreed that Marshal was a small price to pay for his son's mistake. He stood and we shook hands when I left, as though we'd both made a good deal for ourselves.

I don't know why you had to be the one to kill Blue. Maybe Blue knew his time was up, and he chose a merciful friend to end things quickly. We can't always understand what forces are guiding us, but we can try to listen. It's not your fault his world wasn't safe for him anymore. It's no one's fault. There just isn't enough space left to go around, not enough freedom, and not enough wild.

I hope Mother Nature rears up and snatches back what belongs to her. Like a bucking bronco shakes loose the frustration of shackles and the sting of spurs, sending man sailing back into the dust to try to pick himself up again, she will rise up again. Satellites will be left to circle the globe beeping back messages that go unheard. Her claim on our world is not too harsh an answer to the question "Is there enough?" when we have been given so much.

Marshal is doing great. I know I can bring him back, but the only trouble is I don't know if I can bring myself back. I've never admitted to myself, or anyone else, why I quit riding. It wasn't because of Jorge, or losing Marshal. It's because my fear of injury is overwhelming. When I was a kid, I got hurt; everybody does, but I never let it stick with me. If I took a tumble I just got up, brushed myself off and got back on again. Now nausea sets in the second I enter the gate, but it's because I'm more afraid of failing everyone that is counting on me than falling. We are all working for the Memorial Day show. I start training with Billy this week. Wish us luck.

My love is always with you.
Gemcie

She slid a picture of Marshal in the envelope with the letter and sealed it with a kiss.

Chapter Twenty-Seven

Billy was now the head trainer at a facility with a hunt field, sandy jump arena, and a dressage ring. He spent his days grooming a few kids for Junior Amateur rounds. He owned a couple of horses he used with his students. He was lunging an appaloosa with mottled splashes of brown and white on its hindquarters when Gemcie arrived. The horse was wearing a bare-back pad and side reins to keep him in a frame while cantering in a circle around Billy.

"Good mornin', glory," Billy greeted her with a sly grin. "This here is Sammy. You got a lot to learn from him."

Gemcie dreaded starting all over again but promised herself she would do whatever was necessary. She came prepared for endless repetition and the tedium of re-honing skills. She planned to push herself through a rehashing of old lessons without complaint.

"Get those boots off, Gemcie girl, you won't be needin' those today. Did you bring some sneakers like I asked?"

"Yes, but I thought we had a riding lesson today."

"We do."

Billy spoke to her from the center of the circle formed by Sammy cantering quietly around him.

"This guy goes like a metronome. He's a vaulting pony. I been usin' him with the kids here. Come into the circle with me. When I tell you, go up next to him and swing up."

"I'm not working to be a circus act," Gemcie half laughed.

"Don't matter, you do as I tell you, or this ain't goin' too far."

Billy's Gestapo manner caught her off guard. She was too old, and too experienced to be told what to do, but the unwritten law of the riding world is that the trainer is God. Once aboard Sammy, Billy had her cantering about him in a circle with arms extended out, balancing without saddle or stirrups. He brought the horse to a walk, and instructed her to lie back on his rump. As Sammy walked around in a steady, rhythmic motion, Gemcie watched the fluffy white clouds above scud by in a blue sky. Her mind drifted to water. She felt herself melding into the sway of Sammy's warm rump.

"Don't get too comfortable. I want you to get up on your knees. See if you can find your balance in his center."

Curling back to an upright position, Gemcie struggled to balance on her knees, as Sammy continued to walk in a circle.

"Now extend your right leg back, straight like an arrow," Billy called out. She managed to lift her leg and hold it, but the position was a strain.

"Okay, now lift your left arm straight out ahead of you. Look to your hand to keep your balance." She raised her hand, meditating on the tips of her fingers. Once she found her balance, she held the position while Billy moved Sammy to a trot. Her muscles trembled. She couldn't hold herself steady enough to stay with the gait, so she slipped down to a sitting position.

"What are you trying to do? I'm not a ballerina!" Gemcie said, biting back her frustration.

"No, you sure ain't, Gemcie girl. You need to be building your body a lot more if you want to learn from Sammy. You need a workout that strengthens your back muscles; otherwise, you won't be able to hold yourself erect long enough to find your balancing place. Riding in a western saddle changes your seat, works different muscles. You have to retrain your body, and this is the surest, fastest, and best way to do it. We won't be doing any jumping 'til you get this part down. Now, do you want to get on with your lesson?"

Hot humiliation flooded her consciousness. She flushed scarlet but tried to concentrate as Billy clucked Sammy forward and called out commands. His voice sounded like a bossy bumblebee in her ear. At the end of the lesson she was standing up on Sammy's back with knees bent, arms out to the side, balancing at a walk.

"Next time, we'll do it at a canter. This is going to be fun," Billy said. "I think this session went real fine."

"Do I have time to start at ground zero?' Gemcie asked, sliding off of Sammy.

"You don't have much choice, the way I see it," he said,

wrapping the lunge line around his elbow and wrist, into a tidy roll. "I was also checking to see if you were hiding any pain. I didn't see you hanging onto anything, favoring one side of your body or another. We weren't goin' any further if I did."

Gemcie smiled up at her old mentor. He knew her better than anyone, even Sue Ellen. He trained her and Cubby when she was a kid, helped her work out the problems of the rogues she rode as a teenager, trained Marshal with her in young adulthood, and now he was going to bring her back to wholeness. He knew she came prepared to lie to herself and to him. She was grateful he didn't give her the chance.

That night she drug her old riding books out from under the bed, brushed off the dust bunnies, and read until her eyes were bleary and red. She clicked off the light at about two in the morning, settled into her pillow and sighed heavily, realizing how much she had forgotten. It had been years since she had cracked a book on riding technique or tricks to staying on top of the game. She never could cram for an exam; she always had to read each word. She felt pressured knowing she only had four months to groom herself for the event. How could she rebuild her body, and rid herself of those nagging negative images in that short time?

Reminded that riding is eighty percent mental, she decided to concentrate on clearing her mind of the anxiety lurking in her mind, warping her sense of self like the image in a rippled fun house mirror, hiding behind her facade. No matter how strong her body might become, or how finely tuned her skills, if her mind was working against her she couldn't win. Billy could help her with her position, technique, and training Marshal, but she alone would determine her mind-set. She wanted to be like water coursing smoothly to its destination, soft yet strong, yielding, not struggling against circumstance.

The next morning, Gemcie held the turn-out gate open for Marshal. After six weeks of repeated treatments, constant liniments and oils, walks in the creek for a brace, and supplements, Kate decided it was time to test him for soundness. He pranced with pent-up energy, sensing something was up, as she marched him towards the turnout. His coal-black eyes glistened with excitement, while breath vapors steamed from flared pink nostrils, dripping with wet. Once inside the pasture, Kate slipped off his halter. Uncertain that he really was on his own, he snuffed at the dust, snorting loudly. He trotted in a circle until he was sure there was nothing restraining him then he spun on his haunches and galloped to the other end of the pasture, tail crooked high. Exploding into frolicsome twisting bucks, both rear hooves slashed at the sky. Belly low, head thrust forward, he powered himself like a low-slung rocket across the turnout, dashing ahead so fast it looked like he would be unable to pull himself up when he reached the other side. He could easily sail over the fences of his enclosure, but scrunched himself back in time to stop just before smashing through the fence.

Kate puffed on a cigarette, pulling slow and hard on it as she studied his movements.

"He looks fabulous!" Gemcie exclaimed. "He's never looked better!"

"He looks to be sound, all right. I don't see him bobbin' his head at all, or showing any favoritism," Kate acknowledged.

"You've done it, Kate!" Gemcie cried. "When can I ride him?"

"Not for a while," Kate said, still staring at the gelding careening around the pasture at breakneck speed.

"But I've got less than three months to get ready. You know that!" Gemcie pleaded.

"He's got to be completely mended. If he's not, you will reinjure him."

"But he looks sound."

"Maybe he looks that way to you, but you're not thinking about his mind."

"Kate, for God's sake, I don't have time for him to go into therapy. I've got to get him going."

Kate turned stern eyes on Gemcie, "This is my barn, and this is my decision to make. You're not riding that horse until I tell you he's ready."

"You've always loved the horses better than the rest of us. I know that, Kate, but I never figured on this," Gemcie blurted, unable to contain her frustration. Kate's unyielding expression told her it was hopeless.

"I guess I'll have to ride Billy's school horses until you change your mind."

"I guess you will," Kate was quick to say, turning back to watch Marshal flush with vitality, romping like a colt.

"Bobcat will be here this week. I want him to trim Marshal up. Make sure his feet are balanced. In a month I'll put shoes on him."

"A month!"

"At least."

"I hope you know what you're doing."

"Until then, you can hand-walk him to help him relax, but that's it."

Gemcie had to accept Kate's decision. So she went about her business, training her students at the barn next door, working Kate's filly on the lunge, and exercising a couple of the horses at the barn whose owners couldn't get to them. Three times a week she went to Billy's and had a session on Sammy. About three in the afternoon, she arrived at the gym for an aerobics class, a little weight training on her upper body, and a swim to cap off the day.

Stroking rhythmically, slowly and deliberately, she felt the muscles in her back lengthening as she raised each arm overhead. "I'm like water yielding to Marshal's strength, flowing with his energy. My energies are charging freely though my body," she repeated the affirmation as she stroked. Soon, she saw herself on Cosmic Dancer, a gray thoroughbred she rode over a cross-country course when she was fourteen. The mare was light in her movements, responsive and fine. The nip in the early morning air brightened both horse and rider. As they headed for the start gate, Dancer felt lively and eager. The mare bolted at the whistle, attacking the first log fence, charging ahead toward the second, taking it in stride. She landed squarely over the downside of a steep drop jump into a water pond. Her splash stirred a blue heron that lifted at their approach, wafting in slow motion across the dome of blue sky. They met the steep incline on the other side without hesitation, motoring to the top of the hill where they were greeted by an imposing log-jump. Once over, tail flying high, the mare galloped boldly across the crest of the hill, cantering down the steep back-side. When they crossed the finish line, Gemcie's cap was over her eyes. The saddle pad had slipped back to the mare's rump, but they had flowed as one. It was a wild course that took guts, bold strokes, and speed.

"I'm a born rider; graceful and beautiful to watch," became her internal mantra, as she stroked in the water, unaware of anything else in the pool room except her own thoughts.

Gemcie wore tights and ballet shoes for maximum freedom

during her sessions with Sammy. After a couple of weeks of her new regimen she could stand upright on Sammy's back at a canter for as many revolutions as Billy asked of her. She could hold the flag position that was such a strain at first, in every gait. She swung up and hopped off at any gait. She came to love the free-floating feeling when cantering seated, with her arms extended to the sky, finding a balancing place where she was connected to Sammy's center like a Centaur. She was almost disappointed when Billy said, "Looks like you're ready to put your ridin' boots back on, Gemcie girl."

He released Sammy's side reins, letting him walk on to stretch out his muscles before putting him away. "You know, I think you owe this boy a bath. He's probably saved your life about ten times already. He's fixed you to where you ain't gonna come off, less you get pried with a crowbar. Even if you do part company with the saddle, you're gonna be able to get off without hurtin' yourself."

"If that's true, I'll give him ten baths," Gemcie beamed, slipping to the ground as light as a dancer.

When she arrived for her next session with Billy he introduced her to Hardtack, a bony version of Sammy. Gemcie recoiled at the thought of riding a broken-down school horse, after years of riding Grand Prix level mounts.

"Don't tell me. I've got a lot to learn from him?"

"Yep. That's right, Gemcie girl. This boy can jump blind-folded."

Once aboard Hardtack, she found him to be a push-button horse, responsive to all of her aids. Billy started them on a circle around him, instructing Gemcie to rise out of the saddle for three strides, and then sit for three strides, with arms out like an airplane. Soon Gemcie found his center and her balancing spot and they became a team. The first sessions revolved around establishing her jump seat, before Billy moved her up to a surprise.

"I built this chute of jumps just for you," he said, directing Gemcie to a line of six-two-foot jumps placed close to the arena's outside rail. "You can trot the first time in." Gemcie did as she was told. Hardtack bounced through the line without a wobble.

"Good. Now we'll make it a little harder," he said, taking off his bandana and handing it up to Gemcie. "Put this over your eyes."

"What?" Gemcie asked in disbelief. Remembering the handcuffs he'd used on her as a child to keep her hands low, she trusted him, but still felt uncertain of her abilities.

"You heard me. Put this on. I'm going to put you on a lead line and lunge him through the chute."

She felt anxious as she tied the kerchief tightly about her head. Keeping your head up and looking straight ahead to direct the horse's movements is so basic in riding that she didn't know how Hardtack could manage without her guidance. If she fell now and were injured, it would end everyone's chances of getting back in the show ring. Why did Billy want her to take this risk?

"I don't like this," she said.

"Are you ready?" Billy asked, ignoring her protest.

She heard herself say, "Yes," but her mouth was dry. Her pulse quickened when Hardtack picked up a trot. Without sight, her best hope was to feel. She went mentally to the movements of his muscles, sensing his heartbeat, listening to his rhythmic breath. She wasn't certain when he would hit the line of jumps. Billy was lunging her in a circle at a trot then instructed her to canter on softly. She felt her way through the movements, counting on body memory to guide her.

"Okay, we're heading for the chute," Billy said. "You're going to have to feel his takeoff point."

Gemcie knew that horses have almost 360-degree vision, but the stride just before a jump falls out of their field of vision. They must count on their riders to see the perfect takeoff spot for them. She realized, for the first time, how terrifying that must be for a jumper. Suddenly, she was inside the mind of the horse, experiencing the world through his senses, straining to hear what was coming up, acutely aware of odors and sound. Feel and trust were all that stood between her and disaster, as the old campaigner easily navigated the six low jumps. Once through the gauntlet, Gemcie was overcome with hysterical titters. It took her some time to recover her composure.

"That was good!" she laughed.

"Then you don't mind doing it again?"

"No, but let's not make the jumps any higher. I get the point."

Chapter Twenty-Eight

After her lesson with Billy, she headed to the Circle K. Kate was standing at Marshal's stall when she arrived.

"How's the boy?" Gemcie asked brightly.

"He's bored silly, swaying back and forth and cribbing his stall," she said.

"Then it's time for me to take him out?" she quipped, half joking.

"Yep, he's been waiting for you," Kate returned with a smile.

Gemcie grabbed Kate around the neck and gave her a bear hug. "Thank you."

"Don't thank me. You got to thank the boy for wanting to please you."

Gemcie trembled with excitement as she tacked Marshal up. Slipping onto his back felt like sliding her hand into a favorite kid-leather glove. It felt especially good knowing she had earned the right to be aboard her old friend again. She turned him towards a safe trail that wound around a chuckling creek shaded by giant sycamores, to her childhood secret place. He turned his head from side to side, flicking his ears like tiny radar dishes, checking out new sights and sounds. Gemcie wore a scarf to ward off the chill of the sharp March wind, as Marshal pranced through spring-green grass. Bluebirds flashed by in showy jackets while mockingbirds chatted about last night's storm.

Their path led them into the foothills, covered with a silver dusting of flowering sage, past a small lake where mallards with iridescent green heads cruised. Their duff- colored mates trailed behind, while Coots scuttled for cover. Marshal's senses, quickened by the smell of the wild, moved into an elevated trot, prancing sideways. She could feel his massive muscles tensing, preparing to explode beneath her, but she held him in check, steadying him back to a walk. The trail dipped down to follow a spring splashing with fresh energy. Sun streamed through the sycamores, spotlighting sparkling green fern fronds lining the bank.

She followed a tree tunnel up the canyon, until they reached a meadow flush with shooting-star flowers. She let him graze on the emerald grass for a few moments while she spread her arms like an Indian to the sun and absorbed his energy. Marshal, her old friend, was back and she felt powerful again. They could do anything together. One spirit, one body…for this moment they were as one.

After a tender moment treasuring her re-connection to her best friend, she secured Marshal to a tree where she let him graze while she scrambled up a narrow trail to her secret place. Balancing on a down log, she crossed the creek to a waterfall nestled behind a boulder jumble. Just as she remembered it, the shaggy moss monster, with beads of water dripping from his mangled chin forming a stream of droplets that burst into a thousand tiny bubbles when they hit the pool, was standing guard. The liquid amber roots of the trees shading the pool, exposed from years of rushing water, made a good bench.

Her joy of reuniting with Marshal was replaced by a strong sense of melancholy when the rhythms of the water reminded her of her time with Brady. As if a heavy cloak had been placed on her shoulders, she felt tired, desperately alone, and wished she'd never talked anyone into relying on her. Six weeks before the show and she was still not in full training. She needed a hunt field like the one at Mariposa to develop continuity in her ride. No matter how many fences she painted, or flowers she planted, Circle K just wasn't a top flight facility. Even though she knew Billy was helping her to be safe in the saddle, his training was not moving fast enough to get her up to speed. She had no notion where she would get the money for entry fees. All the money she earned from training students went to taking care of Marshal.

She wished time had stopped with Brady on that sunny afternoon in the Sierras. Soon tears came as steady as the moss monster's drools. She sobbed until spent, dried her eyes, resolving to pull strength from the murmuring stream. *Nothing in the world is weaker than water, but nothing is better at overcoming the strong.* Squatting, she hugged her knees with her hand, and rocked back and forth on the ledge overlooking the pool. She tried to absorb strength from the boulders she crouched on, and the giant sycamores swaying overhead. At least Marshal was sound and she had kept her promise to him. The lesions on his lips had healed, his back was no longer sore to the touch, and his proud body glowed with vitality and vigor. If nothing else, she had saved him from insensitive hands.

When she got home that night a small package with a Bishop postmark rested on her dinner plate. She tore into the box, unmindful of her mother's presence. Buried in a mound of white tissue was the crude carving of a cowgirl arced over a crescent moon, whittled in a piece of white pine. It was wrapped in a note with a $5,000 check attached, made payable to her.

"My father always said horses are a real pleasant way to go broke. I earned this money mustangin'. I can't think of a better way to put it to use than setting you and Marshal free. I'm in."

Brady

Now she had no excuses for failure. The universe had found a way. Gemcie tumbled into bed early that night. She had more work to do than ever, and no time to spare in being afraid of the outcome.

Chapter Twenty-Nine

"Good mornin', Gemcie girl."

"Good morning, Billy," Gemcie said, not looking forward to another session on Hardtack, with his sewing-machine gait.

"Figure we better be getting Marshal over here pretty quick, if you want a shot at the Cup this year, don't you?"

"What are you talking about? I can't afford to have him here. I thought you were going to come to us."

"Nope, I talked the owner of the barn into letting me board Marshal here in exchange for training' his kid."

Gemcie jumped up and clutched Billy around his leathery neck, hugging him with all her strength.

"When?"

"Today."

Kate was standing by Marshal's stall with a tack box crammed full of liniments, braces, and sundry medical supplies when they arrived.

"You're sure he's ready?" Billy asked

"As ready as he'll ever be," Kate answered.

Marshal, sensing adventure in the air, pranced with excitement to the trailer. He missed the challenge of jumping, the other horses, and the attentions afforded a champion. Gemcie could see Kate watching Marshal's glossy haunches rock to and fro, tail floating on the breeze, as the trailer jostled through the creek. Kate lit another smoke then went back to mixing potions for geriatric horses, leaving the busy world behind once more.

Marshal's conditioning program consisted of systematic repetitions around the hunt field, beginning at a walk and eventually graduating to a hand gallop. In order to build his stamina and strengthen slack muscles, he needed to be exercised daily for at least an hour.

"Take 'im round another ten times," Billy called through his megaphone from the judge's stand.

Gemcie was weak and out of breath after hugging Marshal with her legs, scrubbing his neck with relaxed arms, and letting him stretch out for half an hour. Even with all the exercise and work she had done to prepare for his training, she was still shaky in the saddle. Marshal seized the opportunity to snatch the bit, clenching it between his teeth, robbing Gemcie of control. He accelerated to the speed of an out-of-control freight train. His Amtrak imitation was not funny to Gemcie, who knew her life was in danger. Even if he did pull up before crashing into the upcoming arena fence, she would be tossed blithely over his head and thrown into the rail. Anger, pent up from a year of over-control, surfaced. Marshal was about to derail.

"Pull him 'round. Pull him 'round!" Billy shouted, but Gemcie couldn't hear anything except her own inner screams. As seasoned as she was, she was scared senseless for a couple of seconds. Weighting herself deep in the saddle, digging down with her heels, she tried to back him off with body language, while reaching down to grab the bit ring. She finally grasped it and pulled with all her might, hoping to bring him into a circle slowly so he wouldn't lose his balance, topple over, and crush her beneath his twelve-hundred-pound frame.

"Stay with him, Gemcie. You just about got him!" Billy shouted.

It took all she had to bring his head to the side, forcing him out of runaway mode. She circled him several times to calm him and walked back to where Billy was waiting.

"I need a breather," Gemcie said, wiping sweat from her brow with the back of her gloved hand.

"All right, but keep him walking on a long-rein. You did right, Gemcie. He was determined to get back at all those spur jabs in his side."

"He's as bad as any rogue I've ever been on, hauling me around like he's never had any training."

"He wouldn't have meant to, but he sure could have hurt you bad. He needs to stretch out those muscles along his top line. He might have felt some pain. He never was cold-backed until that girl got a hold of him. Now we're going to have to work twice as hard to keep those muscles from tightening up. Lots of hand gallop without anybody pulling on his face will relax his mind plus build him up."

"Yeah, maybe so, but I don't want to die in the process."

"Well, Gemcie girl, you said this is what you wanted."

"I do, but that's enough for today."

"Okay, youngun, I'll walk him out for you and put him away," Billy relented, taking hold of the reins, holding Marshal in place while she hopped off.

Gemcie thought she was fit from all the aerobics, swimming, and rest, but it was plain that after a year of not riding professionally she had lost her stamina. She fell into bed that night exhausted, dreading the beep of the alarm at 5:30 a.m. It seemed she no sooner hit the pillow than she was in a deep coma-like sleep. The morning came so quickly she didn't have time for dreams.

After three weeks of conditioning Marshal daily, her thighs and calves were taut, and she could hold her position steady for as long as Billy wanted. It was time to move onto flat work. She arrived at the barn in full, leather-seat riding pants, polished boots, and spurs, with impulsion whip in hand.

"Looks like you're ready for business." Billy said.

"It helps me to dress the part," she said. "Besides, I don't want him to get the best of me again.

Billy gave Gemcie a leg up.

"I don't think you need all that regalia, but we'll see what happens."

The first twenty minutes of the lesson were spent letting Marshal stretch out his top line, relaxing any soreness he may have had in his back muscles. Billy talked to Gemcie constantly through his megaphone, correcting her position, bringing her back to old lessons embedded in her memory.

"Horses aim to please. It makes 'em feel good to think they've done right," Billy said. "Ninety percent of riders overwork their horses, striving for perfection, and take the happiness away from their experience."

Gemcie listened intently to him as she trotted around him in a twenty-meter circle.

"Now take him down the rail and across the diagonal. Try to bring him into an extended trot."

Gemcie weighted her heels, sat deep in the saddle, and put both legs on, squeezing him forward while restraining him from a canter with her hands. He stretched his front legs forward, gliding into an elevated trot. The old sensation now rushing over her of floating across the arena in a cool, soft wind was one she loved.

"Try a leg yield. Let's see what we've got to work with," Billy said.

She maneuvered Marshal into position to execute a leg yield, which called for him to cross one hind leg over the other and move sideways across the arena. Gemcie gave Marshal a nudge with her spur signaling him to move into the exercise. He responded by ducking his head and diving into a rolling buck. Taken by surprise, Gemcie nearly toppled over his head, but she regained her balance in time to ride out the misdemeanor.

"You'd better hand those spurs over right now," Billy told her. "That boy has been poked once too often."

Billy took her spurs off.

"You might as well hand over the whip too. We are going back to basics and work back up to where we can quit for the day on a good note."

He knows best, Gemcie thought, trying not to let her frustration get the best of her.

"If you don't go back down the ladder and come up again, all you're doing is matching your weight against the horse's weight. When you fight out of your weight division, you're going to get whipped," Billy instructed.

Four weeks before the show, Marshal made her feel like she was riding a short-fused powder keg. He would have to relearn the lessons she taught him years ago, only now she would have to ride him with more sensitivity—without spurs, and very little hand pressure. She was left with just her body weight and mental intent to guide him. In order to ride a course, Marshal had to be willing to collect and extend his frame on cue. Tight turns called for fine-tuned immediate responses to her signals. It took months, sometimes years, to bring a horse back from bad training. The challenge seemed overwhelming.

Gemcie's felt over-matched. The chemicals stung her nose, so she backstroked across the tepid pool staring up at the moisture dripping from the ceiling. *Was it a mistake?* Should she have accepted the end of her riding and let it go? She had to learn a new way of containing his energy without interfering with his self-determination. It was too late to train him through his resistances the old way before the event. She determined to be like water, yielding and not struggling against Marshal's great strength, wherever it took her.

Billy placed ground rails for them to trot to help Marshal relax and regain his confidence. Gemcie concentrated on feeling his movements as he bounced through the poles. She tried to key in on his mental state, listening to him, trying to reconnect with her old friend.

"Have to take it slow for his benefit. He knows his job, but he's not sure he wants to do it anymore," Billy said.

After weeks of the basics, Billy had built a double-oxer for them to jump with a ground rail in front of it, to help Marshal find his takeoff spot.

"He ought to be landing over this as soft as a panther in powder," Billy said. Gemcie brought him into the middle of the jump, he snapped his knees up to his chin and rounded his back, went over in a perfect bascule, and landed on the right lead.

"What a good boy. What a good boy!" Gemcie cried with glee each time he took a jump with the ease and grace she remembered. Sensing he was relaxing back into his old form, trusting her again, she was exultant.

"Damn if that horse ain't picture perfect." Billy said. "I swear; he is going to win the World Cup!"

Gemcie stopped in the middle of the exercise, signaling Marshall to halt, and glared at Billy.

"Would you stop talking about the World Cup? I don't give a damn about the Cup. I'm doing one jump at a time."

Billy was flustered. Students didn't speak to trainers in that tone. Students did what they were told, or they found another trainer. Over the years his role of surrogate father while student to teacher had slipped over well-defined lines. It was true he had pushed her to win the Cup for *him*. He scratched at his jaw, sporting a couple of days of beard growth, before answering.

"I'm sorry, Gemcie. You're right. I won't mention it again."

Gemcie and Marshal had exactly two weeks to achieve perfection. They spent it working on combinations Billy set for them in the hunt field. Marshal maneuvered tight horseshoe turns, double and triple combinations, a Liverpool, whatever Billy put in front of him with ease. Marshal responded to her signals telepathically, like a flock of snow geese to the lead honker taking them home. Her mental antennae became connected to the twitch of his ears. Trusting each other's instincts and senses, they flowed like water. They were a team again.

"Don't want to over-train 'im. Let's leave somethin' for the show," Billy said, ending their last session before the Grand Prix.

Chapter Thirty

Everyone in the horse world turns up for the Memorial Day show to get a good look at new talent and size up the season's prospects. The pedestrian crowd filled the grandstand early. Suntanned ladies in halter tops and wide-brimmed straw hats, cowboys in blue jeans and Stetsons, and kids in sweat-stained jodhpurs vied for the best spots in the shaded benches beneath the sycamores to watch the event.

Gemcie arrived early, but by the time she had Marshal settled, the riders were walking the course.

"We'd better get out there and take a look," Billy said.

They rushed to the arena, Gemcie half-running in her riding boots, trying to keep up with Billy's long-legged stride. The course, filled with its five-foot jumps flanked with bright flowers, was designed to trip up the most educated horse and rider.

"These jumps all have an airy look to 'em," Gemcie noted.

"Some brush filler would make it a lot easier to see the distances," Billy said, stretching his step to a yard so he could count the strides to the base of the jump for optimum takeoff. They fell into step behind the other riders walking the course. She recognized the narrow hips and long legs in the tan jodhpurs just ahead. It was Jorge. He was walking with Dominique, whispering course strategy into her ear as he once did with her. Billy noticed her distraction from the job at hand.

"Don't pay them no never mind," he said.

"She's the favorite today. She won Del Mar last week."

"Yeah, she's been doing' a lot of winnin' on Silver Lining. Who wouldn't? He won a Grand Prix at Gesture and did a couple of clear-rounds at the Nation's Cup in Spain before she got hold of him."

"Is that her new trainer?"

"Yea, Helmut Mueller, from Germany. Mostly an eventer. Pushes his mounts to the limit and don't look back."

Gemcie hoped they wouldn't notice her, but Jorge saw her and waved, flashing a brilliant smile. She felt like running out the gate, but she stood her ground when he came toward her.

"I heard you're riding today. I just want to wish you luck," he said, looking at her with bold familiarity. Dominique moved quickly to stand sentinel by his side.

"It's going to take more than luck. Did you see the triple's got a stream linking the elements?" Dominque asked casually.

"Yeah, it will take a lot more than luck today," Gemcie agreed, shifting her gaze to Dominique, who fluttered long brown lashes and smiled, exposing childlike teeth.

"Did you sleep well last night?" she asked.

"Well enough," Gemcie said, remembering the sabotage that caused her crippling accident.

"That's too bad," she said.

Jorge gave Dominique a quizzical look, as though he had no idea why she would say that to anyone. "You look fabulous," Jorge said, turning back to Gemcie.

Dominique fired a reprimanding glance at him as she slipped her hand into the crook of his arm.

"Have fun on that pig of a horse; hope he makes it around without falling apart. Let's go, Jorge; Helmut is waiting," she commanded, tugging on his arm.

"It's good to see you're back," Jorge said, before being pulled away.

"Don't let that vixen bother you none," Billy said, standing beside her.

"Don't worry. Billy. I came to ride: win, lose, or draw," Gemcie said.

"When he gets to that water jump he's either gonna back off or be real careful about himself. You just hug him like a baby and make him feel secure. You'll be fine."

Gemcie continued her walk on the twisting course that called for quick adjustments in stride, tight pinball turns, and enough scope to cover the spread-oxers sprinkled around the field. She had always tried to spot something outside the arena to align to her takeoff point, just before the triple. Meeting the first obstacle in the triple was critical; the rest would come if that were done correctly. While looking for a flag pole or some other solid marker, her gaze went to the crowd in the reserved section with tables, chairs, and umbrellas providing shade for the owners and their guests. She spotted Nelia in a wide-brimmed white summer hat, and a crisp, white eyelet dress draping brown shoulders. The sun glanced off her diamond necklace sparkling in the noonday sun. Heinrich sat dutifully at her side, looking relaxed in a white shirt that was open at the collar exposing a deep tan, sipping a martini.

Gemcie was late to draw a number so was slated to ride last. Not wanting to bring Marshal out too early, she watched a few of the riders go before her. It was a wrenching course. After ten rides there was not one clear round. She was just about to go to Marshal when she spotted Sue Ellen huffing across the warm-up ring wearing red leggings and a brilliant Mexican shirt sporting the colors of a parrot.

"Oh, honey, I'm so glad I caught you. I almost forgot."

"Forgot what?"

"This," Sue Ellen said, pulling a small gold pin melded in the image of a cowboy with hat held high riding a bucking horse, out of her pocket. "Your dad gave this to me. He won it by sticking to a bronco in Bishop so tight they thought he was going to have to take it home with him that night. I think he'd like you to wear it today for luck," she said.

Gemcie held the pin in her hand, turning it slowly in her palm. "I could use a little cowboy luck," she said, lifting her chin up to allow Sue Ellen to secure her stock scarf with the pin.

"Okay, that settles it. You're winning today," Sue Ellen declared. "Did you see him?"

"Who?"

"Heinrich. She must have pulled him here by his nostrils. He never comes to these events."

"Look, mom, none of it matters; I've got to get going."

"It will when you win. They're going to regret pulling that bankroll."

"Okay, mom. Really, goodbye."

Billy brought Marshal around for her to mount.

"Thought you could use this," he said placing her black velvet cap on her head, adjusting the straps to make sure it fit snugly. He gave her a leg up, and then headed for the warm-up ring. They worked mostly on the flat to relax Marshal's muscles and bring him in touch with the aids. Billy talked her over a few four-foot jumps, just enough to wake Marshal up. Dominique, a couple of horses ahead, was warming up Silver Lining, a powerful white stallion honed, nurtured, and bred for this moment. He switched his snowy tail over every jump.

"See that? She's got him jigged up too," Billy said.

Dominique, hearing her name over the loudspeaker, trotted softly into the arena. A sigh rose from the crowd when Silver Lining entered the ring. Proud, prancy, and aware of his great strength, he carried his noble head with nose to chest in a muscled dressage frame. Enormous round haunches gave spring to his step. He was enjoying himself, like a body builder flexing to give the crowd a thrill. He was spirited, eager for the challenge to come.

A bold, aggressive rider, Dominique held him in tight control as she looked to the first jump. Sitting deep in the saddle, pressing Silver Lining with both legs, she powered him through the double combination. He railed a bit against her strong hand, tossing his head just before take-off over the spread-oxer, but followed through by arching nicely. An incredible athlete with agility and tremendous scope, he was at the top of his game. She gunned him over the Liverpool with wide wings of purple flowers on each side of the thirteen-foot span of water, pulling him up sharply to make the five-foot vertical. He was beginning to choke back, lurching forward, trying to get out of her too-tight grasp. Fighting her openly by the time they reached the triple, he sucked back, lurched over and managed to make it through the gauntlet without pulling a rail. After the last jump she let him have his head. He raced ahead like a maniac, nose to ground, tail switching wildly, releasing the bucks he'd held in check over the course. The crowd stood up, giving a standing ovation for the first team to make it over this almost too-challenging course, with a clear round.

A couple more riders went, but no one made it around without a penalty. It was becoming boring, but the crowd woke up when the rider just before Gemcie misjudged the Liverpool. His horse tripped on the front box lip and did a header into the water. The rider flew into the bank of flowers, but stood up immediately and brushed himself off. Neither horse nor rider was injured, but it put an end to their round and reminded Gemcie of her ambulance ride a year ago.

"Gemcie McCauley on Marshal!" came over the loudspeaker. "This is a team we haven't seen for a while. They've done a lot of winning together and we're glad to see them back," the announcer said, as they cantered softly around the infield for Marshal to get a sense of the sights, smells, and noise level of the crowd before approaching the first jump. She felt light-headed, airy, like she would evaporate if she wasn't careful. She imagined a hand outside of her body, guiding her, and prayed it would hold her steady as she concentrated on helping Marshal do his job. He met the first jump, pounced over it, landed lightly then cantered on softly to the next. She let him have plenty of rein. He stretched into his expansive stride, moving up on the next obstacle like a well-oiled jumping machine. She gave him a big release over the double combination. Mind riveted on the course, looking ahead to each new obstacle, Gemcie saw the way to the perfect takeoff spot for him just before each jump. Marshal extended his stride on cue when she put both legs lightly on before the Liverpool. She looked ahead, resisting the urge to look down at their shadow, while sailing over the fateful jump. Landing on the left lead, Marshal was able to make the corkscrew reverse turn without losing precious seconds, but the maneuver risked strain on his old injury. Once over, it was another horseshoe turn. Gemcie called for a quick rebalancing to find their position for the triple combination just ahead. Marshal was so energized, Gemcie felt like she was riding an electric current. Any other horse would be tired facing the triple effort at the end of the course, but Marshal was a champion. Given the opportunity to fulfill his destiny unfettered, there was no more-magnificent an animal. Gemcie looked to the flag pole just behind Nelia, marking the takeoff spot. She lined Marshal up; keeping his stride the same...the same...the same...like a metronome. She stayed light in the saddle. He met the first jump squarely, landing softly and cantering one stride, springing up over the second on powerful haunches with the grace of a mid-flight deer. Then he charged two strides to the last double-ramped oxer, sailing over, taking no notice of the water element beneath him. Gemcie felt he would fly to the moon if she asked it of him. Her heart bubbled with pride. It threatened to thump out of her heaving rib cage as she guided him to the last jump, which he swallowed up easily.

The crowd leapt to their feet, cheering in unison. Cowboy hats sailed in the air. Suntanned ladies sighed. Overcome with exultation, Gemcie stood in her stirrups, letting Marshal have a victory lap around the arena. She didn't know whether she won or lost, but it didn't matter. The union was complete. She had melted into his great strength, becoming one with his flight. Together they had set one another's spirit free. The crowd applauded them all the way around, in admission of their having witnessed the perfect ride. She lifted her hunt cap, revealing a shock of sweat-streaked blonde hair. Clutching hat to heart, she bowed to the judges, then turned to the grandstand with a grin as a big as Texas. Patting Marshal solidly on his neck, wet with lather, she led him to the rail. Children stretched on tiptoes to reach his velvet nose. Relishing the deserved adulation, he nickered sweetly, letting them pat him with praise. The voice over the loudspeaker sounded to Gemcie as if it were underwater.

"Well, folks that's it. Gemcie McCauley and Marshal are back, the winners of this year's Memorial Day Classic! Dominique La Fever, aboard Silver Lining, came in a close second, but they got beat on the time."

Dominique preened for photographers with Silver Lining in the winner's circle, while Nelia and Heinrich accepted their prize money. The judge's attention was pre-empted by Marshal's arrival. Gemcie dropped to the ground. The judge slipped a wreath of deep-red roses over Marshal's immense head to rest on his barrel chest, pumping hard with pride.

Sue Ellen squirmed her way through the crowd.

"Honey, you were wonderful, just wonderful," she said, hugging her daughter so hard Gemcie thought her breasts would pop.

"She was great, wasn't she, Henry?" Sue Ellen said to Heinrich.

"Yes," he said, moving towards Gemcie, taking her hand in his own, and fairly clicking his heels together in a stiff aristocratic bow. He looked into her eyes with a dangerously flirtatious smile. "I've never enjoyed losing until today," he said, leaning over to kiss the back of her gloved hand. Nelia stiffened at this gesture, but remained silent. He'd never acknowledged her winning or losing. Her horses were no more than a game to keep her distracted from his affairs.

"Papa, the photographers are waiting." Jorge interjected, sensing his mother's discomfort. Heinrich relinquished Gemcie's hand and fell dutifully into step beside Nelia, who bristled at his touch when he put his arm around her shoulders for the camera.

Billy pushed his way into the circle.

"You done it this time, Gemcie girl!" he said, wrapping a freckled arm around her shoulders.

He turned to Dominique, wearing a pinched smile behind mirrored shades.

"Good thing *you* were ridin' today; otherwise that horse sure could o' won," he said with a broad grin.

"Next time," she said.

Heinrich and Nelia said nothing, but it registered between them that there might not be a next time for Dominique at their barn.

"You were incredible," Jorge said to Gemcie, patting Marshal on the neck.

"Thanks to Marshal," Gemcie replied.

Winning felt like a rocket blasting though the top of her head, leaving her weak and breathless. Her hands trembled as she received the prize money to be split by everyone in the co-op. For a fleeting moment she thought of Brady and wished he could be there to take his share from her.

"You were wonderful," she heard a voice that sounded like Brady's behind her, but she dismissed it as wishful thinking. There was a tap on her shoulder. She turned to see his indigo-blue eyes, couched in long black lashes, as he smiled tenderly.

Incredulous, she stared blankly at him, certain she was hallucinating.

"It was the most beautiful sight I've ever seen," he said, sincerity in his voice.

Still not convinced it was him standing before her, she grabbed him around the neck to make sure he was real. He clasped her solidly with both arms, lifting her off the ground, swinging her around him like a dad giving his kid an airplane ride. Unable to control the welling tidal wave of emotion any longer, Gemcie gave way to tears.

"Why didn't you tell me you were here?" she blubbered, stepping back to view his face.

"Sue Ellen thought it would upset the apple cart."

Gemcie gave her mother a threatening glance, but instead of chastising her for pulling strings, broke into infectious laughter.

"This time she was right!" Gemcie said. They all laughed.

That night the co-op members hovered around a huge bonfire they'd built at the Circle K to celebrate and count their winnings. The fire cast shadows, distorting their features as they warmed themselves and munched on ribs from the Smoker. Marshal looked on from his stall, still dressed up with his winner's wreath.

"That was somethin', really somethin'," Bobcat exclaimed. "If I live to be a hundred, I bet I don't see a ride that made me feel so good again."

"Those studded shoes sure helped; it was sloppy coming into that Liverpool after twenty horses," Gemcie said. "I saw myself slipping for a second, but I was over before I could get scared."

"I wish I'd been there," Kate said, tossing a bone in the fire. She hadn't attended an event since she bought the ranch and gave up riding for a living.

"You would have been proud," Billy said. "Marshal never looked fitter. You did right proper by him, Kate."

Kate lit a cigarette, exhaling smoke through her nose, and stared into the fire.

"I wished I could a seen it," she repeated her lament..

"Well, next time. Next time you'll be there because with a ride like that, we're going to the World Cup. No doubt in my mind," Billy said, firing up the group for future glory.

"Yeah, the World Cup! We're going for the Cup!" Val, Bobcat, Sue Ellen, and Billy sang out in unison, tapping Styrofoam cups of beer together to seal the deal.

Gemcie held back, clutching Brady's hand.

"I think you should keep your winnings and count your blessings," she said to the group. "No guarantees it's ever going to be like that again."

"My wife don't cotton to bets on horseflesh. She don't like it if I win or lose, so I just as soon keep my share in the kitty. What she don't know won't hurt her," Bobcat announced.

"As far as I'm concerned that money belongs to you, darlin'," Sue Ellen said. "You do with it whatever you please."

"I'm on a roll," Val said, "You damn well better not quit me now."

"Looks like we're going to the Cup, Gemcie girl, whether you, like it or not," Billy said, grinning from one side of his face to the other.

"I just need enough money to cover expenses; the rest stays in the pot," Kate said.

"That money will make more money where it's at than it will in my pocket." Brady quipped as he laughed.

Gemcie felt him squeeze her hand.

"Some people don't know when they are well-off. If you don't know enough to quit while you are ahead, there is nothing I can do about it," Gemcie said.

"That's right!" they cheered.

It was agreed the winnings would be left in the bank, minus costs. Sue Ellen was elected to cut checks from the "Cup Fund" for expenses as they came.

Brady and Gemcie drifted away from the group, settling on a bale of hay beneath a swaying tree canopy. The moon was so bright, they could see the veins of the leaves, like they were looking up from the bottom of the sea and watching them float on the surface. The music of the leaves' frantic rustle filled the warm night air, as their swirling patterns shifted in stout Santa Ana winds.

"I still can't believe you're here. I feel like I'm dreaming," she said. The moon slipped between the clouds, burying Brady's face in shadows. "Why don't you stay a while?" she asked, afraid of the answer.

"I can't," he said, looking up at the star-spiked sky.

"They need you at the lookout?"

"No, it's being shut down. Planes are taking over."

"I'm sorry."

"Don't be. It's been a long time coming. I feel lucky I got to be there as long as I did."

"Then why can't you stay a while?"

Then the full face of the moon broke through the clouds and beamed down on him, lifting the shadows from his ocean-deep eyes.

"Because I'm going to ride from Yellowstone to the Yukon."

"Good grief! That must be over two thousand miles."

"About 2,200, as the crow flies."

"Whatever for?"

"So I can tell people that live near the bear routes about their migration highway, and why it's got to be saved."

"Do you think they care?"

"People might care more if they knew more. My being there will make the route more visible. I'll talk to everyone I meet on the way about linking up the parks so the bears can survive."

"Seems like an awful long shot."

"That didn't stop you from trying, did it?" he said, giving her a squeeze around the shoulders, pulling her closer to him. "The Indians believe that when an animal presents himself to you in the hunt it's a gift. Blue's gift to me should count for something. I can't just do nothing any longer."

"How long do you think it will take you?" Gemcie asked, realizing that this was something Brady had to do.

"Maybe two seasons. I'll start in the spring and see how far I get before the snow flies. I'm not sure yet," he said as he turned eyes, liquid with tenderness, upon her. "But no matter how long it takes me, I know each step I take will be one in the right direction."

"I wish I could go with you."

"I'll be writing to you every night in my journal. You're inside me now," he said. "Just like that moon up there is inside you," he continued, kissing her lightly on the forehead.

She looked up to meet the still eyes of the old man in the moon. She could swear he wrinkled up his wizened face and winked at her. She didn't tell Brady what she thought she saw. Instead, she laid her head on his shoulder, and let herself sink into the sweet shelter of his love.

The End

Author's Note

In the early 90s I had the privilege of interviewing Jimmy Williams, famous for his unconventional training techniques. The article that came from that meeting, *Tips from a Legend,* about his mastery with horses, his ability to speak their language and his unending patience with students appeared in Equus Magazine. At that time (1992), Susie Hutchinson, his prize protégé, was the American Grand Prix Association Rider of the Year. Her skill and daring were an inspiration to me; a fledgling rider. The character Billy in this story was inspired by Jimmy Williams, and Gemcie is a romanticized version of Susie Hutchison who now owns a ranch in Temecula and is a top trainer herself.

The first draft of Cowgirl was written twenty years ago while I was standing up at a computer on my breakfast bar. I was suffering from extreme sciatic pain that would not allow me to sit for any length of time. I was forced to give my beloved mare to Hearts and Horses, a non-profit organization working with handicapped children, and had to leave the riding world until I healed. This was a gut-wrenching decision for me. I truly loved jumping my horse, trail riding and all things horses, but was constrained to leave it behind. Writing this story kept my mind off the nagging pain I was experiencing and allowed me, in my imagination, to achieve the perfect ride I had worked towards with my own mare.

One of the finest experiences of my life was taking a horse pack trip in the Eastern Sierra Nevada. "Once you've been to the mountains they become a part of you, like the kiss from a lover." I don't know who anonymously said that, but I know it was true for me. Gemcie is also healed in the beauty of the "Range of Light" and finds strength in her solitude to face her demons. Brady speaks of the environmental battle that rages for us all. How do we share the planet gracefully with the inhabitants of the natural world? If this book is received well, in my next story I may take readers on the ride of their life from Yellowstone to the Yukon with Brady, and Gemcie at his side.

About the Author

A love triangle of extremes has proven to be a solid base for adventure-travel writer Linda Ballou's writing. From her roots in Alaska she received strength, centeredness and respect for the awe-inspiring power of nature. While living in Hawaii, she found nurturing, a spiritual awakening, peace and a heroine for her acclaimed historical novel, *Wai-nani—A Voice from old Hawaii*. In addition to being available in print and kindle format, *Wai-nani* was released in 2015 in audio format on Audible.com

In *Lost Angel Walkabout-One Traveler's Tales* her travel collection filled with chills, spills, and giggles, she shares her most meaningful travel adventures. You may go to her website wwwlindaballouauthor.com to view a host of articles, as well as her Outdoor Days and blog posts.

Presently, she resides in California and loves to hike in the Santa Monica Mountains and the state's other environs. She shares *Great Outdoor Day in L.A.* in her column on Examiner.com.

www.LindaBallouAuthor.com

Follow Linda's blog at http://LindaBallouTalkingtoYou.blogspot.com

Enjoy Linda's Great Outdoor Days in L.A. on Examiner.com are at

http://www.examiner.com/outdoor-travel-in-los-angeles/linda-ballou

Friend her on Facebook: https://www.facebook.com/linda.ballou.9

Peer reviews are always welcome on Amazon.com and Goodreads.com